The Future Has

a Past

*S*tories

Doubleday

New York London Toronto Sydney Auckland

The Future Has

a Past

J. California Cooper

⚓

PUBLISHED BY DOUBLEDAY
a division of Random House, Inc.
1540 Broadway, New York, New York 10036

DOUBLEDAY and the portrayal of an anchor with a dolphin
are trademarks of Doubleday, a division of Random House, Inc.

Book design by Dana Leigh Treglia

Library of Congress Cataloging-in-Publication Data

Cooper, J. California.
The future has a past : stories / J. California Cooper. — 1st ed.
p. cm.
Contents: A shooting star—A filet of soul—The eagle flies—The lost and
the found.
1. Afro-American women—Fiction. I. Title.
PS3553.O5874 F8 2000
813'.54—dc21   00-034602

ISBN 0-385-49680-X
Copyright © 2000 by J. California Cooper

Dedicated with love to

Joseph C. and Maxine Rosemary Cooper, my parents
Paris A. Williams, my chile
Kiska Ivora Gross, my niece

Other Special People

Ted Lange, Gebby Lange, Juanita Wilson, Hubert Glasgow, William Kunstler, Ron Kuby, Claude O. Allen, attorneys
Irashel Fitzgerald, Bertice Berry, Terri McFaddin, Joyce Carol Thomas, authors
Sharon Elise, poet
Robert Kelly of Los Angeles (& Herman)
Beaver Scott, musician, Oakland
Mary Monroe, author, Oakland
Elizabeth Coleman, author

Other V.I.P.s

All the teachers of the world who love their jobs and children and adults whose minds they are helping to mold. I admire and congratulate and appreciate you so much for what you do with Love. I don't know all your names, but . . . Septima Clark, Barbara Christian, Erin Gruwell, essayist and poet June Jordan and Louis Braille all extraordinaire. You all deserve more. And more money too!

Acknowledgments

I wish to express my deepest gratitude for the assistance in writing this book of the swift intelligence, generosity and patience of Janet Hill and Roberta Spivak, her assistant. I was blessed with their encouragement, knowledge and understanding. I am proud that Janet Hill IS my editor.

I will be forever grateful and beholden to Doubleday–Random House and the people who extend themselves there, always to ensure that good things prevail. Steve Rubin, Gerry Howard, Shioban Adcock and many others. Of those no longer there, Sally Leventhal, Peternelle van Ardsdale and Martha Levin stand large in my heart.

I wish to thank Belinda J. Hughes of Tampa, Florida, for her kindnesses that went far beyond friendship.

I would say a special word to Anita Williams of Washington, D.C., for always being there to rescue me when I needed it and always managing to do it in such a delightful way.

A special thanks to Evelyn Coleman who was so magnanimous and kind when I sought her help. I will not forget.

To my agent, Anna Ghosh, a Scovil Chichak Galen in New York. You have no idea how I appreciate you. Stay.

Last, but not least, I am grateful to the readers of my books. Without Alice Walker and you, there is no me between the covers of books. I do not get the opportunity to see all of you, but I think of you and in my prayers I thank God for you. Just imagine: YOU like something that comes out of my mind. Wow!

Author's Note

I have, I think, written about paths and roads that lead to a future. About the light, quick footsteps on that road—and the heavy, burdened footsteps imprinted there also.

Choices. Decisions . . . Oh, how they form your life. They, finally, make you walk the walk you walk; Run, when you will, and Rest, when you can. I have tried, in a small way, in this book, to remind you . . . Today is Tomorrow taken from Yesterday. Or today is some of yesterday and a bit of tomorrow, too. All are pieces of you. Your life.

If you are old enough . . . you can look back and see your footsteps through the years on the roads you have chosen. If you are young enough you can look ahead, prepare, to avoid or take the roads in your future. As you press forward against the winds of time . . . or are pushed against your will by the winds of consequence. (Which you have possibly set in motion.)

Let us think of the future as a house we are building. A brick or plank a day. Some days we may not have any material, a rainy day even, but we do not disregard the future house. Years pass, and finally, the time is right and the future is built. Our futures we will have to live in during the end of our lives. Will it have bricks or planks missing? Be drafty and cold? Will the foundation be warped and hard to maintain a balance on and will we be able to see the dirt ground beneath us? Will we have windows to see the outside? What will we be seeing; the beauty of the earth or the decaying wall of someone else's future house? Will we be alone? Is there peace in your future? Are there good memories of a good life? Or will we have to take, if possible, a room anywhere we can find it and depend on the kindness of strangers?

As you journey on your chosen roads, think of GOD* and pay attention to the movements of GOD'S garments in the changing winds.

As you move toward your future, look back and** you will see your future has a past . . . because THE FUTURE HAS A PAST.

J. California Cooper

* the Time Keeper,
** if you have good sense,

Contents

The Future Has

a Past

A Shooting Star

Now, you don't know me. And, I know that *you* know that nobody knows everything. But a person does have to go by whatever they do know and every new thing they can learn, to make any good sense out of life. They say love makes the world go round, and I believe that. But, it seems to me, and I already told you I don't know everything, that nowadays sex is making the world go round.

There's another sayin, "What goes round, comes round." Well, I know that sometime what went around comes back around a whole lot different and bigger and worser than what you sent round in the first place.

You got to watch life, cause it's moving all the time, every minute! You have to look all around yourself and see what's happening to you and everybody else. Try to get some understanding of it. But, I notice, some people look at things in their life and never do understand.

I grew up in a fair-size town that had a little of everything in it, I guess. In small communities you just know everybody cause you go to school with em and you usually know their parents cause you know their kids.

You know how growin children talk by the time they get to junior high school; half of the day is spent on gossip, some innocent and some not so innocent. That's when I started payin attention to Lorene. She was one of our classmates and a main subject to talk about.

Lorene's full name was Heleva Lorene Shaky. Her father named her "Heleva" (I don't know how he came up with that name) and her mother put in "Lorene" and that's what everyone called her, til they were mad at her or something; then they would say "Heleva!" like that, for awhile.

Lorene's mother is a real nice, smiling lady from this town and her father was from somewhere in Washington, D.C. Somehow they met somewhere and he traveled back and forth til they finally got married.

Lorene grew up in a nice house and they seemed to be a regular happy family like most other people round here, but what do I know? Her father, Mr. Shaky, was often gone, on business, back to Washington D.C., and her mother was alone a lot so she attended them teas and church socials and some women's clubs. Nice people.

I came to know them pretty well cause my family was kinda poor and sometimes when I didn't have lunch or lunch money Lorene would take me home with her and her mother would have a nice sandwich and a glass of milk for us. Mrs.

Shaky, her mother, always was able to put love in everything she did for Lorene and, in her sandwiches and cookies, included me.

Lorene was a very kind and generous person. I mean, even kind to strangers and anybody. She would make friends with a person in a minute. Her mother was always telling her bout things like that; taking up with strangers, I mean. But Lorene would just smile that friendly smile of hers and keep on being herself.

Lorene wasn't a beautiful girl, but that smile of hers just made her so beautiful like. Just lighted up everything around her and she always seemed to be happy. She knew, at a early age, just how to fool with her hair and make up new styles for herself. Her mother didn't let her wear make-up or nothing, but Lorene didn't mind that either; she could just put that smile on her face and that was enough. She always dressed nice. Clean, too. She made good grades and didn't even have to study hard to do it.

I wasn't always real close to her as a friend because she had so many friends, but they was mostly boys. I always liked her though, but as you grow up you can grow away from some people and still like em.

Now, I don't want to say this, but I have to say it so you will understand Lorene. She was the kind of a girl who was so glad to have a vagina she didn't know what to do. She wanted them boys either to smell it, touch it, look at it, feel it, just anything as long as you did something to it. The boys said she would just be smiling, happy all the time. So . . . she was sorta the object of the gossip of us girls and the object of attention of the boys, a lot.

I can see her now; standing in the schoolyard in her white

and brown saddle oxford shoes, a plaid pleated skirt and a white blouse. Smiling. With boys always somewhere near. She was wearing perfume round that time and puttin on a little light lipstick, too.

Well, I still liked her and sometimes I needed that sandwich at lunch cause my family was still doing poorly, but I couldn't stay close, close friends anymore because she was so . . . conspicuous. Anyway, my mama had heard of some of Lorene's doings and told me to just separate myself from her. My mama may have been poor, but she was very strict. And tired too. She and my daddy worked hard; I had four brothers and sisters. Their jobs didn't pay much.

Now, that made me kind of mad at the girls who were always dogging her and even telling their mamas about Lorene. (That's how my mama found out about Lorene and what she was doing with the boys.) Then I had to miss out on a good friend and a good meal when I was hungry . . . because of them! And who knew what these gossiping girls were doing behind trees and walls?

Lorene found another girlfriend though, Carla, who wasn't just like Lorene in her ways, but did let a boy or two go all the way. But not everybody! When we graduated junior high school Carla was at home having a baby. She came back to high school and left the baby at home with her mother or somebody. Anyway, Lorene and Carla had started having sex with boys when they were about twelve or thirteen, so I heard the boys told, cause the boys always tell.

By the time we were in high school Lorene had gone through all the boys in our junior class and some others that were seniors. High school gave her a whole new load of fresh boys. No boys ever ganged up on her or nothing like that.

They knew everybody was gonna have their own chance and so no rush, I guess. I think they told a lie on my friend though, when they said two boys had gone over to her house late one night and Mrs. Shaky was gone to a club meeting. They said they both had her vagina; one from the front and one from the back, with Lorene laughing between her small screams.

I gasped when I heard that, I didn't believe it! But some girls did believe them boys, so Lorene really did become more of a outsider to us. What I wondered was why they paid so much attention to Lorene and hardly noticed Carla and her baby. Carla was a nice-looking girl, but didn't dress so nice nor look so nice as Lorene. And two or three boys liked Carla, but ALL the boys liked Lorene. I know some of those gossiping girls' own friend-boys went over to see Lorene.

I asked Lorene, one day, because I was her friend, not because I was looking for information to pass around, "Why do you let all those boys do sex to you? Why?"

Lorene just threw her head back and laughed, saying, "Cause they love me! They all love me! I can get any boy or man I want! Cause they love me!"

She was my friend so I felt close enough to be honest with her. I said, "But they don't keep you, Lorene. If they loved you they, at least one of em, would love you enough to stay with you or marry you even."

She hit me lightly on my shoulder, "Well, I'm having a good time. They come to me when I snap my fingers, girl! They love my nice titties. Always reachin for em. They love me!"

I knew the answer to that, my mama had done told me, so I said, "If you put a bucket of food in front of pigs they will all run to it, but that don't mean they love the person who puts it there. Everybody wants something free! And you don't have to be pretty either, you can be ugly and still get that kinda sex." She just laughed again, but not so joyfully this time. We were at school by then and she ran off pretty quick; getting away from me, I guess, and my mouth.

I still stopped by to see Mrs. Shaky every now and then when I was over near their house. She always had some home-made cookies or a slice of cake. That's not the only reason I went either, I really liked her. Mrs. Shaky thought it was nice that Lorene was so popular. She often served the boys cookies and cake, too. She was just a nice woman, a nice mother.

Most everyone had at least one real boyfriend by the time we were in the eleventh grade. I had mine, Neil. Oh, Neil was handsome! and tall! and was a track star! I had all kind of medals which he had won. I wore them all proudly. Everyone knew he was my beau.

When graduation time finally came, many of my girl-friends were engaged and getting married and settling in for life or going off to college. On our prom night, the finest main fellows didn't take Lorene to the graduation prom. In fact, they didn't dance with her much either. They would just stop by for a minute or so to say something to the unpopular fellow who did bring her, Milton.

Milton wasn't in sports or anything, but he was nice; the quiet studious type. But Lorene smiled brilliantly and waved to all the fellows who didn't stop by. Neil and I went over to talk to them because I still felt she was my friend, I don't care how outside she was. Lorene danced most dances with her date and they sat out the others. I heard a couple of fellows asked her to go outside and dance where it was cool, but she just laughed and waved them away. Good!

After graduation, Lorene wasn't engaged and she didn't want to go to college. Her mother told my mother because she was so disappointed. So Lorene got a job as a clerk in a small department store and for her social life she made it on down to the nightclubs and social dances.

That went on for about two years. Lorene went through most of the new men she met and back and forth with a few of the old ones from school. The old ones were now grown and working. But not the married ones. Lorene didn't like married men. "Take yourself on home to the woman you married," is what Neil told me some of the men told him.

I was married to my Neil. My family didn't have the money to send me to college, but Neil was going at night. I was going to go to college when he was finished. Neil had been my first and only man in my life. I had liked a few other heartthrobs, but I always seemed to like and love Neil more. We had a nice, small wedding. I was dressed in white, you know, satin and lace, and I wore a veil, but Neil and I had already made love. I didn't let him wear it out though. Didn't let him get "enough." My mama had done told me about them blues in the night.

My mama said, "Right now, clean and good, you are worth rubies and pearls. But you let someone take that precious pearl and you gonna be the one have to pay the rubies for that pearl, not him. Then, you won't have neither one of them rubies and pearls. Don't care what nobody say, write or telegraph you, the right man wants his woman to be HIS woman.

And, most men, may marry you without that pearl, but he gonna throw it up into your face, for sure, all through your marriage. Believe me when I tell you! Course, I don't think you should want no man who been under too many dresses either, cause that's something of a sign of things to come!"

She hadn't ever lied to anybody, as I knew of, so I believed her. I loved Neil anyway. I knew we were going to get married and that's why I let him. And I was even more than a little curious myself. But, I still never let him get enough. Besides, after I found out what it was, I found out I could wait better. And I'll tell you another thing I found out my mama was right about because our wedding night was exciting cause Neil could finally get to the lovin and the lovin was good, and special, cause we had waited for what was ours only!

After marriage, too soon, I had a baby and was taking care of my first child, working part-time. I worked part-time to help Neil stay in school. I wanted him to finish so I could get started. I was so proud, and Neil was so proud of us, too.

My mama helped me by baby-sitting because the one thing she wanted for me was a degree in SOMETHING instead of a house full of hungry children I couldn't feed lunch to. That way I could take two nights a week at junior college to find out what I really wanted to do. Honey, sometimes I was so tired I was sure I didn't want to do nothing but stay home and care for my child, but I had already lived that life with my mama and daddy so I went for the education. Besides, at junior college, I was learning how many different kinds of worlds there are to live in and I wanted a better one than any I knew. Having and making choices! I could do it!

Well, you know, I told you about the social clubs in our

town that gave dances. Sometimes they had a good big band come down from New York, Chicago, California or somewhere fancy. Every once in a while, we would get a baby-sitter and Neil would take me out to dance.

It was always crowded, crowded because this would be a really hip band. I would see a lot of old friends and some of my main buddy-friends. Once I saw Carla when she came in with her boyfriend. She was happy to be out because she had two babies now and hadn't married yet. But she was holding on with both arms to her man. "Maybe he will be 'the one' for her," I thought.

I saw Lorene come in. She was alone. But she was smiling and looking good! All dressed to the T's. She still had her nice shape with those beautiful legs, and of course she was still young and very nice looking. When I waved to her and started over to speak with her, she waved back and pulled a fellow toward the bandstand. Lorene loved to dance and could do it good, too!

But in that short bit of time I noticed just a little sad droop to her eyes as she looked to see who I was with. Her eyes flicked on Neil, who was talking to somebody else at the moment, then her eyes flicked away. Quickly she was smiling and waving to other people as she moved her hips to the good music and her body toward the band.

I wanted to get a chance to talk to her, tell her what I was doing and see what her plans were. I remembered her really good grades at school and I wanted to tell her how college could be exciting. And there were many men in college, too! More mature. But, somehow, we never connected at the dance.

Anyway, we all had a good time and I was sorry to see it end, but there was plenty work waiting for me when we got home. Early morning homework.

The band had been so good they were held over to play a few more places before they left town. Before the band left, Lorene had gone through half of them. When they did leave town, Lorene quit her job, packed and left with one of the fellows in the band. Smiling and happy.

When I saw Carla again, about four years had passed since the dance. It was a coincidence that I saw her on the very same day I saw Lorene again.

It was a lovely day and there were a few things I had to buy for my son's schoolwear and a few little things for my house. Neil was just finishing his master's degree and had a very good job and we had bought a house. (Smile-smile).

I still had a part-time job, though a better one at a veterinarian's office. I was studying now to be an assistant, which means I could get a job anywhere, anytime, because people really do love their pets and spend a great deal of money on them. I loved helping animals. It also meant I could take off to be with my children when I needed to. The pay was good, also. I had two sons now, four and six years old. Our parents fought over who would baby-sit each week, we were very blessed.

I love secondhand and antique stores. One day I went into my favorite secondhand store and looked up and there was Carla, hollering at about a nine-year-old daughter and holding the hand of about a two-year-old, with a four-year-old holding on to her skirttail. I patted her shoulder and hugged her where possible, with one arm. She smiled and laughed a little, "Girl, where you been? I ain't seen you since I don't know when!"

I laughed with her, pleased to see her. "Carla! (I lied a little) You look good! Are these your beautiful children? (That was the truth.)"

"Chile, you see em don't you!? Yeah, girl, they're mine."

Then, with my foolish self, I said, "I haven't seen you in so long! Who did you marry?"

Carla twisted her mouth and turned her lips down. "Girl, I ain't thinkin bout gettin married. I don't want none of these do-nothin, no-count men. How you doin? I see you got two kids yourself."

"Yeah, these are my boys."

She rubbed the head of one of my sons, saying, "I bet you married that Neil of yours. You didn't let him get away, did you?"

I smiled and answered, "No, I sure didn't! We got married."

She turned back to the clothes rack after hollering at the running son and said, "Well, that's good, girl. Glad for ya. I better get on bout this clothes business. Glad to see you again."

I started to move away, myself, then stopped because I wanted to ask her, "How is Lorene? Do you ever hear from her?"

Carla laughed a little again, turned to me saying, "Yeah. She's back now for a short visit with her mama. Her mama's kinda sick. I went to Chicago and visited with Lorene once; she sent me a bus ticket. Girl, she have a ball! A natural ball in that Chicago! But she be in New York and Detroit and all like that. She knows a whole lot of bands now! All sharp, fine men! She ain't stuck with no kids like us. She's lucky!"

I started to say I wasn't stuck, but I knew what she meant. I was stuck, but I guess I didn't mind it at all. I didn't say anything in reference to being "lucky" either, because I did know how she meant that, too. I just smiled and hit her lightly on her shoulder, then moved on away to look through the things I wanted to look at.

I don't mean to say I think everybody should be married, but . . . what are you going to do if you don't get married or get an education? Where is your home, or your life, going to be? I have learned there is very little playing around in the very serious game of life. You can play, but it should be after you have done what you need to do for yourself!

Later, that same day, I was going into the department store Lorene used to work in and that's when I saw her. She did a little scream, so did I and we hugged. I really did like Lorene. She was fun and alive. What she did with her life was her own business and even though I thought it was a sad life and a waste, because I like real love, steady love, it was her choice.

I knew Lorene looked good enough for any man to be proud to marry her, if she wanted to get married. But, I remembered my mama telling me, many times, that respect is the foundation of love. That without respect there will be no love, long. Check it out! Self-esteem is loving yourself! But . . . you can only get self-esteem by doing things you are proud of. And I don't care whether you go to church or not, God has made it so you KNOW when you are doing wrong. Wrong things can destroy your life. Look around!

Anyway, we stood back from each other and looked each

other over, smiling. She was the first to say, "Maisha! You look good!" I told her right back and it was true, "Lorene, girl, you look great! All the latest clothes and that hairstyle! You look beautiful!"

She grinned happily as she looked down at my children and asked, "Oh, are these your boys? Aren't they handsome! Whose babies are they? Who did you marry?"

"Neil, you know Neil."

"Sure, I remember Neil. He was handsome!" Then she giggled, "Girl! You got yourself a good one! Sure have! You all stayin together?"

I nodded as I smiled, "Yes. And I'm getting a degree in college; night college, but still a degree."

Lorene laughed sweetly and waved her hand at the air. "All you smart married people bore me, but I am happy for you, old friend. Well, I have to get home to Mama. Stop in and see her for me sometimes, will you? She likes you."

As we hugged again, I was thinking I did need to go to see Mrs. Shaky, just been so busy. But I was also thinking, "What does Lorene mean, 'I got a good one'? I knew I had a good one, but how did she know?" I brought myself together to ask about her mother.

She answered, "Oh, Mama is much better. She is just lonely, girl, cause Dad still got his travelin jobs and she misses me. So I come check in on her when I can, you know, come home. Cause there really is nothing like home anyway."

"No, there really isn't. Nothing. Did you get married? Are you in love? What are you doing now?"

She laughed, with an exquisite perfume lightly filling the air all around her, and said, "I'm always in love, girl. Isn't it grand?"

"And marriage?" I had to ask.

She pushed my shoulder a little as her laughter stopped, "Marriage! Marriage is for old people. I'm not old. I'll . . . get married when the time comes. Been engaged lots of times though."

I had to ask. "Don't you want some pretty babies of your own?"

She didn't laugh, just looked at me like I was pitiful, but it was her face that looked sad, not mine. She said, "I don't . . . have much time for babies, right now. That's all in the future. I don't want to worry about anybody's future but mine, right now. I never have tried not to have children. But I never have tried to have them either. I guess I lost a few without knowing it. I have . . . enough to think about, for the day."

Then she put her arms around my children and they let her pull them close to her. "Someday, I want two babies just like these. Just as healthy and handsome and sweet. And I know they are smart! Just look at those eyes! Someday! I'll have my own! Two. Maybe more! Who knows?" We laughed and I hugged her, close.

"Maybe so," I answered, "but what I really worry about is somebody's life." She let that pass and we said a few more words, her big smile beneath the sad eyes brightening the moment, then . . . she was gone, with me standing looking after her as she sashayed down the street. Not vulgar sashay, but just life sashaying.

As I went home, I kept thinking about what she had said, "You got a good one!" because I did have a "good" one, a whole good husband. Later, I asked Neil about it. "Did you . . . sleep with Lorene?

He looked slightly uncomfortable, but he answered, "Sleep with her? I never 'slept' with her."

"Did you have sex with her? Neil, you know what I mean."

He rubbed the back of his neck before he answered me. "Well . . . sure. Everybody did." (At least he didn't lie. I was glad.)

I remembered him saying when we were younger, "The love that is only yours." I was older now and knew a little something about life, but I was hurt. "Oh, Neil."

He didn't apologize or plead, he just said straight out, "Honey, it was free. I was young. How could a kid let that pass by? There it was on a platter. Everybody did it to her. But there was never any thought of 'love' as you and I knew it. It was just a piece of tail lying there, waiting for you. Calling for you, even. Anybody could have it. And did. Just nobody wanted her to get pregnant and have to be a father of a baby mixed up with everybody's stuff in the same baby."

"Ohhh, Neil." It was all I could say. I tried to understand. I did understand; so that passed.

Well, time went on. I am always engrossed in my family and my work. That is what keeps me going on. I love them. But, I kept thinking of Lorene, now and then. I even went by to see her mother. She was lonely even with all her clubs and teas. She wanted a grandchild. Someone to take Lorene's place; someone new to love.

Lorene went back to Chicago, or Detroit, wherever. Over the next three years she came home every once in a while to see her mother. I always missed catching her at home.

We were all going on thirty years when I did happen to see Lorene again. She was still quite attractive, but there was something shabby around the edges. Used. Tired. Hollow. It reminded me, fleetingly, of a print I had seen by Salvador Dalí, of a beautiful woman obviously used and ruined by life. Still, the vestige of beauty was still there. Strangely, the thought didn't all come from her body, it came from her eyes. The sparkle . . . the light . . . was fading. But her smile was still brilliant as it tried to shine through disappointed, hurt eyes.

Please don't think I am being cruel. I truly liked Lorene. And I do not think my life is the only or perfect life to live. But, my life was helping me to live, adding to my joy in life, giving me pleasure and love to hold on to. Lorene's life didn't seem to do that for her and I hated to see that happen to my friend. If you are going to choose a certain way, at least be happy as possible, satisfied, with it. Maybe she was satisfied even if she wasn't happy. I don't think so.

My children were standing on the edge of teenism when I was thirty. All of a sudden it seemed as though I was getting old. Just being a mother and sometime part-time worker and all the talk of "doing your own thing." Liberalism and feminism made me think life was passing me by. Oh, I had no complaints about Neil. He was still a good, fine husband. But the world is so big and full of so many things, I wondered if life might not be passing me by or something.

Then . . . Lorene came home again.

Only this time . . . she did not step off a plane or a train or a bus. She was carried off . . . in a coffin. That Lorene. Oh, Lorene. Dead at thirty. Coming home for the last time.

I knew Mrs. Shaky must be in misery. Her daughter, her only, young daughter, was dead. I went by to see her, but her house was full of her neighbors; come to see what had killed Lorene. I went back home, planning to see her later. But life can be so full sometime you don't get a chance to even breathe deep. You push your way through. I did check with the church for the place and time of the funeral. I don't like funerals, but I was going to this funeral!

I spoke to Neil about the funeral. He was shocked at Lorene's death, of course. But when I asked him if he was going to the funeral, he said, "Well, gee." Shaking his head. "I . . . ah, oh, I, gee, well . . ." Then, "Honey, I have to work. I didn't even hardly know the girl." (She hadn't even grown up, to him.) So I knew he was not going.

Still, I said, "You slept with her."

"I didn't sleep with her. It was just a . . . a . . . a quick piece. It's not like we were even friends."

I lost a little respect for my husband that day.

So the funeral day came and I went alone. Somehow I got the time wrong, or they changed it, but, anyway, I was early. I entered the little chapel at the mortuary with the sad organ music playing in the background. It was dark in that room the casket was in, so I couldn't see clearly all the seats. I was looking straight at the casket, anyway. I hesitated to go toward it, but my feet kept going, slowly, and I finally reached the coffin.

Mrs. Shaky had dressed Lorene very prettily, as usual, but

in a dress Lorene might not have liked. The peach color was pretty on her, but the bodice was high up to cover her neck and long sleeved so no part of her showed except her face. There was no smile, just a pitiful, grievous, defeated look, as though she had seen death coming and had been sad to meet it.

Lorene was still lovely, though. Her hair was neatly done and whoever had made her face up, made her look so natural. She was young, so young, and my feelings for her made me press my hands to my heart in sorrow for her. The tears began to run down my face for the woman I had never come to really know.

After several quiet, thoughtful moments, I leaned over, close to Lorene's ear, and whispered a question that was suddenly important to me. "Oh, Lorene, Lorene. Did you find what you were looking for?" Then her life, as I knew it, flashed through my mind and I whispered another question. "Sister-woman . . . Was it worth it?"

In a moment I heard a rustle among the seats, so I began to move away from Lorene, drawing my hand, slowly, along her casket as I went to take a seat.

I cried, silently, all during the service. There were about twenty people there, but I didn't hear anyone crying. Perhaps because Mrs. Shaky was hurting, moaning and crying out so. I guess she might be the one I was crying for. She had no grandbaby to hold in her arms to fill the empty place that had been Lorene's.

When the service was over I was trying to prepare myself with which words to say to Mrs. Shaky. I knew there were no words to express my feelings for her loss. What can you say? Words are so small, can be so empty and inadequate to replace a warm, human loss. A child, at any age, is still your child, your baby. I was crying for many reasons and I don't know them all.

The people were filing out, straggling. People were trying to move Mrs. Shaky away from the casket which the undertakers were trying to close. I went over to help and Mrs. Shaky turned and saw me in her distraction. She recognized me, not as me, but as one of her daughter's friends. With open mouth, she let go of the coffin and opened her arms to enclose me, grasping me. She pulled me to her and buried her head on my breast, crying, almost screaming, "My baby, my baby, my baby! She's gone! Gone! Gone!" Then she moaned in a deep, low voice, "Forever gone."

I tried to console her as they moved the coffin off its stand and out of the chapel. I lead Mrs. Shaky out behind the coffin. As we got to the outside door, Mrs. Shaky, beside me, still holding on tightly to me when the sunlight hits the coffin and us blindingly. I am blinded as I hear Mrs. Shaky crying, "Oh, Lord, oh, Lord. Give me my baby back. It ain't supposed to be this way!"

She turned her tear-stained and sleepless face to me and asked, "Do you know what happened to my baby? Do you know what happened, child?"

I shake my head "No," because my mouth is too full of tears for her and I cannot speak.

We were still stumbling down the steps, trying to see through the tears, following the coffin in that blinding sunlight. She shook her head in sorrow as she said, "She met a man." She is holding my hand so hard I feel even more of her pain. She continued talking to me. "She met a man. She took him as a friend. My chile was so friendly, so friendly . . . even to strangers."

I could only nod and hold on to her. I didn't want her to fall and I wondered where Mr. Shaky was.

Her pain was mixed with a little anger as she continued, "I don't blive anybody knows where he was from. I always told her about strangers like that, but she was too friendly, too nice. My baby was such a sweet, kind girl."

I continued to guide her down the steps toward the people waiting down there; they were watching her . . . and waiting to hear more.

Mrs. Shaky, as I held her, still leading her in our walk behind the casket, kept trying to tell me the story in her frustration and heartache. "Well, child, he took her to a hotel . . . some hotel. I went there when I went to get her precious body. I saw it, but they wouldn't let me in the room where they found her. they wouldn't let me." She turned her face up to mine, "You know what the police say, chile?" She didn't wait for an answer; I had none anyway.

"Those policemen said . . . they said they went there to make love, make sex. My poor friendly daughter. Oh Lord. Make love. She loved love . . . so she didn't know he didn't have any for her. They told me, the policeman say he couldn't enjoy making . . . sex with someone who was alive; they had to be dead. Dead! And, so, that man who don't know nothin bout no love killed my baby. Strangled her! Strangled my child who I love. She was so pretty. He strangled her and kept her there five days . . . dead . . . just usin her body. Oh! Lord! Usin her body without her knowing it. Then, the people in the other rooms smelled something . . . and reported it and that's when he left . . . In the night."

There were no words, there still are no words to express my horror of such a thing being in life; no words to say to this poor woman because I know she was picturing it, would be picturing it for the rest of her life. I led her around the people gaping at her, straining to hear her words. I led her to the limousine the mortician was pointing at and helped her get in.

I had not planned to go to the cemetery; so much sorrow when one is lowered down into a grave. I had just known Mr. Shaky would be there. But, as I tried to back out of the limousine the mortician whispered to me that I might stay with her; she needed help from someone who cared for her. I whispered back, "Where is her husband, Mr. Shaky?" The answer was he had suffered a mild heart attack when he heard of his daughter's death and was in the hospital. Mrs. Shaky didn't have anyone else. So I went to the cemetery in the car with Mrs. Shaky and just let her talk herself out.

And she did talk. "They broke the door down the next day, the sixth day, and that's when they found her." She reached her hands toward the hearse driving in front of us, saying, "Oh, Lord. Jesus. He killed my baby . . . not for no love . . . just for sex."

When the end of the funeral was over and we drove Mrs. Shaky to her house, her husband, Mr. Shaky, bent over a little from weakness, came out of the house to meet her and took her from my arms. He didn't say a word, just patted her back, put an arm around her and led her, the two of them leaning on each other, back into their home.

I stood there watching until their door closed, then got into the limousine for the ride back to my car. Ahhh, my heart was full of heavy sorrow like a huge weight.

When we reached the funeral home Carla was there with her children; late. She came over to me and said, "Well . . . she gone."

"Yes, she is gone."

Carla shook her head and said, "I tole her bout goin off with people. Now, look! She done got killed. She liked that lovin; but you can't fool with some people. That sure is a shame!"

I turned to her, already tired of pain, and I didn't mean to be mean, but, I had to say it. "Yes, she got killed. She is dead. But you like 'that lovin' yourself. She got killed, but you got five children by different men while you were looking for love! Why didn't some one of them love you enough to marry you and stay? Your life ain't living either."

"What you talkin bout? What you got? We all women. We all need some love! You like love your own self!"

I had to answer, and I heard my mama's voice, "Yeah, but I waited long enough to know he loved me before I let him use me up! Everybody might want to screw you, but not everybody wants to stay and marry you if you love em! What you feel isn't all there is to it! What he feels is important too! Now you got babies and the men got some nooky and they probably done forgot all about your stuff and maybe the babies, too!" I hated to sound so righteous, but I wasn't being righteous, I was trying to use some sense in what I said. I didn't want to hurt her, but I knew the men in her life had.

As I started moving away toward my car I hollered to Carla, "You need to read *Waiting to Exhale* by Terry McMillan; it's actually about many women in the world who want love. You don't have to settle for just ANYthing! Life can get better!"

I said to her as I stepped into my car, "I got a man and two babies who belong to him. I got a life I choose. Didn't nobody leave me with it or make me take it."

As I drove home I was thoughtful about life. I thought about my friend, Lorene. All her life she was so proud, glad to have a vagina. People, men, used it, might have abused it. Must have. I know they did. She abused it herself. She never did seem interested in anything else, but "love" or sex. Far as I know, she was never anything BUT a vagina to most of the men in her life. And because she never developed anything else in her life, in herself, to wrap that vagina in . . . That's all she was. A vagina. And that vagina was so helpless that even when she was dead it was still being used. And by someone who could do anything they wanted to do with it. And still not love her. A vagina needs a brain to control what happens to it. Be responsible for it! Hopefully with the brain it was born with at the top of your body.

I thank God and my mama for any sense I have in knowing I am more than just a vagina. There is more to life. Your vagina, my vagina, is very, very important to me, but it is not my whole life or your whole self. Love does make the world go round, sure does. But, when sex makes your world go round; look out! And when some women use it to make money off it, just let some years go by and you are gonna have to spend most all of the money you no longer have trying to get your behind back to some kind of useful, healthy shape. If you can. Everything wears and tears if you don't take care of it. My mama told me and I believe her.

See? People, men and women, come into your life with free pretty words and actions and they ain't there except to steal somebody's happiness. A liar is a thief who will steal from anybody. And a liar ain't but a second away from a physical abuser and a murderer. Lorene is dead because that man stole her life. Sure did. Lord, bless her. But, did she give it to him? Her choice, wasn't it? Not to die, but she put herself out there. Poor Heleva Lorene.

And time won't wait for you to catch up and learn. You have to love your own heart and body! Love is LOVE, and LOVE protects what or who it LOVES. Believe me. If somebody is not there to HELP you, what else are they there for? Answer me, please.

Well, I was talking to myself, but I was practicing for my children. Boys have to be careful too.

I brushed all that off my mind and new thoughts came into it. I rushed home and picked up my babies and the cake I had made earlier to take to the Shakys' house. I headed straight there. I meant to give Mrs. Shaky some part-time grandchildren. She might not love them as much as she would have loved her own from Lorene, but she was full of love for just "youngsters," as she would say.

I wasn't trying to pay her back for the many times she fed me when we were poor and I was growing up. I wanted to give her back some of the love she used to put in those sandwiches and cookies and everything else she gave to me. And others. Cause love does make the world go round. Sure does.

Poor Heleva Lorene Shaky.

A Filet of Soul

Part I

ife is so big, so big . . . so huge, with so many things in it sometimes you wonder why some people get so little out of it and others find a way to get so much. But, then, I reads a lot and I read where your character is your destiny. Well, that means that the life that makes up that character is just too downright important not to think about.

But, is it something else, too? Something born inside you, that shapes and sifts the things that happen to you when you are young? Things that shape your thoughts about life and how you reacts to it? Even your dreams? Your choices? Now, I have seen a lot of things in my life and I know most everybody has a dream to love somebody and be loved by that somebody in return. That may go to character too! Like, how lonely are you? How much in need are you? After your character is born and grown, how slim or how great are your chances? For happiness?

Luella cried last night. Again.

This town is a little, ole place, I reckon like a many another little ole town in the world. A few well-off, maybe wealthy rich folks and a heap of poor folks. The people who has the most live on one side of town and us, we live over on this side of town. They white, we black.

But we have a clean little town on these four or five blocks; not all of it, but most of it. Cause some folks you can't teach em nothing much; but that kind live on both sides of town.

Lining our streets we have great big ole tall, beautiful trees. Some planted by our grandfolks or our parents, so they old, old and big and wide and beautiful. They set off the streets with the little, mostly wood houses set back from the street. And peoples here take good care of their lawns and all. Plant flowers and such.

But it seems like it's a old folks town. Ain't too much to do after your day's work but eat and sit out on the porch til you go to bed. Young people leave here bout soon as they get out'a school. Going somewhere else to college or something, or just going somewhere else, period.

I still live in my parents' home, rest they souls, they dead now, both of em. Me and my husband took care our parents

til they died. I married after I graduated school. Had children; they grown and gone now too. Husband dead; worked hisself to death. Sometimes I ask myself: For what?

Anyway, I'm alone now. Yes, sir. And I get lonely . . . sometime . . . but I'm so glad not to have nothing to do but what I want to do that I just keep to myself and mind my own business. I ain't old yet so I work two days a week, sometimes only one; just depends how I feel.

See, it's too hot here to get too busy at anything in the summertime. Even the flies and the mosquitoes buzz a minute, then sit and rest a couple of times on their way to bite something. It's that hot! Yes, mam! I work my yard, food and flowers, in the evenings or early mornings. Once that sun near bout hit the middle of the sky, I'm gone on in and pulling my shades down. And in the winter it's too cold to think of bein lonely when you trying to keep that wood stacked outside and in the house and finding ways to keep from going outside. Sides, I read books. I always did love books. They keep my mind full.

My neighbor Luella cried last night. Again.

See, some of these little houses sit mighty close together and sometime you be in your neighbor's house without trying to be. Luella's family house sits on the corner of Hope Street and Wayward Lane, and my house is right next to it on Hope Street. Her other neighbor is Mattie, she on Wayward Lane. My house has a long backyard, so my land runs the length of Luella's and Mattie's. All these houses started out belonging to our parents. Now . . . I am not a nosy person, but I can get interested some-time. A little fence and a thin wall . . . things carry.

Luella cried last night. Again.

Luella's mother, Sedalia, was in the same class in school with me and Mattie. She was a nice girl who could have been fast; if you know what I mean. Cause she was cute and the boys teased her a lot. She was a thin, nervous-type girl, always watching everything and everybody but her books. I loved books, but Sedalia seemed to like boys more, leastways one or two. She was poor, a poor family, but we was all poor. Don't care what you say though, she washed them two dresses she had so they was clean every day she came to school cept one or two times her daddy had beat her so bad she could hardly move. But she made it to school in a dress, then torn and mended by unlearned hands, but clean. I magine she rather be at school than at home no matter which way she had to come.

Oh, she worked too, from the earliest days, helping her mother wash clothes for others. Her mother was a thin, nervous woman, too. Sickly. Her father looked strong, but he drank; a lot. Sedalia was their only child cause they just didn't seem to be able to make any more children. Prob'ly was a good thing.

Then Sedalia started doing other folks' clothes on her own. Was always two or three big tin tubs half full of clothes sitting out back of the house. And she takin care of babies or the neighbors, whenever she could, cause they poor too. Her mama took the money, had to, cause her daddy didn't provide. But, enough of that, cause I done had enough of sad songs. Most everybody got one to sing.

But, now, I members just plain as day, we were in our last month of school and everybody was getting ready for the prom, such as it was. But, Sedalia, she knew she wasn't going because she had no prom clothes to wear. Nobody had asked her to go with them anyway. Scared to, I guess, scared of her papa.

The night of the prom Sedalia came anyway, still in one of her mended dresses. But, she didn't come in the brightly lighted, decorated gym where the prom was held, she stood outside, watching everybody else go in. When it seemed everyone was in, she sat on the grass, just looking at the building, listening to the blaring music, I guess.

Some of the boy-men, after a few stolen drinks of somebody's cheap wine, hatched a trick-plan to send a fellow out to play a little joke on Sedalia and ask her to dance on the grass. One of the boys she had liked and stared at all the time while he was with other girls at school volunteered to go do it. I'm shamed not one of us girls spoke up to shame them from doing it, I guess we wanted to laugh too. Thought it was all in fun and I even thought she might like to dance at her prom even if it was outside on the grass. It must take common sense to be a decent person, cause none of us had any.

That boy, Wiley, went out there and a flustered, needy, pitiful Sedalia smiled up at him and when he held out his hand, she reached for it. He was, maybe, supposed to run off then, but he didn't. Maybe cause of the tears in her eyes, but he didn't run off, he danced with her. Slowly, even though the music was a swing dance. He must have made her very happy because hope rose in her little wrung-out heart and when he stayed to dance a second time, she clung to him, even as he danced her across the green grass to the darkened trees, into the black of the night.

We few who had watched, finally lost interest when we

couldn't see them no more and we went back to our own heartthrobs and dancing. I was with my future husband, chile.

When Wiley finally came back in, a little rumpled with grass sticking to his clothes a bit, he was smiling. A few people gathered round him to hear and laugh. He sure could talk, that boy could. He had us laughing so hard, til I realized Sedalia was still out there by herself and I got sad for her. I went to look out the window to see if she had enjoyed being part of the prom anyway, but didn't see her anywhere; she was gone and I could only see the blackness of the night off up under them trees.

Then . . . graduation was over. Sedalia didn't attend, but I thought it might be because of a graduation dress. In all that flurry of school ending and life, at last, beginning, I forgot about her because soon I was sayin good-bye to my fiancé, my beau, and going off to that junior college my folks had saved so hard for.

When I came home for vacation, I saw Sedalia. I saw her walking home from the big market in our area, owned by a white man. Lord, she was big with child. I ran up to her, like a fool, asked her, "Sedalia! When did you get married? Did you marry Wiley?"

Sedalia stopped and shifted her brown paper bags and just looked at me. Hard. With angry, hurt eyes. She never answered me. She just turned and continued on her, now weighted, uncomfortable way.

I learned Sedalia had her baby at home. A girlbaby. That was Luella. Her mother helped her with the cord cutting and such, while her father cussed her out. Sedalia gave birth as she cried. Wiley didn't show up to see his baby girl. Never. When Sedalia got up from there she just went right on outside and began her life of bending over them tin tubs washing clothes for a living for her and her baby, Luella. By herself. I heard Wiley left town bout that time.

Now Mattie . . . Mattie was fast as they come. She was a nice girl, but a fast girl too! She was cute as a button and the boys surely liked her and she liked them back. I think she been married two or three times now. Got about five kids; three of her own, grown and gone out the house now (cept off and on), and two grandchildren. But, she don't have no real man. Yes, she's alone now. Raising them children for her daughters. Oh, she has a man-friend, but he don't stay there much. He says it's too many children and too much noise for him. Mattie had plenty brothers and sisters, a big family. But Mattie done run them all away now, cause she needs that house. They all still kinda friends, but Mattie done let them know there ain't no room in that house for them. They tried to sell it a few times since the parents died, but Mattie goes down to that city hall and cry and slobber and yell all over them white folks and they want her to leave so bad, they give her her way.

Anyway, two years of junior college was enough for me. I was closer than ever with my fiancé-beau and it seemed like I was pregnant, so we got married. He had a decent job and I got a job as an assistant teacher of kindergarten. We moved in with my parents cause I'm an only child myself and I didn't want to leave my mama no how! It's what people do in this little town anyway, cause we need to put our money together to keep the family going and keep the taxes and upkeep on the house they done sacrificed for already. You know, family.

As I be going to work or something, I would see Sedalia going out with baskets of washed and pressed clothes and coming in with bags of dirty clothes. I had Saturday and Sunday and holidays off; she didn't, except for church on Sundays. That preacher kept her coming to atone for her "sins." But, she would have gone anyway. She told me often, "God is the only friend I have, sides my mama, sometimes."

Her mother still tried to work, but she was tired and she was sick. Then she began to drink a bit herself; weary and disgusted I guess.

Then Sedalia's father died. He got a pauper's funeral because they used the little insurance money for a down payment on that house they had been renting that was already falling down.

The years continued to be hard years, passing slowly, for them. Then when Luella was about seven years old, Sedalia's mother died. Sedalia did use the little insurance money to bury her mother as best she could. It was a decent funeral and, Oh! how Sedalia held on to that little wooden coffin her mother was in. Seemed she hadn't held on to her mother enough when she was alive cause they was too busy surviving, but, to me? . . . There is always, always, time to take hold of the ones you love! Make yourself think about them! Do it! Fore it's too late!

Of course they went on living in that house. That was their home! It was rather decrepit now, cause never no man come to see them, but the preacher sometime. But he never ate there so that will tell you about their money and their times.

Sedalia still worked hard, even harder because she took over her mother's jobs. And when Luella was about nine or ten, Sedalia began to work her too. Luella missed a lot of school. No one ever bothered Sedalia about it because Sedalia would look at you with those hard, red-brown eyes and that deep frown on her thin face and tell you right where you could go in a hurry . . . and stay!

It was natural for me to watch Luella as she grew up. She was a real sad little girl who tried to smile. And when she did smile, her whole body smiled, she was so happy for the kind attention. She was not thin like her mother because Sedalia did feed her own and she kept a good kitchen. Sedalia even got that house painted, one side at a time, every six months or so, until it was all white at last and if one side was brighter for a while, then another, well . . . so what?

I had younger children and Luella seldom got to have playtime, but I gave her books so she could sort of keep up with something. I had cousins about her age and when I gave her dresses they had outgrown, I would get that smile as she pressed them to her little, plump body. Luella would run home with the dresses and things, then she would come back with them in her arms, quietly crying and say, "My motha'dear say she don't need no char'ty. We doin alright with God's help."

So, I began to get her to do little chores for me, sweep the porch and stairs Saturday mornings, things like that, and I would pay her. Sedalia never sent that money back.

I knew Luella liked other children, even little boys, child-like, you know, but Sedalia hated everybody but the preacher and no one could visit that house. Sedalia ran them off if they happen to forget and come visit anyway. Luella would watch them leave, looking through the windows as long as she could see them, then just looking out the window at nothing until her mother called her for chores or something. I had seen her with her hands on her narrow hips, and heard her when I couldn't see her, say, "You betta remember what I'm tellin you, girl! Leave peoples alone! Ain nobody ever gonna love you but me and yourself! You is ugly! Just ugly, that's all! They just gonna take vantage of you, leave you with somethin you don't need! Nor want! It's just you and me! Blive that! Cause you ugly and your mama is all that's ever gonna care bout if you eat or live! Me! So you keep your eyes on me and offa them boys! And them dumb girls, they don't mean you no good neither! They'll do mean things to you if you don't watch um!"

Over and over and over, through the years, Luella heard these words, almost daily.

Luella cried last night. Again.

Needless to say, Sedalia dressed Luella dowdily . . . clothes from the secondhand store, even when she started high school. The young woman still tried to smile. She was not ugly and the boys seemed to like her, as a friend, because she was always so . . . so worn looking, so sad. Hair just brushed back over old braids, always braided. While other girls wore bangs and curls in their smoothed hair. Her shoes, run over when she got them, ran over even more and soles soon slapped the ground as she walked, so she just stood still as much as possible or took them off. To hide the holes in her socks, she took them off too and went barefoot, saying, "I like my feet out . . . free!" But some of them stupid kids laughed, pointing fun at her feet. She still tried to smile, sometimes through tears she angrily brushed away, like the joke was with her, not on her.

Graduation time came and Luella had fair grades and was going to graduate. A boy in about the same shape Luella was in invited her to the prom. Sedalia seemed to go crazy when she heard the word "prom" and screamed at the top of her ragged voice, "Prom! Prom? You ain't going to no 'prom'! Are you crazy, with your plumb ugly self? That boy ain't gonna take you nowhere!" Then Sedalia broke into her own tears and ran to her small bedroom and slammed the door behind her.

Luella swallowed the huge lump in her throat, and fighting tears, told the boy she guess she better not go. He, the boy was named August something, turned to leave, saddened also, because who else could he ask? Luella leaned way out the door to watch him leave. "Everybody's always leaving. But not never me."

She missed the prom and started right to work on the jobs her mother had found and had ready for her. Said, "Get you some money! That's what we love! That's better than a man cause it won't leave you like a man will! It's all you ever gonna have, chile, cause ain't nobody else gonna love you like me, and do you right! That and the fact you just ugly. You ain't got nothin womanish and soft about you. That's what a man wants. He don't want nobody lookin like he do. Like a man do. Like you do!"

Luella would look through her tears at the cracked, shadowy, mirror in her little room and she didn't see she was ugly, but she began to question herself. "I ain't ugly, am I God? Why you had to make me ugly and everybody else pretty? Even Mama, she prettier than me. Oh, God, I don't want to say it, but I wish everybody pretty would die, just die, so somebody would just HAVE to love me and take me way from here."

So Luella turned to wanting a pet, a kitten. Even a bird.

Sedalia, hands on narrow hips, said, "Not here in my house! We don't need another mouth to feed round here that don't do no work for nothin! They full of germs anyway! I don't want none in my house!"

So Luella asked for a puppy, hope in her voice, "He can stay outside in the yard, Mama."

"No, she sho can't! Make noise and dogs eat plenty! Ain't I enough comp'ny for you? I'm mostly here when you are."

"Yes'm."

Luella finally stopped asking for things that were alive and would love her. She stopped crying too. She just worked. She set her heart aside and went straight ahead to the next job, to work, to work, to work. Sedalia took most all her money, saying, "You know this house needs things. I can't do it all. This house gonna be yours someday and it gonna be all you ev'a have, so we better keep it up and save for what it needs. What you need a dress for? You already got a church dress. And I don't see nobody running round here to ask you out, so where you goin? You don't need no new dress. You ain't goin nowhere." The prom boy, August, was already thrown out of Sedalia's mind. Dismissed.

Times went on like that and I heard and saw and felt so sorry, so low over Luella.

Then I got busy marrying my daughters off and my son coming home from college and moving away to the big city. One of my daughters' husbands took her away to the city too. But, you know, I didn't mind because I was tired of the busy life. Getting people up and off to school or work, then going myself. Washing and ironing all those clothes, cooking all those breakfasts and dinners and such. Finding money for all the special little things people getting grown need. Finding time for each one to have the piece of you they need. No . . . I didn't mind the change of pace in my life. Me and my husband could rest a bit.

Wasn't too long though before he liked to died from a sickness and I nursed him well and I told him, "Darlin, you just might as well get well and get up from there, cause we ain't had much of a life and I don't intend to spend the rest of my days as a nurse. You get well. We need to do some more living in this world and this house we worked for . . . now that the kids are gone. And we better hurry cause they may decide to come back!"

Well, he got well . . . and we had about five good years more, together, then he died on me. I was shamed for a while for telling him I wasn't going to be no nurse for him. If he was here . . . I'd be a nurse for him, gladly.

But . . . he's gone . . . and I'm still here . . . so I'm making a life for my own self now.

And Luella still cries, sometimes, at night.

It's a true shame bout all this death, but what are you going to do? Death happens whether you want it to or not.

Luella was about twenty-five years old when Sedalia got sick. Sedalia was an old woman before her time, not even forty years old. Luella nursed her mama all day every day and did her washing when her mother fitfully slept. I don't know when that chile slept herself. I didn't hear no crying though. I guess she was too tired to cry and just went to sleep when her head hit that pillow on the pad in her mama's room.

Even Sedalia had to see what a treasure she had because I was there helping her when I heard Sedalia tell her, "I don't know what I would do without you, Luella. I just don't know."

And I heard Luella answer, "You ain't supposed to know, Ma'dear. You ain't never gonna have to know."

That's when Sedalia told Luella in that, now, soft, raspy voice, "See the preacher bout the money, daughter. And I got death insurance for us . . . don't want to be no burden to ya, cause you gonna be alone . . . soon."

That's when I broke in, saying, "You gonna be alright, Sedalia. You gonna get well," cause Luella was bout to cry.

Sedalia died. And Luella spent every dime of that money on her mama's funeral. It was a very nice one and since all Sedalia ever did was go to church, all the church members came to the funeral. I helped Luella with the reception afterward. The little house was clean and everybody brought food. It was sad, but it was nice.

Luella took her mother's death hard because her mother was all she really knew in this world and Sedalia had made that girl think nobody else would ever love her. So? But Luella began to smile at the reception. Grateful that people had come. Most came to eat, but . . . they came.

The next few days, Luella was sad, but she brought a kitten home, and a puppy, and a bird, too. Happy things were running around her house and she laughed out loud.

Every Sunday, after church, Luella walked the three miles to the cemetery where her mother was buried and just sat there. Sometimes, most times, she would cry; other times, she would just sit there and think. She was always dressed to look nice at church. "I dress specially nice to go visit my mama cause she always said I was ugly."

Luella still cried some of those nights.

Anyway, that next Sunday we went to church, during the sermon I noticed the preacher kept looking at Luella and he seemed kinda nervous, stumbling on some of his words and thoughts. I thought it was because he was kindly aware of her bereavement. Later I wondered if it was because he was wondering how much she knew of her mother's business; and I remembered Sedalia had said among her last words, "See the preacher."

Later that same evening, the preacher, Preacher Watchem is his name, he came to what was now Luella's little house to see her. I was already there because we are friends; we have talked a lot over the fence, over the years, and she is like a daughter to me. I did not leave when she invited him in.

Preacher Watchem a'hemed and a'hawed round with words and it came out that he has some papers from Sedalia to do with business at the bank she had given him for safe-keeping. And ... he said . . . "A'hem and a'haw, round five hundred dollars, a'hem to give to you, Luella, at this time of her, a'hem, passing on to heaven. Now . . . I don't a'hem have it now, but I will have it in a day ... or two, church business, you know, we always helpin people. We gonna be hard put to it to get that much money cause the church need it so bad . . . a'hem, that be why Sister Sedalia wanted us to have it, a'hem and a'haw."

Luella mighta thought he was clearing his throat, but I knew he was having trouble getting his throat to bring them lyin words up to his lyin lips.

He handed Luella the papers as he cleared his throat again, "A'hemmm, these papers here have to do with Sister Sedalia's savings which she has put your name on. I know, a'hem, she would want the church to, a'hem, have some of this money cause she was a faithful daughter of God. A'haw, and since you gonna have most of this bank money, maybe you will see your way, praise God, to let the five hundred dollars, a'hem, stay in the hands of the Lord, thank You, Jesus."

Well, I knew Luella was still weak and soft from all she had been through, so I spoke up and I lied. "No, Reverend (I hated to call him that because I don't revere no one but Jesus and God and the twelve disciples)." But, I said, "No, Preacher Watchem, Sedalia told me . . . she wanted her daughter to have all that money and the money in the bank. Luella is a young woman without a husband, at this time, and no one else in the world to depend on."

The preacher spoke right up, "Well, she can depend on the church, Sister."

I spoke up, too. "Well, you just saying how the church don't have too much cause you got so many to help."

He spoke again, leaning toward me, "She got you, Sister."

I leaned back at him, "Preacher Watchem, you are right. I am her friend and she can depend on me for whatever I can do, and with that and God and the money her mother left her, too, well, she might can make it. But, she needs all the money possible, owed to her. Like her mother, Sister Sedalia, planned for her."

He leaned back in his chair and smiled at Luella, then a little drier smile at me, and said, "Sister, you know, money, a'hem, is the devil's weapon and he seems to be using you mighty strong to try to keep God from . . . (he tried to think of a better word, but couldn't) from . . . getting it."

I didn't lean back, I just said, "I'm trying to see that Sister Sedalia's money goes to who she wants it to go to. You are fighting for the money to stay in or go to your church; God, you say. Who is 'god' at your church? Cause I feel in my heart that if God had the money, He would give it to the neediest of all . . . Luella . . . and, by rights, it's already hers by her mother's words."

Well, the Preacher Watchem got tired of fooling with me and words, so he just said right out, "I knew Sister Sedalia as well, no, I knew her better than you! The church was highest in her mind, above all things! And I ain't 'fighting' over no money, I'm trying to do what's right!"

I didn't say anything. Just looked at him.

He asked, as he looked at me, slyly, "A'hem, she . . . only told you . . . what she wanted to do with this money?"

I lied again. "No . . . I blive there were two or three of us there. A little private prayer meeting while she was sick."

Luella had been looking back and forth at us as we talked, now she stared at me . . . and smiled.

Preacher Watchem wanted to stand on that money. "Did she, also, tell you . . . how much she had given me . . . the church?"

I asked God to forgive me as I lied again, "She kept account of it. I blive it's in one of her drawers. Luella ain't had time to look yet, everything so sudden and all, you know. When she finds it, we'll take these papers, and her list, to the bank . . . I don't know. I'm just tryin to do the sisterly thing like you would want me to do, Reverend. And, I'll probably go with her to the lawyers so the bank won't give her any trouble . . . either."

Preacher Watchem stood up, said, "A'hem, well, praise the Lord, Sister. You are an angel in our church. To speed you all along I will look through my papers and have the money here for her day after tomorrow . . . or so. Take her that long to get ready to tend to money business anyway, after such a loss as a mother."

Luella spoke, "Yes, sir."

Preacher Watchem gave her a look I can't explain and said, "Well, I'm gonna get on along now. Got more errands of the Lord's to tend to." He started toward the door, just a few steps away, then turned back to Luella, "You remember how good the Lord been to you, young lady, and give back to the church."

Luella smiled, gently, "I preciate you, Reverend Watchem. I can never forget the church." Then Preacher Watchem a'hemed and a'hawed his way out the door and on down the walk. Away.

As I went home, through a few broken slats in the fence we hadn't bothered to fix since it was a shortcut between our houses, I noticed them tin washtubs were empty of all clothes and dried out because Luella hadn't gone to pick up any washing jobs. Luella was not working. These were her first days off in more than eleven years. Except Sunday for church and now her cemetery visit.

The next day Luella asked me to go with her and we went to the bank. Wellll . . . at the bank, Luella was beneficiary to $4,308.10. Not a lot by some standards, but . . . Her mother had saved it, nickel by nickel, dime by dime, to leave to her child. Obviously. Because she never spent it on herself. I wondered, at last, did the woman, Sedalia, really believe all the terrible things she had told her daughter? About being ugly and unlovable. Was this another way to prepare her, Luella, for a bleak life? An empty future? I would have hated everyone who had set someone's life on this foolish path to a solitary, lonely life. But I didn't hate Sedalia because I knew whoever would do that, they must be in pain.

The money changed things a bit for Luella. The future did not seem so dark or bleak, even if she was alone, because she had a little nest-egg and it proved to her her mother was thinking of her. "I'm not gonna rush and spend it. I'm gonna wait for the money the preacher give me and then I'll do something round this house."

The house was full of secondhand furniture and castaway furniture given to Sedalia by people her mother or she worked for, except for her grandmother's trunk. They all had been proud of that trunk, no one could touch it, so it must have come to her new. Now it sat in Sedalia's old room with the imitation cream lace scarf across the top and a blue, slightly chipped vase filled with imitation flowers sitting in the middle of it. Luella kept the lace scarf washed and pressed and the chest dusted and oiled. Her heirloom. All the furniture was bits and pieces of different times and styles but all wood.

She still bathed in a tin tub and, being slightly plump made that very uncomfortable and she couldn't sit and soak in the hot water heated on the stove or lean back and drowse on a tired evening. She had to kneel in it, get on with the bath and get out. So she decided she would spend some of the bank money and build a real bathroom. She had started calling her neighbor-friend, "Aunty Corrine," and she asked her to help her work it all out.

Workmen were called and the bathroom was put in on the outside, an appendage to the old house. Luella went in that bathroom twenty times a day to look at the shiny new bathtub with polished brass fixtures. She hung new, pink fluffy curtains and threw an almost-new, round, pinkish rug on the floor beside it. Where she used to bathe once a week in that tin tub, now, for awhile, she bathed every day. It seemed to take so little to make her happy.

Time passed, quieting her pain, but not her loneliness. The kitten, puppy and bird were loving and wonderful, but they couldn't talk. Feeling guilt for spending money, Luella bought a little radio and, holding the package tightly under her arm, she rushed home to plug it in and turn it on. To have sound in the house. She dared not listen to it play the blues on that one little station, her heart and her body responded to it so strongly it kept her awake nights. She cried quietly those nights and couldn't understand what was wrong with her because she wasn't thinking of her mother.

But she could listen to quiet music in the evenings. Then she heard a different quiet in her house and realized how wonderfully serene it was. She would sit for hours, stroking her pets, just listening to the little radio that added a beautiful facet to her life.

But, then, there was Preacher Watchem; every Sunday he shook her hand and told her he was working on the money, but, "A'hem, times is hard, Sister, give the Lord time." Finally she thought she should speak to him herself privately.

In the meantime, though their lifestyles kept them from being friends, exactly, Mattie had gone to school with Sedalia and when she saw the bathroom being put in, she came tipping over to look at it. Mattie ohhhhed and ahhhhed as her fast eyes looked over the house, seeing the radio and the other little few things Luella had bought for herself.

Luella didn't want to be bothered with Mattie and her foolishness. She was trying to keep Mattie standing so to lead her back to the back door when Mattie sat herself down. "I surely don't mean to worry you, Luella, but I'm in such a fix right now. Not goin to last long, but, well, here it is now. I need to borrow ten dollars til a week or so. You know, I got these childrens over there I got to take care of. Lord, it's so hard sometime, but I do my duty, thank the Lord. So . . . I sure would preciate it if you have ten dollars . . ." Her voice dwindled off.

It so happened that Luella had started washing again for two of her best customers and she had twelve dollars in her purse. She gave ten dollars to Mattie, who left soon thereafter to go buy a pack of beer and a carton of oatmeal, then stuck the change in her own cache. Later she sat down with a beer, smiling and thinking about Luella's money. She didn't know about the bank money, but she did know Preacher Watchem was supposed to give Luella something.

When Corrine heard about the loan, she nodded her head thoughtfully and said, "You know, Mattie gets help from the city and a little bit more help from her daughter. It is not your job to take care of her responsibilities."

Luella smiled in sympathy with Mattie. "Well, it was just ten dollars and she gonna give it back."

Corrine laughed a short laugh, "You'll see Jesus walk in your front door before you'll see that ten dollars again. You hope she gives it back. Don't forget the way your mother saved that money; a very little bit at a time. Bending over them washtubs! And she didn't never borrow anything from Mattie and she was raising you all by herself. And it does not take long for money to be gone! For good. All of it!"

Luella nodded thoughtfully as she smoothed her dress. "You right, I'll ask her for it back."

"You can do that, but I would use that ten dollars to keep

from 'lending' her any more money. Tell her to pay that money back first! And Mattie talks to a whole lot of people," Corrine mused. "Have men started calling on you yet?"

Luella smiled sadly at the very ridiculous idea.

Several days had passed since Mattie had borrowed the ten dollars and she had had several visitors to drink up her beer and she had talked about Luella and "all that money her tightfisted mama left her!" A few fellows had leaned over the fence to see if Luella was working in her garden. Several, if Luella wasn't in her yard, would knock on the door, hard, as if they had a right to do it.

"How you doin, Luella? Girl, I haven't seen you since the other day. Why you always hiding your fine self away?"

Luella would answer, standing at the door, "How do? No, I haven't seen you since school days. I ain't hiding. I'm just livin. Ain nowhere to go to get out none."

"Oh, it's places to go, Ms. Luella! You been to the Hi Ball Inn yet?"

Luella laughed, "No, I have not! My church would put me on a cross if they was to think I . . ."

"Church don't have to know everything, Luella!"

Something in her brain told Luella this was not what she wanted. She had never thought anything special of the men who came anyway. "No sir, I don't blive I'm goin to the Hi Ball Inn."

When she saw the men, any of several, fix his body to step inside the house, she spoke quickly. "It's too soon after my mother passing for me to think thoughts like that . . . and I'm not taking company."

Once a man came by, she knew him from frequent, casual, public meetings in passing, and she let him, hesitantly, into her house. He pulled out a half-pint of gin and set there, drinking it all; then ate the food she had on her stove for her own dinner. After his dinner and returning to the living room, he commenced to take off his shoes, til Luella stopped him.

"Oh, Sam, you got to go now. Aunt Corrine will be here soon and I got to get ready to go to church with her."

A little drunk and full of food, all he could say was, "Huh?" She helped him up and into his jacket, all the while he sputtered about he would wait for her, "take a nap whilst you gone." His body wanted to lie down real bad.

But Luella persisted, doing everything to get him to the door. "You want me put out of church, Sam?! And ain't you still married to Dolly? No, I think you better go."

It was right after that that she decided not to talk to all who stopped "to holler" at her, out in the yard.

Corrine and Luella, in the end, laughed and talked about these men, Corrine thought she was showing mature good sense. "Any woman with a house can always have a man, cause most of em are always looking for a home."

Until. One morning, early, Luella stepped off the three little steps leading down to her backyard to do some work in her vegetable garden. A tall, brown, broad-shouldered man with his hair slicked back was shining in the morning sun. His overalls had been laundered and even had a crease down the front of the pant legs. And there he was, digging in her dirt! Had small, little piles of weeds he had already picked along the row. When she appeared, he smiled up at her with even white teeth and said, "You up awful late this morning, Ms. Luella. I looked over your fence and saw you needed some help with this here beautiful garden of yours." He worked as he spoke, slowly, lazily.

"You know, workin a garden relaxes me, so I thought I'd just hop on over your gate and get in a little work and pleasure fore I go to work on my job. I sho hope you don't mind?"

Well, Luella didn't know just what to say even if she hadn't been flustered when she looked at his grand smile lighting up his face and, then, into the deepest, dark-brown eyes she had ever looked into. She forgot there hadn't been many she had looked into anyway and especially none, as he stood up, his hands covered with her dirt, none looking down at her with such bold admiration.

She stammered, "Well . . . I . . . who are you? Do I know you?"

"Well, mam, no you don't. I ain't been in your nice little town long." He knelt down again. "My name is Silki Gains. Hey, come on down here, let's get to work on these here weeds."

Without another thought Luella looked around for her trowel and garden gloves; they were near him. She moved to reach for them and his hand closed around hers. "If these all the tools you got, let me finish this row. I got to go anyway; got to get to work, then you can take over."

He gave her a job. "Here," he let go of her outstretched hand that hung in the air a second in time. "You gather them little weed piles up and put em wherever you put em." Luella did as he bid her to do.

He finished the row, asked to wash his hands, went into her house, washed them, came out, put his hot hand on her shoulder and smiled and left for his job at the factory, saying over his shoulder, "See you next time!"

Luella was left standing in a now darkened garden with a trowel in her hand which she held tighter, trying to feel him as she remembered his smile, those eyes, that smooth skin, that thrilling voice.

She was up and out early the next morning. Hair brushed and tied back with a bright pretty kerchief. Dress, not new, but flowery fresh and too nice for yard work. She worked in her garden longer than she had worked in it for a long time, even under the steadily rising heat from the sun.

But . . . he didn't come.

Luella did that every day for a week. Silki hadn't come back. But the garden was doing grandly. Better than usual. The collard greens and mustard greens, onions, tomatoes, okra and a small plot of corn fairly flew up out of the ground. The vegetable garden looked healthy and smelled wonderful.

Things were growing inside Luella, also. Feelings. Thoughts of Silki made her heart thrill a little. Questions every young girl thinks about, only for Luella more so, because she was not such a young girl anymore. When she bathed, she rubbed the rag slowly over her body, looking at the skin on her plump arms and legs. Feeling the texture of the hair under her arms and everywhere. She examined her feet, her toenails. Her hands, her fingernails. "I will stop biting them."

That week she spent a little more bank money for a bottle of perfume with matching cologne and body powder, a pale lipstick and a jar of perfumed Vaseline for her skin, face and all. She thought of the money Preacher Watchem had of hers and she determined to put her foot (now with the polished toenails) down. "Preacher or not!" she spoke to the kitchen walls. "I need some new clothes! Spose he ask me out? I didn't see no weddin ring on his finger!"

Now, Luella didn't know, but Silki had been watching her

every morning. Corrine had noticed him, now and again, but didn't have time to just stand and watch him from behind her curtains, so she thought he might be in the area waiting for someone else, waiting mongst the trees for shade. But Silki had a plan.

Silki had given himself his new name. Actually he was born Cecil Ray Picket, the fifth child of nine, in a sharecropper shack in Mississippi. Even his busy mother noticed he was different from her other children; he was a dreamer, always staring off into space, sucking his tongue dreaming up ways to stay out of work and out of the sun out in the fields. Of the year or two he was allowed to go to the one-room school, he made good use of the time by learning to read and count. He was not far ahead of his class, but with more interest because the stories in the books were so different from his life and he hated his life.

Silki found every excuse to stay out of the fields with his father and was often "sick" enough to stay in the house with his mother. He was smart enough to do everything he could to help her around the shack; sweeping the floors, raking the tool- and junk-filled yard, feeding chickens and weeding the house garden and . . . holding a baby and reading to his mother as she worked. The woman was so proud to have a child who could read, her whole soul fairly fluttered to each word pushed through his lips by his determination.

As poor as they were, the mother gave him any change she could filch from the meager money for little things they just had to buy. He would, now and then, steal a penny, nickel (never a dime), when possible, slyly whispering to his mother it was one of his brothers who had stolen it (if it was missed) and that one would get a whipping. Needless to say, his brothers and sisters grew to hate him. Already having hard times and somebody gonna lie on you, too?!

Cecil Ray loved to go to town with his mother and once he stole a cheap magazine. He would have paid for it, but he just didn't have the money. The magazine was full of pictures of what looked like rich white life and movie stars. He loved the clothes on the men and the painted, fast beauty of the women wrapped in furs. It set a love of clothes on him for all his life. For pretty women too, though the ones he knew were not pretty in the same way the white ones in the magazine were. He did not know the white ones in the magazine were not pretty in that way either. He thought their beauty was natural.

He didn't know much about make-up beside lipstick. He stole a tube of lipstick for his mother and because she loved her son, the helper, she put it on for him when his father was not home because she did not want her husband to worry about the money.

She believed her son had stolen the lipstick. She was a Christian woman and did not want her son to be a thief. But Satan is a wily ole devil and he knows the human heart pretty well. The mother had never, never, ever had a tube of red lipstick or any other type of thing to make a woman pretty . . . so she kept it and pretended, as he said, he had found it. But, now, when her son stared off into space, she raised her eyes over her chores, watching him, and wondered and worried about his future, his life. She prayed for all her children, but especially Cecil Ray.

Even in the country, people find some way to have a little relaxation, so there is usually a place called a juke joint where you can get a little drink and socialize. There are people who look for places like this to gamble. They take away from the poorest of people what little has been left to them after their toil for the first somebody, their bosses, who kept all they could get away with from the poor laborers. Passing the juke joint on his way to and from errands run for his mother sometimes, Cecil Ray met other young men who did not like to work. Suitcase Brown, Cadillac Jim (though he didn't have a Cadillac, he had seen a rich white man in one when he was riding the rails into some town), Big Red, Little Black, Broadway were names of some of the passing gamblers. These men and others gambled for a living. They even took money from women and you must know how little the women made in such company.

Only a poor Fool would be caught between a rock gambler and a hard place woman, but the Fools came back every week for more of the same cheatin and lyin. Fool's gold glitters too!

Some of the gamblers had women they carried around with them, to keep the one or two dollars coming in to gamble with. Occasionally these men had cars, some old and gasping, but still running. A few of the men had a fine, sleek, new model automobile, but they usually didn't stay more than one night in a small town like the one Cecil Ray lived in.

These men became Cecil Ray's heroes. Not his father, who worked hard, wearing washed-out, faded overalls every day, sometimes unwashed for a week or two, and didn't have but one old threadbare suit he wore to church every Sunday. Had no automobile. Had a mule and a cow. And worked for the white man, who cheated him. Regular. He was what Cecil Ray called a fool. But the father lived and had nine children and a woman he loved.

Cecil Ray didn't hear, but seldom, about the gamblers shot, stabbed, starved and dead after they passed through the juke joint. He just saw what looked like "the good life." That's when he changed his name, secretly, to "Silki."

When he was fifteen years old he began to sneak out and stay out til the early morning hours. He had even had his try at nooky because he was good looking, and with any money he won he went into town and bought clothes or won a jacket or shirt off someone's back. When he was sixteen he kissed his crying mother good-bye and left . . . for good. Never did plan to come back, ever.

In his moving around from place to place he came to Oscum, where Luella lived. Doing poorly right then, he took a job at the factory there in order to make friends and beat them out of their paychecks.

He was a juke joint man, so he had met Mattie, Luella's neighbor. Hers was a place to go for a drink or a light poker game sometime. There, he had heard about Luella coming into some money from her mother's death. Then he had watched her, just in passing, until he knew her rhythm. Then one morning, that morning, clean and fresh because he had a lady who washed, lightly starched and pressed his overalls, he appeared in Luella's yard.

After that first morning he had arisen early or had not even gotten to bed the previous night, passed by and sat in Mattie's yard behind the wild shrubbery to see if Luella looked for him. He was pleased with himself when he saw she tried to look better when she came out of her house to work her garden. He saw her looking over the gate, up and down the quiet street, looking for him, he was sure.

About seven days later, he was in her yard when Luella

came out, less dressed because she had given him up. Her heart leapt in her untouched breast. Joy filled her mind and slithered on down her oiled body to her fingertips and toes.

The garden was well taken care of because she had done a lot of work just to stay outside, but Silki found things to do that made him decide not to go to work. He had been having a little trouble there anyway.

Luella just stood there, enjoying looking at the young man, looking into his deep brown eyes. Since he was already working at something that didn't need anything, she started working herself. He had taken his shirt off so as they passed each other in the garden or exchanged tools, she felt the smooth skin of his arm, his shoulder, his hands. He knew every move she made and why she made it. He bumped into her many times on purpose. You know.

As the sun rose higher in the clear, blue sky, Luella asked, "Don't you have to get to work, Mr. Silki?"

"Sposed to, but I am enjoying myself right here with you. They can get along alright without me one day. Sides, I left my lunch at home anyway and it's too far to go back."

"Ohhhhh."

Silki smiled at her, squinting in the sun which made him cuter, "I'll just help you round here and then I'll go find somethin to eat and somethin to do with the rest of the day."

Luella frowned and repeated, "Ohhhhhhh."

"Say," he spoke, "you got a hammer and some nails? We can shore up and steady your shed." He laughed, "It needs some help. Fact is, I see lots of things round here could stand a little help."

He saw her look around the well-kept yard.

Silki laughed, "Not a lot of help, but a little help, so things don't get worser."

Later, he hummed a little as he worked. A man sound. He hit his thumb a few times which meant he could sit down and rub it until it felt better. This was not his line of work, but he did do some good.

Luella had been running in and out of the house, preparing his lunch so he would not have to leave. At last, everything was ready and it was time for lunch. "Lunchtime," she called from the back door.

Silki struggled up with a frown from the spot he had quickly slumped down to when she ran into the house. The frown turned into his bright smile as he strode around the shed and into Luella's sight.

"Lunchtime? Lord, has it been that long? I guess it has because my stomach just told me I'm hungry! Girl, you didn't have to go to no trouble for me. I coulda found somethin somewhere."

Luella's heart felt like a wife's. "Come on in and wash your hands." He went in like he had done it a thousand times.

Luella had set a lovely table for him. Garden vegetables and a crisply fried pork chop that was tender in the middle and hot bread. "I know this ain't as nice as you are used to, but I hope it will do. Butter beans out the garden, and rice. I got some gravy for them pork chops. And plenty butter for that cornbread. I buy it fresh from the cow man. You want buttermilk or red soda?"

Silki thought a short minute. "I love iced tea, but red pop will suit me just fine."

Luella wished she had made iced tea. There wasn't even

any tea in the house. "Well, there sure will be next time," she thought to herself.

They talked and laughed as they ate and Luella saw he had two side teeth missing; she smiled because she had the same two missing, one on each side. But that didn't take anything away from his charm. When he smiled he had a way of tightening his cheeks so dimples came in them and the missing side teeth were hidden. Luella decided to practice that smile to hide her own missing teeth.

After lunch, Silki just had to sit a minute because "the house I live in is so noisy and I don't get a good night's sleep at night, sometimes. Lemme just sit here a minute, Ms. Luella. My stomach feels so good and my mouth is so happy! I'll just close my eyes a minute and draw in all this good feelin you got in your house."

Luella nodded her head, grinning, "You just go on and rest. You been workin in that sun all mornin! I'll just go on in the kitchen and clean up a bit."

Silki fell asleep because he hadn't been to sleep at all last night, he'd been gambling. When Luella came out of the kitchen, drying her hands, she smiled at him sleeping. She tiptoed to her bedroom and got a pillow and took a quilt from her grandma's chest. She covered him and inch by inch got the pillow under his head. He seldom slept well because he was always around people he could not trust enough to sleep soundly. So not fearing Luella, he slept deeply all the rest of that day far into the evening until even Luella got worried about what her neighbors would think.

When it was plumb dark she woke him up. His eyes rolled round in their sockets, because it took him a minute to remember where he was. He had trained himself not to call out names, so he didn't say a word until he was sure of where he was. "Oh! Ms. Luella! I done overslept. I got to go. I didn't mean to stay here on you all day."

"Mr. Silki, you ain't done nothin wrong. Just it's late and I don't want my neighbors to think I'm doin wrong up in here."

"No mam! Ms. Luella!"

"You need to just call me Luella, not Ms. Luella."

"And you need to just call me Silki, not Mr. Silki. Can I stop and see you again, Ms. Lu—ah, Luella?"

"Why sure. You been a big help to me. I preciate you."

Silki took her hand and led her to the door, thrilling her. He kissed that hand as he went out the door. Thrilling her some more. He went out and closed the door behind him. Luella leaned against it, smiling that smile that lit up her whole body and just thrilling all over her whole self. "Silki," she whispered out loud. "And Aunt Corrine can't say nothin bout you cause you worked and helped me."

Now, Silki thought Luella was nice, but he didn't like her for himself and he certainly didn't love her . . . or plan to. She was not fly enough for him. "She ain nowhere near them pretty women I done seen. But she can cook!" The women he did have, or know, were the make-up, baubles and bangles, straightened and curly hair slick with scented pomade kind. They wore tight red, green, yellow, blue or purple dresses; some sparkled. Most of these women "made" money, the little that was out there. They could cook, too, when they had time and the inclination. Silki got some of the money, some of the time, from one or another.

Silki was selfish and it extended to his loving. His love-making. He satisfied himself first and always. Well, a woman, good or bad, gets tired of that. But some good women don't know it could be better, while the others knew it could be and would be, because they didn't keep Silki very long. First the money began to dribble in, then stopped. And a beating from him didn't improve things. He got cut once or twice on his behind. Until at last, they were gone or he was gone.

That's where he was now. Kinda on the outs. He knew he could do better in a big city. Memphis, Birmingham? Atlanta! He wasn't ready for New York yet, he thought, but maybe soon . . . Chicago. He just needed some money . . . big money.

Lunch at Luella's house came to be a regular thing. He said, "Luella, I just can't help it! I just can't eat that slop at those cafes no more. Your cookin done spoilt me."

Luella would smile and serve him, day after day. It was his one good meal a day; sometime the only one a day. The money from his job, he gambled away, always losing. He was a dumb slick and all the fellows knew it, so they always set him up and played on him together. Cheating, like he was trying to do.

Corrine had, of course, noticed Silki and his growing friendship with Luella. She didn't know or understand Silki, but she had a good idea what he was doing. She knew Luella was starry-eyed and spending her money on plenty food. Luella was even getting plumper because of all the cooking she was doing for Silki. Now, she even fixed him a bag of food for him to take with him and eat later. One thing he never did, he never asked her for cash money. He had his plan.

On one of Corrine's visits through the fence to see Luella,

she asked her, "Has that Preacher Watchem paid you your mother's money yet?"

"No mam, and I sure do need it."

Corrine cleared her throat, "I reckon you do, feeding that young man like you do."

"Well, I eat, too."

"Yes, but you the only one payin for it."

Luella smiled in spite of herself, "Well, he works round the house and yard."

Corrine took a moment before she said, "It would cost you almost nothin to pay somebody to do what he does."

"But . . . I like him, Aunty, I think I love him."

"Why? How?"

Luella squirmed a bit in her chair. "Well . . . it's just a feelin. I think he loves me too."

"Why? How?"

"He's nice to me."

"Luella, sweetheart . . . you don't know what nice is. Or what love is." Luella turned her face away from her friend. Corrine continued anyway. "You know, Luella, people think you got money."

"Wellll . . ."

"Well, you don't. You got a little savings your mama and you worked for. It won't last long. I'm not going to ask you how much you have left in that bank, but you be careful because it will be gone and something tells me Mr. Silki will be gone, too. And all the food and comforts you have spent your money on will have been flushed down the toilet. You know what I mean? And you will have nothing to show for it except empty toilet paper wrappings. Even the doodoo will be gone."

Luella hurried to answer, "Oh, no, no. I only spend what I make washing clothes. I started picking up my old customers again. And he don't never ask me for no money, no way."

Corrine shook her head sadly, "He don't have to. He's eating and sleeping all day. Free."

Luella looked into Corrine's face and she looked so pitiful to Corrine when she said, "But, Aunty, he's talkin bout takin me off to a big city cause they don't pay nothing in that factory here and his foreman don't like him noway."

"I guess not. They like people to come to work."

Luella reached for Corrine, holding her hand out to her, looking so pitiful, begging to be able to believe her love had come. "I'm thinkin bout goin with him to see about it. I ain never been to no big city. Picture shows, big stores, pretty parks and things. I can even get a better kinda job." She smiled a combination of sad and happy. "We gonna be married and buy a house up there. Just think, Aunty, I'll have a husband. And a whole new life!"

Corrine felt like crying for her friend. "Oh, Luella, sweetheart, ask yourself a few things. You have a good life here. Someday some man will come along who will really love you. He'll help you keep what you have and help you build on it. You are a nice-looking woman. You are plump, but you are built real nice. You are going to be loved for yourself." Luella turned her face away again and Corrine knew she did not want to hear about some other day. She kept talking anyway.

"Luella, you talk about love. Let me tell you . . . You know all those plants in your yard? Your trees? Well, the seed came first, long, long before the leaf or the fruit. Learn a little about what it is to love. First the seed, then the soil, then the rain, then the sun, then the care, and even after all that, it still has to ripen so when you put it in your mouth to chew, the taste is not bitter, does not make you want to spit it out. Kindness, honesty, truth all go into making love. You don't know the first thing about Silki after he leaves your yard. Have you been, ever, to his house? Has he ever handed you a dime and thanked you for doing what you do for him, by doing some of it for you? He could take you out to dinner."

Luella hastened to say, "Oh, he don't like that cafe food."

Corrine hastened to say, "Well, let him take you and let you see if you like it! Instead of you always in that kitchen, no matter how hot or cold, cooking your food, bought with your money, cooked on your stove in your pots served on your plates which are later washed with your hands. What does he do for you?"

"He . . . loves me."

Corrine didn't want to hurt her friend, but the truth is the light. "I bet you if you don't do any of all the things I just said to you, you givin him, I bet he won't come back."

Luella didn't want to hurt Aunt Corrine. She wanted to tell her to get out of her house, but couldn't, so she cried. Aunty took her into her arms. "Oh, baby, I didn't mean to hurt you. But it's some things you just have to think about. If Mr. Silki so sharp and smart and hot, what's he doing in this little town? Why isn't he in some big city already? Why you have to feed him? I bet he has to use your money to even get to the big city."

Luella spoke into Aunty's shoulder, she didn't want to move from the warmth of Corrine's love. "Married people do that."

Aunt Corrine lost some more of her patience. "Fools do it too! And you are not married to him yet! All you got from him is talk! He gets good food and you even wash his clothes. He bathes in your tub and sleeps during the day. What he do at night, Luella? All night?"

Luella didn't want to think about that. This was love walked into her dead and dreary life. LOVE, and she was going to hold on to it if it was the last thing she did! She straightened herself out of Aunty's arms and made up her mind to go see that Preacher Watchem and get her money ... before Silki decided to up and leave without her.

And that's what she did ... the next Sunday. She sat through the sermon and when church was out and Preacher Watchem was standing in the wide-open doorway, shaking hands with his parishioners, Luella was in line and when it came her turn, the crowd was still milling around.

Luella frowned and said, "Preacher Watchem, I have waited all these months for you to bring me my money my poor dead mother left with you for me. You promised her, and you promised me, my five hundred dollars! I need my money! I am all alone now. I'm washing clothes to live, just like my mother did. I need my money!"

Silence dropped on the crowd like fog and everybody turned to hear his answer.

Preacher Watchem sputtered and spit as he tried to find words to make everybody look some other place, but Luella stood her ground.

People mumbled, "Five hundred dollars?"

Other people, women said, "That chile sure is washing clothes for a livin'!"

So they closed in around him, their beloved preacher, and he said, "I am truly sorry, daughter, the Lord's work keep me so busy, I forget sometime. I will be there directly tomorrow."

Luella didn't move, said, "No, Preacher Watchem. I need my money today. Can't wait no more. You said that three, four months ago. I waited for you every evening after I got through my hard work. Today, Preacher Watchem, today!"

Now, I will tell you something; it was her love of Silki and his needs that gave Luella such attitude and nerve. She might not have done that to the preacher if it was just for herself.

Preacher Watchem made a few quick a'hems and a'haws and said, "I'll be there today, then, directly, daughter. You must forgive me for taking so long, but so many people in my flock need so much. I just didn't—"

Luella interrupted him. "I'll wait right here, Preacher Watchem. I won't go home til you repay me what is mine."

Wasn't too much going on in that town anyway, so for some reason the whole congregation waited with her. Well, it was something new to talk about, "how that Luella talked to the preacher! that way! My, my, indeed."

But . . . Preacher Watchem paid Luella that day.

Five hundred dollars seemed like a million dollars to Luella so she gave Corrine one hundred dollars to keep for her and put one hundred dollars in the bank. Then, Luella put the rest of the money away in her grandmother's trunk. Her heart was full and ready to tell Silki they could get ready to go.

Part II

Silki's life was at one of its lowest ebbs. He had lost his last $1.50. It was 9:30 P.M. on Friday night. It would be nine and a half hours before he could go to Luella's. He had lost his job a week ago because he was never there anyway. His last woman had moved her new man in and put his own suitcase, not on the steps, but on the walkway by the gate near the street. He was ready to cry, but, instead, told himself, "I am a man and a man don't cry."

Mattie had been back several times to borrow money from Luella and the woman could beg so good, Luella had relented and loaned her neighbor some money. Five dollars, then ten dollars and once, when Mattie cried so hard about feeding her grandchildren, twenty dollars. So, now, it was a regular item on Mattie's list to go over there once or twice a month to borrow whatever she could.

Mattie had, also, been at church when Luella spoke with Preacher Watchem and knew Luella had five hundred dollars. Five hundred dollars!! But she had had too many gins and beers the night before and had slept late on this day. She had stuck empty, sour milk bottles into the mouths of her grandchildren, three and four years old, so they would be quiet and let her sleep. "Shet your mouf up so Granny get to sleep one more minute." Around eleven o'clock the four-year-old got up and went to see what he could find in the dirty kitchen on the greasy stove; the three-year-old followed him, leaving Granny in bed on the gray pillow, her mouth open dribbling saliva from the corner of her mouth.

The persistent sounds of pots falling, dishes breaking, finally woke Granny Mattie up. She was angry. She reached out a hand, feeling for the babies in the bed and they were not there. "What the hell you basta'ds doin in there?!"

So, Mattie's day had begun. She had intended to go over to Luella's and get "a little money to feed these kids, they hungry!" She was hungry, too, and had left last night's beans on the stove all night in the warm weather. "Sour! Ugh!" Mattie sat down a minute to get her thoughts together.

Silki had picked up his suitcase during the night, out of sight of prying eyes. He washed up in the cafe bathroom and smoothed out his clothes as best he could, put on his freshest shirt and made it on over to Luella's house, carrying his cardboard suitcase in one hand, a large paper sack in the other hand and two cheap suits, on hangers, over his shoulder. "Hell, if she love me, she gon help me or I'm gonna leave her ass alone, too!"

You cannot imagine . . . the fear that flew out of his mind and the joy that flew in and took its place when Luella met him at the door, throwing her arms around his neck saying, sweetly, "Silki, my darlin. We can leave and go on way from here. Now! Preacher Watchem gave me my money! Five hundred dollars! We can get married!"

You already know Silki had never even seen, much less had, five hundred dollars at one time. Nor two hundred, not even one hundred dollars. The most money Silki had held at one time was seventy dollars, which he took to bed with him, clasping it to his chest and thinking all the night about how his future was changing, looking up, getting somewhere. At last! This, until he went out that night and lost it back to his world.

Now, Silki said, "Five hundred whole dollars?! Baby? Darlin!"

The plans for the trip rushed right on in.

First, Silki wanted to go down to the little town section and buy a few things for the trip on the way to pick up the tickets to some place he hadn't decided on yet. "Baby, I . . . we need to pick up a few things for the trip! This gonna be the best thing you ever done. This place too small for the life I want to give you!"

Luella blushed to her toes because he had never held her so tight before. It was love! "I know it. Aunt Corrine gonna take this house until we decide where we gonna live. There's gonna be much better jobs in the new city for us and we got to get married right away so our dreams can start coming true!"

With the money on his mind, Silki continued, "Baby, we got to take care of first things first. First, let's go get something to pack so when we get to the city they don't think we are country folks. We got to look good! I want my baby to be the best she can be; you already beautiful. We . . . you just need some clothes that fit your looks. So, arm in arm, hand in hand, we can get off the bus lookin good!"

At that moment, Mattie knocked at the door. Luella peeked out of her window, "That's Mattie!" Silki answered the door because, now, he was the man of the house and he was sure he knew what Mattie was after.

"Hey, Sister Mattie! How you doin?"

Taken aback for a few seconds, Mattie answered, "I ain doin no good, Silki. I need to talk to Luella for a minute." She winked at Silki, but he didn't wink back.

Silki stepped back to let her in, but said, "Well, we in a important talk right now. You got to come back some other time." He had a second thought, "Or you can tell me what you want."

Mattie thought that might be encouraging because she had told Silki about Luella in the first place. Mattie asked, "Silki, my kids is hungry and I am sick and I ain got no food from the city for the week and I don't know what I'm gonna do. I need five or ten dollars . . . just til I get some money from my daughters . . . a day or two."

Silki answered, "Oh, Sister Mattie, you have caught us at a bad time. We just sittin here tryin to figure out our own way. We wish we could help you, but we just sure can't . . . right now. Try again in a few days and things might be better."

Mattie got angry, "Well, she just got . . . Preacher Watchem just . . ." but she couldn't say it for some reason. So she decided to say, "Well, okay. But, you know how it is to be hungry!"

Silki smiled, "Not for a long time, since I . . . Mattie, we can't do you no help today. We'll see you in a few days."

Mattie frowned at her former friend, then turned to walk slowly away. She looked back at the closed door. Her mind was going more than a mile a minute. "I am goin to come back! That's my friend's money, not that Silki's money! I hope she ain no fool bout him cause he sure don't mean her no good!"

It is so hard to look, talk and think between the people that pass through your life leaving sugar, sometimes, and shit, sometimes. Sometimes it's hard to figure out what and who have thoughts that will not hurt you, will not take from you your life, or the pieces of things that make up your life. Like your love, your heart and your mind. Must you, yourself, become hardened? Do you need a certain amount of larceny, malice and greed in your mind to perceive it in others? And even then, you are still only human, subject to error. So Luella was not smart . . . nor was she a fool. Luella was human.

When Luella and Silki returned from shopping in the late afternoon, he was already dressed in his natty, cheap, new suit and was stepping gingerly along the dusty street. Luella was loaded down with a box and several bags of her new finery, including nightwear for her wedding night. They were both smiling, but only Luella was sweating. She was proud of Silki.

She was proud of her house when it came into view. Proud of herself. She was a woman. Still shy, but excited, she spoke, "Let's go in the front door this time. We goin first class, like you say, so we'll go in the front door!"

They turned in the front gate and there on the front door was a black, funereal wreath; forgotten because the front door was seldom used. Silki pointed to the wreath as he hesitated on the front steps, "I don't like them things to be nowhere round me. I gets the creeps or somethin!"

Luella laughed, happily, juggled the packages and loosened the wreath. The wreath fell to the floor of the porch. She stepped over it, looking back at Silki, who had taken his new handkerchief from his pocket and was dusting off his shoes. She said, "Come on in, Silki. That wreath ain gonna bother you none. It's just a sign my mother is gone; rest her soul. This gonna be your home now."

Silki stepped over the threshold, looking at the wreath distastefully. "Just the same, I don't like bein round death."

Luella, still laughing happily, "Well, close the door, darlin, and you won't see it. Sides, ain't no death in here, only me and you, and we full of life and gettin ready to live." She set her packages down and reached to hug him.

He let her touch him a moment, then backed away looking at his new watch. "Yeah, baby, yeah, and we don't have much time. That bus leaves at five-thirty this evenin and it's three o'clock now. You shoulda done your shoppin by yourself, cause I got plenty things to do fore I leave here."

Luella turned back to her packages, opening them. Still

happy. "I just wanted my new travelin clothes to have some class, like you say." She held up the red dress he had picked out. "And with you there to pick em out. I'ma look good for you, Silki, you ain't gonna be shamed of me." In a softer, placating tone, she said, "You ain't gonna be sorry."

Silki shook his head as he looked over her shoulder at the mirror, "I know I won't be sorry. I'm too young to be sorry." He smiled at his image in the mirror.

While Silki and Luella had been talking, Mattie had come from her house next door and was creeping around the side of Luella's house trying to hear what was going on inside. Adjusting his new shirt collar, Silki was oblivious to everything else. At the same time, that little something at the back of Luella's mind was worrying her.

"Silki? You sure you don't think I'm too . . . old for you? For to be your wife? After all, you are only twenty and I am twenty-four."

Still looking at himself in the mirror, "If I did I would'na fallen in love with you, would I?"

Looking at him with all the long, unused yearning in her eyes, Luella asked, "Say it again, Silki . . . Do you really, really, really love me?"

Silki finally gave Luella his attention and took her face in his hands and lied. Anyone else in the world might have seen the lie, but Luella was blinded by her need and feelings for him. Yet . . . it wasn't really him; he was just handsome and the first man to really give her even such attention as he had. He stood to her for a chance at life. He said, "I really, really, really love you!" as he stepped back from her.

Luella held the red dress to her breast and in a pathetic voice only a lukewarm, hard heart could ignore, said,

"Nobody . . . just nobody ever said that to me before. Not one man. Not nobody."

Silki let her hug him again. "Well, you got the man of all men now, baby! When I say it, it's enough to last you the rest of your life!"

Overcome, Luella dropped the dress and tried to hug him closer, saying, "I blive I love you . . . I KNOW I love you!"

Disentangling himself from her embrace, Silki said, "Look babe, I better get on down the road and get some things done so our trip to the big city will be what I planned for ya! You know, when we get to the city bout nine o'clock tonight, we gonna check into the hotel, then I got a special club I want you to see and a whole lot more things." He kissed her forehead, then stood back to see how that worked. He had never been intimate with Luella. At all.

It wasn't that Luella was not attractive . . . she was. Even her plumpness was not fat, it just gave her a fuller, softer look. But Silki had never asked her to sleep with him, nor touched her in any way suggestive of making love. It was a perverse thing that he had no interest in making love to someone who was not trying to use him in some way. Like a hustler would do.

Now, he said, "Oh! I forgot; you got all the money ready?"

Luella frowned because she had promised Corrine not to tell him all her business until he proved hisself and she hates to lie. "Well . . . Preacher Watchem didn't give me ALL the money. And they wouldn't let me borrow on this old house, like you said. All the money you said we needed, seven or eight thousand dollars." Her eyes and mouth opened wide at the very thought of such an amount of money. She hadn't needed Aunt Corrine to tell her about that! "Til Mama's business is all settled and everything is in my name, they wouldn't lend me nothin."

Silki's face was distorted with disgust.

Luella hurried to tell her man, "They let me have three hundred dollars and we done spent over one hundred of that, but we got bout two hundred left, and that will hold us til we get married and find out for sure that we want to move to Memphis," she almost whispered, "won't it?"

Silki's face was two folds full of disgust and chagrin. "Awwwwww, I wanted to show you the best time of your life. I want to be the first one to make you really live. Really show you bout life!"

With stars trickling all over her eyes, Luella grabbed Silki around his neck, but Silki pulled away, angrily. "Well. . . . that's messed up! I betta go!" Then he had another second thought and put his arm around her waist. "Say baby . . . you betta let me carry that money." He laughed softly. "That's a man's job, you know."

With Aunt Corrine's words ringing in her brain, Luella looked nervous and said, "I don't have it all with me. I was scared to carry ALL that money cause I ain't never had more'n five or ten dollars with me all the time Mama was living and then I was goin to get somethin for her."

Silki took his arm away, abruptly, "How much you got wit cha?"

"Bout a hundred and fifty dollars left from shoppin and the tickets."

"Where is the rest of it?" Silki held out his hand for the money.

"Aunt Corrine is holdin it for us til I come by."

Silki rolled his eyes to heaven, "Well, you betta hurry on

by there then! We got to be at the bus station at five o'clock straight out! I'll meet you there. Now . . . give me the money you got."

Mattie had been listening at the door and chose that moment to knock on the door. "Ooooo, Luella? You home?" She knocked again and said, "It's me, Mattie!"

Annoyed, Luella whispered unnecessarily, "That's Mattie!" She started to put the money back into her purse, hurriedly. Silki heaved a great disgusted sigh, and said, "I know," still holding his hand out for the money.

Mattie decided to try the back door knob and the door opened. With an obvious, deceitful smile on her face, she says, "Oh, I didn't know you had company! I could come back another time."

Silki said, "You still can." But Mattie ignored him.

Luella was uncomfortable and flustered with so many things happening so fast around her. "No need to do that. We in a hurry anyway. Silki was just leavin." She looked at Silki's hand which is still reaching out to her for the money and is ashamed to give him money in front of Mattie. Luella sighed and opened her purse again, saying, "Ahhh, yes, well . . . here," handed him a few bills, "this is just a little somethin for helpin me with all these packages."

Mattie eyes weren't big enough or quick enough to see all she wanted to see, but she saw the money, the boxes, the bags and the red dress. "Sho musta been a lot of help. And I ain't never seen that there suit before either, Silki. And new shoes!"

Silki dropped the money Luella had just given him on the floor, on purpose, so Mattie could see what a man he is.

Mattie did. "SHO musta been a lotta help . . . or somethin!"

Silki smiles a satisfied smile, even with the little money, fifty dollars or so, he has in his hand. "Okay, baby, I'm gone now. Don't forget to give yourself plenty time to get to Aunty's house and everything. It's most four o'clock now."

Momentarily, Luella is happy. "Alright! See you at five o'clock." She watched Silki as he crossed the yard to her backyard gate, his head bent, counting the money. She sighed, deeply, and slowly closed the door.

Trying to ignore Mattie, Luella began bustling around the room. Clearing the boxes, folding her new clothes, running to her room for her grandmother's cardboard suitcase. Glowering, Mattie just watched her, standing with her hands on her hips. Finally Luella said, "Well, how you doin, Mattie?" She didn't wait for an answer, she just asked, "What do you want? You can see I'm in a awful hurry. I got a lot to do . . . I got a pointment at five o'clock."

Mattie raised one hand in the air, "You sposed to be a church woman. Your mama raised you right and took good care'a you. Now . . . you ain't showing no principleations. You ought to follow in her footsteps! Yeah . . . she was a good woman! You ain nothin but a fool!"

Luella had been changing clothes and was now in her new slip. She stopped and looked at Mattie, surprised. "I ain't in your shoes and I am not in your house. And, now, I'm supposed to help myself! I'm takin care of me and I'm gonna be a real woman with a real man, and if you don't like it, don't stand there and watch me be something I always wanted to be . . . somebody's somethin!" In a gentler tone, Luella added, "My mama wasn't ever anybody's woman."

Mattie misread the tone. "Girl, you too old to be a fool . . . talkin bout bein somebody's woman! Huh! And your mama musta had somebody cause she had you! So what if he left? They all leave. At least, she didn't go off with him, like you doin!'"

Luella tried to continue preparing her clothes and talk to Mattie at the same time. "I ain't too old! And I ain't no fool! And I am somebody's woman! I want a man who won't leave. MY man! And I GOT one! Now . . . you stop tryin to tear me down . . . make me sad . . . and lonely again."

But Mattie was too selfish to hear. "Girl! Money is important. You ain sposed to give it away! To no man! What would your mama say?"

Exasperated, Luella said, "My mother dear is dead. I ain't. I'm standin here, breathing . . . right in front of you. I am ALIVE. I'm alone. You had you somethin to get your children with. I ain't got nothin but some little money . . . what won't give me no babies . . . and a big empty life. So don't you tell me what I'm sposed to do . . . you go do what you sposed to do. And pay me back my money."

Mattie didn't really want to hurt Luella and ruin her chances for some of that money, but she wasn't all that smart herself. She said, "You twenty-five years old!"

Luella gave pound for pound, "You forty-eight years old. Why I got to be better'n you? You ain't been so smart. Ain't no man at your house, that blongs to you. Ain't no man waiting on you, workin for you." Again, Luella's tone softened because she meant nobody any harm. "Mattie . . . I'm me. I want to be me. I don't want to listen to nobody no more, but me. And (lying), I'm twenty-two years old."

Mattie, encouraged by Luella's softer tone again, "You buyin that man! And bought men ain gonna stay no longer than the money. When it gone . . . they gone too! You ain got nough money to hold that Silki man long enough to write 'my man' on a cupcake!" Mattie looked at Luella's sad, little profile as she turned her head away and she realized she was hurting her own chances. She changed her tune to a friendlier one.

"You ought to save that money and help some of your friends that you can count on when you down. Now, I don't need," Mattie stopped to smooth her dress and straighten her shoulders, "no help. But . . . I could use some. And . . . and you could do it. You don't need nothin . . . you got everthin. And you ain down . . . You young. You ain't got no kids. And me? I am down, right long in here . . . now. If you could give . . ."

Sadly, Luella answered her, "If I could give you my dreams, you wouldn' want them . . . wouldn't even want to hear bout em. Nor my loneliness . . . nor misery. Not my pain in my soul." Becoming annoyed again, she said, "You don't care bout those things of mine, you just keep talkin bout my money. MY money! What you really here for, Mattie? You one of my friends I can count on? You want me to be the friend YOU can count on. Are you my friend to tell me what I don't need? What I do need? What I should buy? With my own money?!"

Trying to scoff at Luella's truth and not knowing much to do with the truth, Mattie said, "Stop talkin foolishness, girl. Sure, I'm one'a your friends you can count on. Ain I always been? Ain I been your mama's friend? Your mama loved me! (Lying) She always helped me."

In the meantime, Corrine had come home and she could hear them when they spoke loudly. She did not go over to Luella's house, she just sat on her porch and listened to hear Luella's mind work.

———

Luella looked at her kitchen clock and started trying to dress again. She took a girdle out of a bag, studying it. She put her hand on her hip and looks at Mattie, "My mama didn't allow you to come over here. And I know she never gave you no money. She never gave anybody any of her money cept the church. And since she been dead, I ain't never needed you, but you always need five or ten dollars. I let you have it, but I want it back. I ain't never needed you before and I don't plan to, cause I'm gonna be married with a husband takin care of me."

Mattie made a last try. "I just don't want you to be no fool, girl. You need to count on . . . a friend. Let me tell you what to do with that money the preacher gave you. How much you got?"

Luella started to put on her girdle, but looked at Mattie like she was crazy. "Practice on your own money."

Mattie couldn't quit. "Somebody sure goin to take vantage of you!"

Luella sat down, breathless from struggling with the girdle which was still just over her thighs. She was very sad because she wanted to think happy thoughts, love thoughts, and Mattie just would not leave her alone to be glad about her future. Sadly, she said to Mattie, "That's what my mama always tellin me. Says, 'Luella . . . don't be no fool, girl. You ugly. You ugly and ain't nobody ever gonna love you but your mama. So you betta work hard right here with me, get you some money and save it, put it away, and when the hard days come, as you get old, cause you sure gonna be alone when you get old, too, chile. Ain't nobody ever, EVER gonna wanta marry you! You just ugly . . . like me . . . and you ain't even shaped right neither. But . . . if you gets you some money . . . you can pay somebody to come in here and take care of you if you ever sick. And stick to the church.' "

Mattie relished the thought, "She was tryin to be a mother to you, just like I am. Tryin to be a mother to you."

Corrine, on her own porch, almost fell out of her chair.

Luella's mind was lost in the pain of her mother's world but she spoke out loud, "Mama always say, 'Don't think bout no love, chile. No man.' Then she would laugh that tight laugh of hers. 'Don't you even think bout no love cause some things ain't meant for love and you one of them things wasn't meant for no love.' "

Mattie fell under the spell, said, "I guess I wasn't neither. All my mens leave me!" But her attention snapped back to her own plight. She looked at Luella closely, said, "That's why we got to stick together, girl."

But Luella snapped back to the present herself. "Least you had some, Mattie. Leastways you know what men are like. Mama say all a man want to do is drop a baby in my belly and if that baby come here lookin like me, be a shame fore God. I don't blive God's shamed of what a person look like."

Mattie nodded her head, "Ms. Sedalia was a good, wise, Christian woman. I'd do what she say . . . if I was you."

Luella was lost in the pain of her mother's words again, "Said she woulda been shamed to have any more children. Say she didn't want no more if they all was goin to look like me." She breathed a deep sigh and was silent a moment. "But I knew she couldn't have no more if wasn't no man around. My daddy was gone and didn't nobody . . . nobody . . . no other man come for her."

Mattie shrugged, "I don't blive Ms. Sedalia let em. And you ain't ugly, Luella . . . I don't think you ugly," she laughed.

Thoughtfully Luella said, "I do. You know, I'm still a . . ." she paused, then said softly, "virgin?" She looks at Mattie and realizes all she has said and became brisk again. "But, now, I'm goin."

She got up to go into her bedroom, shuffling with the girdle around her knees. "I'm goin with Silki. My Lord! This girdle thing act like it's fightin me!"

While Luella was in the other room, Mattie sneaked a peek in the rest of the bags and starts toward Luella's purse as Luella returns, the girdle in place. Mattie opens the shoe box instead and holds up a pair of red shoes, then tries to try one on. "It's too small!"

Luella sits down holding her sides, exhausted. "Whew! Well, I got that on!" She lifted the red dress, then put it down as she reached for her new perfume. She sprayed it everywhere; under her arms, down her bosom. After putting the dress on, she sprayed under it, too. Finally she looked at Mattie as if she had forgotten her.

"Oh! You better go now, Mattie, cause I got to go. It's gettin late," she said while having a little trouble bending over to put on her new shoes.

Mattie, persistent as ever, asked, "Why you got to give him so much of your money? Where you goin anyway?"

Happy again, Luella answers, "Memphis! A big city!"

"Well, you betta leave some of that money with me so you won't be broke when you get back! Cause you comin back! Alone! And broke! Blive that!"

Luella goes to the door, opening it for Mattie, saying, "I'm coming back with a husband! You won't have to worry, Mattie. Thank you kindly."

Mattie slowly goes out, saying, "I'll sure pray for you."

As Luella watches Mattie leave, she mutters to herself, "I magine I would need more than your prayers, Mattie." She gathered her things in her bag, looks around her little house and goes out of the front door, and as she does she spies the black wreath. She picks the wreath up, saying, "You dead now, too. Just like my mama." She places the wreath carefully on a bush. "You lay here on this land my mother loved so much, with both our lifes." Luella went back into the house to get the kitten and the bird, Corrine already had the dog. She looks back at the house. "This is goin to be a house of life now. And I'm goin to get me some love!"

Unused to the high-heel shoes Silki had picked, Luella teetered as she walked over to knock on Corrine's door to leave her pets and to say, "I'm goin now." Corrine looked sad, Luella looked happy. As she was leaving, Aunt Corrine stopped her at the door, saying, "Luella, sweetheart, you have made up your mind to go to Memphis with him, such as he is, and I'm not going to try to stop you anymore. But I want to say one last thing, please." Luella waited, shoes already hurting and girdle choking her, too.

"You know, you got a good heart, girl. A good, soft heart. And you gettin ready to be amongst a world of hard-hearted people. A good-hearted person is never safe around hard-hearted people because they are always looking for a way to creep inside it, take advantage of you. You. They can come at you more ways than the wind, and you know we never know how the wind is going to come. You be careful, baby. Because they all will be in need. They poor, most of em, and being poor is dangerous to some people. All kinds of people can make lies sound just like the truth, but it won't be the truth. You guard your heart, you hear me? Guard it with your mind.

And let me know if there is anything I can do. And ... you come on home where you already know you're safe. I'm not saying you can never go away, I'm just saying, there is a time; and there is a way to go." She said a few more things as Luella carefully made it down the stairs to the gate, then they said their last good-byes.

Corrine watched from her window as Luella, carrying her suitcase, teetered and stumbled down the street. "Lord, please answer my prayers, please. Watch over Luella."

Part III

Silki and Luella met at the bus station. He had wrapped a belt around his suitcase because it was packed fuller than it had ever been and it wasn't too new. He grumbled a bit because it was getting late, but they boarded the bus and were soon on their way. As they were settling in their seats, Silki asked, "Did you get the rest of the money?"

"Oh, I forgot! After you left, Mattie worried me so."

Silki snapped his head around to her, "Forgot?! Now how we gonna do what I planned for you?" His turned his face back to the window and pouted, angry. "You let that cow mess up your mind!" Then, after a moment, "Well, how much you got then?"

"One hundred dollars. You still got the fifty dollars."

Silki had only lost twenty dollars in a crap game. "No! Told you was some things I had to do!" He turned again to the window, then back to her. "Well ... shit. Give me the money so I can carry it. It ain't safe with you."

Luella looked around the bus, said in a low voice, "Not now. Not out here in the open where people can see."

"What I care bout these people?"

Luella didn't answer so Silki turned back to the window and said very little all the rest of the way, except, "You better clear up in your head who the boss is." Soon he fell asleep. Luella slipped her shoes off, they were killing her feet, then she dozed a bit. They arrived in Memphis at nine forty-five that night.

The bus station was surrounded by bright lights and people milling around. Silki was grinning, walking in front of Luella. Luella was between smiles and frowns. She had had a hard time getting her shoes back on her sore feet and she had to trot every once in a while to keep up with Silki.

Finally, he stopped to ask a black man in a rickety cab where a good hotel was.

"Can take you to a good rooming house," the man replied.

"Take us then. Get in, Luella."

Silki and the cabdriver talked and Silki learned where the places were he wanted to go to.

When they arrived at the rooming house, Silki left Luella to pay the cab while he took his bag and checked into the room. The landlady, Ms. Ready, looked them over and, seeing Luella looked respectable, showed them her nicest vacant room. "Five dollars please, in advance." The room usually went for two dollars a night.

Silki turned to Luella, "Give me the money, Luella, I ain't got no small bills." Luella opened her purse, glancing at Ms. Ready, who was taking account of everything, and gave him twenty-five dollars.

Silki shook his head. "Give me all the money, Luella." She gave him twenty-five more. He gave a disgusted sigh, but handed Ms. Ready five dollars. "We gonna see if we like it here, then we'll pay the rest of the week."

"It be due tomorrow mornin'," said Ms. Ready as she handed him the key and left.

Silki began to bustle around the room, getting settled. He put on a fresh, new shirt, shined his shoes with a thin towel from the face-towel rack. Said, "Come on now, Luella, we got to go, it's gettin late! After ten o'clock."

Luella wanted to take off her girdle and the red shoes. She was numb around her hips and her feet really hurt, but she felt she couldn't. Her feet felt as though they had claws gripping them. Half her body was numb and the other half was in pain. But . . . she had to follow her man.

Ms. Ready recognized Silki's type when she first laid eyes on him, but she couldn't get Luella right clear. She thought Luella obviously didn't belong with Silki. "She dumb, but must have somethin. Prob'ly money."

Silki, grinning, took Luella to the Blue Blew Inn, a jazzy bar with a dance floor, naturally. Seemed like a thousand colored lights to Luella, but the place was still dark. She tried to become excited as she tripped over people and tried to wave the smoke away from her face. Through smoke that wouldn't be waved away, she saw more people in one place than she had seen at any time in her life, except church. But this crowd beat the church crowd. The music was the blues and it was low-down and lower. The people dancing seemed hardly to be moving, just clinging close as they could.

There was a couple just leaving from a table near the bar. Silki pulled Luella, stumbling, behind him as he headed for that table. He was happy. He was in his element. After they sat down, Luella leaned heavily on the table, trying to ease her tired, hurting body. Silki primped and styled, his feet eager to dance to the good music.

He waved a hand with money in it at the overworked waitress, who looked at the sharp-looking Silki and took his order with a smile. When the drinks arrived, Silki sipped at his a few minutes as he looked around the room. Then he grabbed Luella's hand, pulling her up to dance. She followed him, reluctantly, trying to smile. In pain. Her dancing was not quite up to date, but she leaned on him, which she liked and which made the dancing bearable.

Silki paid Luella very little attention, he was too busy watching himself and all the other people in the club. When the music finally ended, they returned to their seats and he waved more money to catch the waitress's eye for another drink.

At that moment a fine-looking, flashy-dressed woman entered the Blue Blew Inn as Silki was waving his money. She saw the money before she saw Silki. The bartender called to her, "Hey She-She! Com'ere girl!" and she went to take a barstool vacated just for her. Silki turned to look at who the bartender was talking to. Silki liked what he saw.

Luella hadn't finished her last drink when the new drinks arrived. She was happy to be with Silki, but she was also miserable. Everything was happening too fast. But, oh, her feet and her numb behind.

Silki reached for Luella to dance again. Luella, feet in too much pain, bowed her head.

"Come on now, Luella! Let's dance! We in the big city now! You can't lay back on your ass like this! I done spent all this money!! Trying to show you somethin bout life! Come on! Live!"

As Luella started pulling herself up, she felt a rip begin in the seam of her tight, red dress. She quickly put her hand over the ripping seam and started to sit back down. "Silki . . . we been travelin so long . . . I am tired. I just gotta rest my feet . . ." But Silki is not looking at her, not listening to her. She looked to see where he was looking. He was looking at She-She.

For Luella's benefit, Silki started looking around the club to see if he could find someone to dance with as though he had not already chosen She-She. "Well . . . then . . . damn. I'll just have to dance with somebody else." He started walking away, calling to She-She, "Say there . . . young lady! She," he waved his hand back at Luella, "tired. Come on, let's dance!"

She-She crossed her long pretty legs and leaned back on the bar. "I dance better when I've had a drink. Adds a little fire to my blood." She smiled up at Silki. "And I step a little higher."

Standing over her, looking down at her, he answers, "Well, get you a drink! Get two! Add a little MORE fire to your blood. Bartender! Two drinks here. Ah . . ." points to Luella, "give her one, too. If she can wake up long enough."

Luella looked at her man, slowly and sadly. She wiped her forehead and looked like she was going to cry. She slowly nudged her shoes off, then she picked up her glass and drank it all down.

She-She looked at Luella, then smiled up at Silki, saying, "That your mama? Look like she need to be home. Better get some more money from her, quick, if that's where you get it from, cause it looks like she is gonna go to sleep."

Silki took affront at her words, "After all," he thought, "I am a man." So he said to her, "That ain't your bizness to worry bout! Let her go to sleep! I got my money! Now! You ready to dance or not?"

She-She threw her head back and laughed, throwing her hair as she said, "I stay ready! Now, you sure you got some money? Cause I don't like no 'po' nothing! No how! No way! No time!"

Silki pulled her into his arms as he said, "I ain't never gonna be 'po' again. I done found my callin. Now, I'm callin you. You better hurry up and answer. Come on now, let's dance."

But She-She liked to tease, "Are you sure you can dance? I don't like nobody messin up my feelings on the dance floor!" She stood as she hollered over her shoulder to the bartender, "Give us another drink, Ju Baby!"

As they moved to the dance space, Silki told her, "My name is Silki, baby. If I ever mess with your feelings we won't be dancing! Say . . . I could ask you, if you don't like 'po' what you doin in here? But, mama, you look so good, I don't even care!"

People stepped back as Silki and She-She held the floor in a very sensual dance. Not too slow or even too close, but extremely sexual movements. It was like a dance symbolic of all the Silkis and She-Shes in the world. Promises, lying promises. A sensual, false-true longing and unaware loneliness and Promises. Were the surface scratched, it would reveal the underlying fear that he was getting broke and might not make it. Anywhere. Fail. Her fear that time was already passing her by, she couldn't reach out and touch it any longer. It was changing her value in her world. She would, inevitably, be less to nothing. Promises that would be difficult for them to fulfill for themselves, or for them to fulfill for anyone else.

One never looked away from the other's eyes. Oh, those lyin eyes were on the promise. Even when they made dance turns, their eyes sought and found the other's without a second lost. They came to an uneasy understanding during that dance. When the music stopped, they stood together waiting for it to begin again, and although the music was faster this time, they danced at the same slow rhythm. Silki wanted She-She. She-She wasn't sure if she wanted him; she had already had many of him. Ahhhhh, but . . . the promise, the promise. It was "love" they wanted, but "love" was breaking the rule of the game they wanted to play. To the Silkis and She-Shes of the world, love was a weakness. It cost you. Their need was so great they possibly couldn't afford to pay.

Near the end of the third dance, Silki stopped and pointed to Luella with his thumb, then made an outside motion, like pointing to the rooming house, then pointed back to himself and then at the floor. As if to say, "After I get rid of her, I'll be back!"

Sitting at the table over the watered-down drinks, Luella was wide awake and sleepy by turns, but she had been watching Silki when she could hold her eyes open. She looked at what she thought was the beauty of She-She and it looked ten thousand times more beautiful than it actually was. She looked at She-She's tight yellow dress and felt her own dress ripping even more. The girdle was choking her soul that wanted to breathe. Her heart was like something that had been washed and stretched all out of shape, never to be whole and good again.

When she saw Silki coming back toward her, her poor little heart got ready to leap for joy. He took her arm and pulled her up. She asked him to wait until she could put her shoes on again, but he pulled her out the door as she dragged her feet trying to get her heel to go down into the shoes; they wouldn't, so she just clopped out to the cab. They had to take a cab even though the rooming house was not far, because Silki was embarrassed by her, and she absolutely could not walk and struggle with the numbness of her behind.

Silki helped Luella undress, but not with lover's hands. With hasty hands. He put her to bed. Through a yawn, she asked, "You comin?" A yearning for the knowledge of love still struggled for awakening in her tired pained body.

He didn't answer for a moment, then said, "You go to sleep, I be here directly." So she relaxed and went to sleep. When he had finished fooling around, wasting time until she was asleep, he was packed again and his bag was by the door. The last thing he did was go through Luella's purse which was on the dresser and remove all the money that was left. "That'll teach her she shoulda brought all of it, then I coulda left her some!" Then he was gone, tipping down the stairs so he wouldn't wake Ms. Ready. Ms. Ready saw him anyway. It was her business to see everything and she almost always succeeded in her business.

Part IV

When Luella woke up the next morning, it goes without saying, she knew Silki had not stayed the night with her. In this strange city, she was alone. It felt as though the girdle that had caused her such distress the night before was now wrapped tightly around her heart. She hurt with every fiber of her body. But she did not cry. Too hurt to cry. Just out done, finished, tired. Her mother's words of her never finding love kept running through her mind. "You just ugly! Nobody ever gonna love you but me! Your mama!"

The third day she couldn't understand why she couldn't cry and why she was more worried about her situation, being broke and alone, than she was about Silki. She wished she was home, Silki or not. But . . . there lingered the thought, the hope, that he would, he might, return.

The fourth day Luella was still sitting in a chair looking pathetically through the one window in the small room with the one mirror, one chair, one bed all as simple as possible, with marks of people gone through and by. One sign on the wall said HOME IS WHERE THE HEART IS, another said ANY-WHERE I HANG MY HAT IS HOME. The smell of bar-b-que chicken rising up from the cafe next door to the rooming house continuously nauseated Luella because her appetite, usually so good, was gone.

She had still not seen nor heard from Silki. But that worried her less and less. The landlady, Ms. Ready, had fed her, some, and had not put her out because she could not pay . . . yet. Somewhere in that run-over heart of Ms. Ready was a little tiny soft spot remaining from all her strife in life.

Luella was lost in her thoughts looking at the steady movement on the street outside. She jumped, startled, when the knock sounded at her room door. Ms. Ready came in without waiting for an answer from Luella.

Ms. Ready was annoyed about her money, but tried to sound kindly to the confused, lost young lady. "Honey . . . it's nine o'clock at night and you been sittin in that window four days now, lookin for that man. Even YOU ought to know he ain't comin back! You been here four days and I ain't got a dime more from you than that first five dollars. This room is for RENT! And when it's rented it ain't hardly for sittin in. Now you got to do somethin! I got to have my money or make way to let somebody else take this here room that can pay."

Luella, tired, worn from worry, and sad, smiled wanly at Ms. Ready. "You ain't gon lose by me bein here, Miss. I got some money. I can send it to you."

But Ms. Ready didn't want to hear that again. "Everybody always want to SEND me my money! People talks bout sendin way more than they sends."

Luella turned to look out of the window again. "I just thought he would be here by now."

Ms. Ready felt sorry for Luella, but this was business. "I know you musta thought somethin like that. Otherwise, you be a fool to just sittin and lookin out windows!" She looked at Luella's sad face. Her voice softened, "Honey . . . that little piece of a man who brought you here don't know what he gonna do from one minute to the next. He done done you a favor really, and you ain't got sense enough to know it. Sometime when they leave you . . . you lucky."

Luella hung her head. "Don't say that. Please don't say that . . . He be back. We got plans. Silki is my future. My man. I still got my dreams."

"Yeah . . . but he got the money!" Ms. Ready walked the few steps to the bed and sat down on it. "Woman, where you from?"

"Boville . . . You prob'ly ain't never heard of it."

Ms. Ready laughed, "If I have, it was easy to forget. That where your man from, too?"

"No. He's from some bigger place. He didn't tell me yet."

Ms. Ready opened her mouth in slight shock. "Well . . . then, woman, how long you known him?"

Luella shrugged her shoulders and felt dumb. She also did not like telling her business, such as it was, to a stranger, but owing Ms. Ready money and needing her help made Luella more amenable. "Oh, bout three, four months."

This time Ms. Ready's mouth opened even wider. "Three, four months?! And you say you put all your money in his hands?" She laughed a strange little laugh in sympathy. "You sure was a fool! What was wrong with you, girl?"

Luella turned back to the window and said, slowly, "I wanted to see if life . . . to . . . to . . ."

"Well, he sure is showin it to you, honey, from the bottom, ass up! TOOK your money! Well . . . now I know he sure is gone. So . . . now, whatcha gonna do about my rent? I got to have my rent TODAY! You got to do somethin!"

Luella did not know what to do. She had told the woman she had no money left. "I . . . I guess I'll borrow my bus fare and go home and mail it to you." She got up heavily from the wobbly chair and went to pick up her traveling bag. As she picked it up, she sighed deeply. Resigned.

Ms. Ready got up from the bed and grabbed the bag from Luella's hand. "No, no . . . we can't do that! See, I can't believe . . . I don't believe you, cause I done already seen life a little myself, a couple times around."

Luella stepped back from the woman, worried aloud, "Well, what can I do?" She pointed at the suitcase, "You want these things? I ain't got nothin else."

Ms. Ready shook her head, "Nooooo, I don't! What I need is money!"

Confused and bewildered, Luella asked her, "Well, if you don't want these things and you don't want me to leave and send your money back to you, I can't see what else I can do." Now she felt like crying. She wished for Aunt Corrine, she even wished for her mother. For anybody who knew her and knew she would pay.

Ms. Ready set the suitcase down and then walked slowly around, looking Luella over, good. "Spose I would think of somethin else for you to do? You a good, strong, healthy girl. Nice lookin too."

This information seemed to excite Luella. She turned to face Ms. Ready with anticipation in her pathetic face. "You mean you might know where Silki is?"

Ms. Ready laughed that strange little laugh again. "He don't know where he is hisself! I hear he with She-She! That's the biggest barracuda outside the ocean! You can forget him! Honey, she done chewed him up and spit him out anytime now! I bet he ain't got your money no more!"

Ms. Ready screwed up her face, like she was thinking hard, but that was for the benefit of Luella because she had already thought of what she was going to suggest to her. Her handyman had come to set a screen door in for her that very morning and the idea had come to her then. "But . . . I may know where someone else is. Have you ever had a 'date'?"

The look on Luella's face and the sound of her voice was somewhere between hope and fear. "Well . . . Not a real one. Only this one . . . with Silki."

The landlady scoffed at that. "That don't come under nothin! I mean . . . you know . . . been to bed with somebody gonna give you some money? Slept with somebody for some money?"

"Only person I ever slept with was my mama. Sometimes."

Ms. Ready was aghast, "Your mama?! You mean . . . you didn't even get what you paid for with that Silki of yours? Didn't even give you nothin?!" Ms. Ready thought for a minute, then said, "Well! That happen to me once . . . more'n once, I reckon." Her thoughts returned to Luella. "Anyway, sleepin with your mama ain't what I'm talkin bout. I mean . . . you ever been to bed with a man . . . for money?"

Luella was shocked, but growing curious. "No, mam. No love or money either. Who gonna pay me?!"

The landlady, in her business, less than seldom met women like Luella; grown women who had never slept with anybody. She didn't believe Luella. "Ain't no need to lie to me, honey!"

She looked at Luella, carefully, as she pieced her own sly thoughts together. Thinking, too, "I don't want no problem with this woman." Finally, decided, she asked Luella, "Spose . . . Spose I know someone, maybe, who might pay you a little somethin for your . . . time?"

"You mean somebody I ain't never even said 'hello' to . . . or . . . or nothin?"

"Oh, shit woman . . . don't play no games with me! You need some money! And I got to have my rent money they gon give you to go to bed with them. You need to take it! Then I'll be paid and you can go on and get out of here!" Her voice softened because Ms. Ready remembered her own past, "And go back to that little home you done told me about."

Well, Luella was not the kind of fool not to see which way things might have to go, and, too, she was still thinking about love because sex, to her, meant some kind of love. She knew about business, now, too. "How much do I owe you? Who goin to pay me?"

Ms. Ready didn't have to count because she already knew down to the last dime, but she counted on her fingers for Luella. "Now, let's see here. You been here four days now, five dollars a day, but, because you alone, I will reduce it to three dollars. I fed you four times now, it's your business if you didn't want to eat it; so that's two dollars a meal. Now . . . that comes to twenty-four dollars."

But, Luella was a working woman, so she could count. "That comes to twenty dollars."

"I knew you wasn't as dumb as you make out to be!" The landlady smiled.

"Who is goin to pay me that much money?"

Ms. Ready sat back down on the bed beside Luella and said, "Why you think so little of yourself? You worth more than that, I betcha, cause you a nice-lookin, nice woman. But that is all 'I' need. All you owe me. I'm thinkin of my own business and what you got to do is think of your own business; you need a bus ticket home so you need money for that too. And you might want a bite to eat on the way. You need to come to yourself!"

The landlady looked at Luella carefully as she spoke, and she spoke persuasively, "Now, I blive I know a real nice man who will do it." Luella, excited, started to speak, but Ms. Ready held her hand up for silence. "Now . . . he ain't the best-lookin person in this world . . . and he do have his problems . . . but that's why he will take care of this here business for you. And I know he won't do you no harm and I want you to leave here just like you came."

Brightening at the prospect that someone will care enough for her to pay for her, Luella said, "Who is he? Do I get to meet him first? What's his name?"

Ms. Ready, pleased that things will work out, rose from the bed and walked to the door. "You sure got to meet him first, cause even thin as these walls is, you can't do nothin through em. His name is 'Turtle' and I'm not gonna tell you nothin else. You meet him and talk to him for yourself. BUT, remember, no matter what . . . we need that money!" She paused to let her words sink in Luella's sometimes slow, sometimes fast, mind. Then, "Now . . . I'm goin down here now and splain to him why he got to help you."

With those last words, Ms. Ready opened the door, preparing to leave, but Luella reached out, grabbing her arm. "Spose Silki comes back?"

Ms. Ready shook Luella's hand off, "I don't care who comes! I got to have my money. But, honey . . . that's your littlest worry, him comin back. Now . . . I'll be back soon as I can."

Luella's lethargy had zipped right out of her body. "Wait a minute! Shouldn't I take a bath first?"

The landlady turned back for the last time, "What you askin me for? Can't you smell your own self?!" She was already out the door as she spoke the words, but you could hear her as she walked away. "Good Gawd almighty. I can't do everything!" She hollered over her shoulder, "And towels is extra!"

Luella stood with her hand on the door a moment, then closed it slowly. She turned around, slowly, to face the room and look at the bed. Her face is registering, first, alarm, which graduated to fear; then wonder replaced the alarm and fear and brought with it a slight smile, then a wide grin.

Then . . . alarm again. "Spose . . . he says 'no.' " The grin returned slowly, with, "Spose he says 'yes'? She starts removing her clothes and takes the chair from the window so she can use it to look into the mirror, the grin and the fear alternating across her face and in her heart.

Part V

Turtle was the unkind nickname given to him by unkind, unfeeling schoolmates and it held to him even with adults. When he was born he was given the name Sidney Wish Wayes. The fourth child and youngest son of Otis Wish and Lucille Wayes.

His mother, Lucille, had lung problems from a youth spent in poverty. There was no money to pay a doctor for what could have been easily cured, so it progressed steadily into TB. His parents had loved each other and married young and, soon, began having babies. The fourth, Sidney, was the last and Lucille was glad because, though she loved all her children with all her heart, she felt it was her fault, her illness, that Sidney was born with a hunched back, a growth on his back between his shoulder blades. It probably could have been helped by surgery or some medical attention, but they could not afford that either.

Lucille, the mother, died when he was ten years old, but, for him, they were ten years of love, warmth and family security.

The two older brothers had died along the way, so Sidney and his sister, Dora, were even more loved and cared for. Dora learned to cook from her mother early in her youth, she had to. Sidney began learning early in his life to do small carpentry jobs around the house, helping his father. He also learned cooking and housecleaning because both he and Dora had to help their mother.

Sidney liked wood work and furthered his progress in doing special things; engraving, carving and such. He loved wood. He spent most of his time alone, without playmates, to avoid their laughter and thoughtless remarks. He liked to read. The mother made both her children go to school. "You must learn how to read about life."

On his own, Sidney studied and knew all the different types of trees and their wood, even those he had never seen and never would see. He made many beautiful things for his mother, even after she had passed away. He made strong but lovely furniture for the house and his sister, even after she was married.

Otis Wish Wayes, his father, had passed away when Sidney was twenty years old. By that time Dora had married and, with her husband, had remained at home to care for her father and brother.

Sidney was thirty-two years old now, and lived in a bedroom and bath he had built for his own self on the rear of what he now considered his sister's home because she had a family and he was very sure he would never have one. He had never even had a girlfriend. He was a slender man of medium height, well-built in proportion, except for the lump between his shoulders.

He had liked several girls, but they never knew it because

he did not want their laughter or rejection. Over the years he had learned to laugh when others laughed at him. It made their laughter hurt less. In time he grew, almost, not to care what others thought or said behind his back or when he passed them by. Truly, most didn't bother anymore because they were used to him. But, always, there are some fools around somewhere.

Now, Sidney was a normal man. He had tried, as puberty came and stayed, unfulfilled, to visit secretly a prostitute or two, but they called him "bad luck" and refused to have anything to do with him. But . . . you know . . . sometimes one or two, in dire need, would sneak and do what they called a "quickie." It cost him much, was never truly satisfying and happened very seldom.

What brought him to Ms. Ready's mind was that Sidney, at this time, was putting a new screen door on her back porch. Ms. Ready was not totally hard-hearted, just had her own need to hold on to that rooming house she and her husband had sacrificed and struggled to finally acquire. Mr. Ready worked as a redcap at the railroad station and she ran the house. They were getting old; it had taken their whole life just to get the rooming house. They had to make it pay. Now, Ms. Ready was not an angel, so she rented two rooms, located in the basement, to prostitutes when her husband was at work. (She thought he didn't know. He preferred it that way so when they went to church on Sundays he wasn't the one to have to struggle to look innocent.)

Ms. Ready knew Luella was not a fast woman and she would not have suggested any man just looking for any woman, to her. But she knew Sidney, and her husband had used him for carpentry jobs for years. She didn't know ALL his problems with women, but she was a good guesser. And, "Another thing," she thought to herself as she went downstairs to see him, "he is clean . . . and kind . . . and a churchgoin man. And I need my money." So . . . she talked to Sidney.

When Ms. Ready got to the back porch Sidney was just finished and cleaning up around his job. He looked up at her and smiled. "You just in time, I'm through. You can check it out, see if you satisfied."

"Oh, I know you done a good job, Turt—Sidney. I know I can count on you." Still, she looked the work over, then set down in a rocking chair. "Sidney . . . I want to ask you somethin."

"Yes, mam."

Ms. Ready thought, carefully, a moment in the afternoon silence of the backyard. Deciding she knew where to start, she asked, "Sidney? What do you think about loneliness?"

Sidney was momentarily taken aback. "Loneliness?"

"That's what I said."

Sidney took his handkerchief from the back pocket of his overalls, wiped his face and put it back as he wondered why he was being asked the question. "Why you ask me that? You ain't lonely, is you? You a married woman with a good man."

"I ain't talkin bout me, I'm askin you what you think."

He smiled before he answered. "Well . . . Ms. Ready . . . what I think is loneliness is one of the worse things in the world. It got to be pretty bad cause even God gave Adam, Eve, cause he saw that loneliness was hard on the fellow."

"What's so bad about it? What it feel like to you?"

Sidney looked down at the ground, lifted his hammer in the air and let his arm fall back to his side. "Wellll, to me, it just mean nothin."

"Nothin?!" Ms. Ready leaned forward in the chair.

"Yeah. Like my daddy always say, when I was growin up, I was a king. But I ain't got no woman, no family, cept Dora and her youngens and they hers. So, if I'm a king, I'm just a king of nothingness."

"A king of nothingness?"

Sidney made himself laugh, "Yeah. If you really want to know, I just go on with my life, but I ain't got nothin no other man got. They got women, a wife. Every night . . . I go home . . . I go home to my dog. I feed him and I'm done for the day. I pet him, but I don't want to kiss him none." He stopped laughing. "Loneliness is never havin nothin to look forward to. You wake up in the middle of the night and ain't nobody there. Bed is cold. Night is dark, don't care how bright the moon is. Sun shine, but it don't mean nothin too much. I mean, I'm glad to live another day, sometime, but what am I livin it for?"

Ms. Ready sat back in her chair. "For yourself."

Sidney laughed, softly, "Yeah, but I can't hug and kiss myself. I can smile at myself, but what do that mean? To me? I can hold my own hand, but what do that mean to me? Don't get me wrong, Ms. Ready, I'm doin alright, I ain't cryin. But, just seems to me, with all the love they say is in the world and good as God is sposed to be, why am I the king of nothingness? Why ain't I got a normal life? But I guess I should be satisfied, cause I got my health and such."

Ms. Ready started rocking in the squeaking chair, very slowly. "Well, you honest, Turtle—Sidney."

"I don't care bout you callin me Turtle, cause everybody does anyway. I'm used to it." He smiled, "But I like 'Sidney,' the most."

"I need you to do me a favor, Sidney."

"Why, sure, Ms. Ready, what can I do for you?"

"It's not for me . . . exactly, just in a way."

"Yes, ma'am?"

"I got a lady-friend here who has been . . . Some sucker has done her wrong and left her high and dry here in Memphis with no way to get home. He prob'ly got her cause she was lonely."

Turtle took his handkerchief out and wiped his face again. "Lord, have mercy."

"Please, Jesus. But she been here four days now and only paid rent for one. I can't keep her here on that. We broke, too."

"You mean . . ."

"I mean, she ain't no fast woman, I know that. She got a home to go to. But, she got in her mind that she gonna have to get some money from somewhere . . ."

"Lord, have mercy."

Ms. Ready pursued her goal. "Now, I don't want her to step out here and run into trouble and all what is out here in these streets."

"No, Lord, not here."

"Not anywhere for a nice woman. So . . . I thought if I was to let her see anybody . . . it . . . it be you. Oh, NOT for that . . . but because you got a good, kind heart."

"Well . . ." out came the handkerchief again, "I don't have no whole lot of money . . . but . . . how far she live away from here? How much she owe you?"

The rocking chair stopped. "She owe me twenty-two dollars . . . today."

The handkerchief was busy, "Whew! well . . . four days . . . twenty-two dollars?"

"Well, I been feedin her, too. That woman love to eat."

Turtle began putting his tools away, slowly, thoughtfully. "Well, let me see if I can get some money together and kinda help her long her way." He wondered if he was being used by his friend's wife; did his friend think of him as a fool?

Ms. Ready kinda read his mind, so she leaned forward in the rocking chair, "Well, no . . . I know you got the money, but I know you got a good heart and will prob'ly give her the money and help her. But . . . don't you see? Her. She need somebody. The man who talked her into comin here wasn't never really nothin to her and sure didn't mean her no good! And she hurtin in her heart. She need somebody to talk to . . . and you know this house don't give me no time to sit round and talk. Ain't you got a evenin, like this evenin, where you can come talk with her? Friendly like. That way she won't mine takin loan-money from a stranger like we are?"

"Well . . ." He picked up his toolbox, ready to go. "You say she lonely? You say she a good woman? What a good woman doin bein lonely? I'll . . ."

Ms. Ready leaned so far over toward Turtle that the rocking chair gave a loud screeching squeak in protest. "I'm tellin you, she IS a nice-lookin woman, sure is . . . but, she think she ugly!"

"Say what?"

Ms. Ready knew she was treading on serious ground, all up in Turtle's business, messin close to his own personal feelings about himself. "I'm tellin you! She think she ugly and won't nobody ever love her, or like her neither. You know, like a true friend?"

This was giving Sidney plenty more to think about. His own little heart was getting involved. A woman . . . felt ugly? "Wellll . . ."

Ms. Ready waded right on in and closed the gap. "Oh, thank you, Turtle, Sidney. Now, time is passin. Can I tell her you comin this evenin?" She didn't wait for an answer. She was up and heading into the house to finish everything up, but she stopped and turned back to him. "And, Turtle, you can go on and try to have a piece if you want one. Prob'ly be doin her a favor."

Sidney, standing in the yard, holding his toolbox, confused, curious and thrilled all at the same time, said, "Hush your mouth, Ms. Ready!" But . . . all good intentions said and being done, Sidney went home in a glowing, fearful daze.

When Sidney reached his home, his sister could tell there was something, not wrong with him, but something had happened to him. As you know, they were very close and talked about almost everything together. He told Dora of his conversation with Ms. Ready and that he planned to go back over there to meet this woman, but he didn't know the woman's name.

Dora, being the loving sister that she was, called Ms. Ready to see if this was some kind of joke or trick being played on her dear brother; she was even kind of angry. Ms. Ready assured her it was no joke and since women can talk together sometimes, she told her exactly what kind of woman Luella was, as far as she knew and she knew pretty far. Well, anyway, when they finished talking, Dora went and got all her husband's colognes and shaving creams and all that men use, that her brother, in his simplified life, didn't have. She pressed his suit, which didn't quite need it, and ironed a fresh shirt for him. At 7:30 P.M. Sidney was ready to go and go he did.

Luella had bathed and dressed in her red dress. She had forgotten the rip and it was too late to fix it, so she planned to just keep that side turned away from this man. This man! She had put on her red shoes and as long as she didn't walk in them, too much, they didn't hurt too much.

Ms. Ready knocked on her door and came in without waiting for an answer, as usual. "He'll be here in a minute! You look mighty pretty, Luella." Then her heart turned on her again. "Now, don't you forget! That money belongs to me! You got to work up on your own fare home!"

Luella was scared and dewy-eyed at the same time. She hesitated, "Did he try to say . . . no?"

Ms. Ready softened again. "No . . . Honey, you a good woman . . . he's a good man. I feel like I'm doing one of them good deeds. But I think everything will work out alright. Just let it get along on its own." Her heart hardened again. "Don't you let nothin change your mind . . . No matter what!" Then she went out and shut the door behind her, muttering to herself as she went down the hall.

Luella was very nervous, but she had sense enough to be thoughtful. "Well . . . I sure hope he ain't got no gonorosis or sylphilrita or nothin! Lord! If I can just get home one more time." She got up, holding the rip, for the hundredth time to look in the mirror, fixing a hair here, a wrinkle in her dress there. She was so anxious about the coming evening she couldn't do anything for too long. So she started talking to the Lord.

"Well . . . Lord, I don't want to do this, but what else can I do?" She looked up to the heavens. "Drop me a ticket home and the money to pay this woman with and I'll go right on home right now!" She moved to the opened window, looking out. "No, Lord, I'm lyin. I want to see what life is all about. I'll never do it again, but just this one time, Lord. You know, this may just be my last chance to know . . . I didn't make myself, Lord, so . . . I'm a woman, Lord, a human, flesh woman. I ain't got a lotta hot blood, but . . . it's pretty warm." She shook her head as if this was no way to talk to the Lord, then decided to explain to Him.

"Now . . . I done got some money my mama left me. I got a home. But, I ain't got no love . . ." She got down on her knees by the chair. "That's what I want, Lord. Now . . . I know this ain't love . . . real love . . . but if I pretend realllll hard . . . Lord, you know I ain't never gonna have no house high up on no hill . . . with no bedroom where I steps into paradise and no high romance. I ain't gonna get to live on no romantic island with the palm trees wavin at me. Ain't never gonna have no livin room like no ballroom and no bedroom with all them yards of silk and satin. I ain't got nothin but myself . . . here in this dusty, cheap little roomin house . . . and a possible man who may change his mind . . . and not come at all . . . Oh, Lord, if he do come, forgive me, but I got to take this chance . . . cause who gonna love me sides my mama and You . . . and my mama's dead, gone. So, who gonna love me sides You?"

Then . . . there came a knock, soft, but firm, at her door.

She was on her knees as she answered in a voice which sounded all wrong to her. "Co . . . com . . . come in?"

Turtle turns the doorknob slowly, opens the door, sticks

his head in first and comes inside the room and tries to hide his back by keeping it close to the wall. "How do?"

Luella did see his hunched back, but tries hard not to let him know as she rises from the floor. "How do?"

"I'm Turtle."

"I'm . . . Luella."

Then both of them, shy and embarrassed, start speaking at the same time. Turtle points to the chair, asking, "Can I sit down?" Luella points to the bed, saying, "Sit down, why don-cha please?" They laugh nervously, too long, as, still facing her, he set in the chair. Then the laughter stopped and a silence falls between them until Turtle asks, "How old are you, Ms. Luella?"

Luella tried to smile as she answered him, "That ain't no good question to ask no lady. Why do you ask me that?"

Turtle did smile, "Cause I know you been havin company long enough to say more'n 'have a seat'!" They laugh together again, grateful for something to fill the void.

Luella, in the middle of her laughter, said, "You can talk, too, you know."

Turtle's laughter dwindled as he looked at her, this woman, his date. "Yes, I can talk, but I thought maybe you might want to say . . . somethin special."

Luella frowned slightly, "Special?"

Now, Turtle frowned, "Well, yes . . . like . . ." He is truly embarrassed and nervous. "If you want me to leave . . . Ms. Ready, the landlady, say she didn't tell you ALL about me . . . So, if you wants me to go . . ." He got up from the chair and started to the door to leave.

Luella held out her arms as she got up from her seat on the bed. "No . . . I don't want you to leave. You just got here.

Why do you want to leave?" Then she thought it might be because he didn't like the way she looked.

But, Turtle was already moving back to his chair, smiling as he did so. "I don't want to leave, but you know . . . sometime . . . people, they look at me and . . . then they just . . ." His voice trailed off.

"They just what?"

Turtle looked directly into her eyes, "They, some people, just want me to hurry up and get away."

"No, no! You sit down. I don't want you to leave. Why would somebody want you to leave?"

Turtle took a deep breath, "Don't you know what everbody say? A humpback is bad luck?"

Luella set back down on her bed and, with a wave of her hand, said, "I ain't never heard that in my life and, anyway, if I had, I wouldn'ta believed it!"

As Turtle slowly set back down, he asked, "You wouldn't? Why?"

Luella shook her head as she laughed softly, "Cause bad luck don't come in humps . . . It comes in people's ways."

Turtle relaxed and set back in the chair. "That's right! I know that! I seen people have plenty bad luck and I ain't been nowhere near em!"

Luella relaxed a little more herself and smiled her lovely smile again. "Me, too! Why, there's a lady, ole Ms. Johnson, she live in Boville, where I come from. She married to a handsome deacon in the church . . . Every time a new baby born there, she scared to look it in the face. Scared that baby is gonna look like Deacon Johnson . . . and most times it do!"

They laughed, together. Then Luella said, "But that ain't really funny . . . it's sad."

Turtle added, "And it ain't bad luck . . . just a bad deacon!"

They laughed, together, again.

As Luella nodded her head "yes," saying, "There's all kinds of bad luck. It mostly comes from bad thinkin. Humps ain't got nothin to do with it. I ain't never seen one before and I'm having plenty BAD luck!"

Turtle didn't laugh, he became serious. "I done seen too much of one."

Luella sobered at his seriousness. "What's it look like? What's it feel like?"

"It don't feel like nothin, til somebody else see it."

Softly, Luella asked, "Can I see it?"

Turtle is hurt, embarrassed and ready to run, wishing he had not come after all. But he wanted to stay where he was, too. "Wellll . . . if you want to . . ."

Slowly, Luella got up, held her hand out as she walked over to him and touches it, tenderly. His face showed his pained feelings. This was his! He didn't want her to see it, much less touch it, and make it more real.

Luella's voice was very gentle and soft. "It's warmmm."

"I'm alive!"

Then, to add misery to his soul, Luella lifted his shirt collar away from his neck and put her hand inside and down his back, still gentle. "Why, that ain't nothin. Just you got more back than somebody else."

Turtle looked up at Luella, gratefully. She said, "Now, you're gonna have all good luck! I have took all the bad luck away. I have so much already, a little more ain't gonna make it nothin."

Turtle smiled, still looking up at Luella. "It feels better. Ain't nobody ever touched me but my mama and my pa and

Dora." Lest Luella think he had a woman, he hastened to add, "Dora my sister. But, it seem like you done had enough bad luck of your own. Why you want some of mine?"

Luella went back to the bed and sat down, dejectedly. "Why not? I got so much of my own, that little bit of yours ain't gon matter one bit. Beside, I like to see you feel . . . better."

Turtle, feeling lighter and brighter and happier than he had in years and years, asked, "What kinda bad luck you got? A good-lookin woman like you? You got everything you need to take you anywhere you want to go."

Luella began to fidget, nervously. "Well . . . I ain't never been one to talk much . . . But, people? They seem to all be playin some kinda game all the time . . ." She searches for words to explain her thoughts, "A game . . . you . . . can't get into it, if you don't . . . fit . . . the things . . . they are. Their . . . rules . . . or somethin."

Reflectively, Turtle nods his head. "I know those games."

Luella, caught up in her thoughts, continued, "When I think . . . of all them days I spent . . . alone, cause even if I was with my mama, I still was lonely. Sundays, holidays, night-times, meant for . . . people . . ." She laughed at herself a little as she fidgeted with her fingers. "Well . . . it gave me plenty time to think of all the things I wanted." She almost whispered, "That I would never have."

She raised her voice a little and continued, "All the things I wanted. All the things I needed." Then, in an almost angry tone, Luella finished her thought, "and all the things I had to settle for." She sighed and the anger seemed to leave her voice as she looked at Turtle. "I had dreams . . . I have dreams . . . but most of them have done gone on away now." She laughed, lightly, at herself. "See . . . in them books and magazines? They always showed me what I was missin. So I had real big dreams. Them dreams was my only happiness. But . . . it really wasn't happiness." She sighed, then smiled, sad, in spite of her trying not to be. "I never liked to look in mirrors after them books."

Turtle was leaning toward her, listening with all his attention and all his heart.

Luella paused for a moment, then decided to continue expressing her feelings. "You know, I wanted to blive there was someone in this world who wouldn't think of nobody but me. Wouldn't make love . . . to nobody else on the side . . . and I wouldn't either." She laughed in embarrassment. "Well, I was young then." She corrected herself, "Younger!"

As if Luella just thought of it, she said, "Some girls get married four or five times! . . . I never even got a Valentine card!"

Turtle's body jumped as though startled. "But you so pretty . . . them boys in your town musta been blind!"

It was Luella's turn to be startled, "What you sayin? Are you crazy or something? I am ugly." She spells it out for him. "U G L Y. Ugly."

Turtle, his voice strong, disagrees with her. "No you ain't! No you sure ain't. I done seen plenty women in this city . . . and you ain't no ugly woman! No sir! You damn nigh beautiful!" Then he lowered his voice, as though ashamed of what he was taking a breath to say. "I don't like that red dress though."

Luella was shocked. "You don't like my red dress? I mean . . . I know it's torn a little bit, but . . ."

In a stronger voice, Turtle added, "I don't like them shoes either! Red ain't your color."

"It ain't?"

Turtle softened his voice because he could see her feelings were hurt and he knew she was trying to look nice. "No . . . it ain't. Maybe a . . . a light rose color . . . or a pale, pale green. Even a light, light blue. Or cream." Then his voice became serious again. "But, no . . . not red. And I bet you don't need to wear no wig either."

Luella's hand flew up to the bedraggled wig that seemed to set askew atop her head. "It ain't? I don't?" She loved the color red. "Not reeeddd?" She challenged him. "How do you know so much bout what's good bout colors?"

Turtle took a moment to answer, then said, "I done watched the sun rise a lot . . . and I watch it set most every day it's out. I'm up deep into the night, and I get to see the sky in all the dark, beautiful colors. The clouds are different colors at night, too. I love the black clouds shot through with gray, floating across the sky. In the daytime, I see the grass and the trees . . . changin . . . all the time changin, all year round. I keeps a garden of flowers. Sometime I work it at night, if the moon is bright, and I can still see the colors. I don't sleep too good, you see."

Luella didn't always sleep too good herself, so she wondered why he didn't. "Why?"

Turtle tilted his head to the side, "You really want to know?"

"Yes, I really want to know cause I don't sleep too good either."

Turtle decided to just go on and tell the truth. "Cause I don't have no woman . . . of my own."

They were silent as they thought about his answer.

Then Luella said, "Maybe that's why I don't sleep too good . . . cause I don't have no man of my own."

Turtle waved her words away, "Well, you could get a man . . . but I have a hard time gettin a woman . . . the kind I want."

Luella waved his words away, "It ain't all that easy to get a man either."

Turtle chuckled to hisself, "The funny thing is, some of them who think they don't want me . . . don't know I really don't want them!"

They laughed together, happily.

Luella said, through her laughter, "You know, I never thought of that! Some of the women in my town? They feel sorry for me . . . but I really wouldn't have the men they got!"

This, of course, interested Turtle. "No? Why?"

"Well, take Mr. Brasen . . . he so lazzzzzy. And Mr. Fred, he always chasin after women; little ones, middle ones and old ones too! Got in trouble once! And Mr. Crimp, he married, but he sleep with everybody in town but his wife!"

Turtle added his two cents, "And the prettiest girls in this city, who feel so hotshot, can be mostly had for twenty dollars! They be sneakin, but even if you sneakin, you still bought! I don't want that!"

They nod their heads at each other, beaming with smiles.

Luella pointed her finger at him as she smiled, but she was serious. "Now see? A man like you got some sense."

"I hope so. And if I do, that's all I got!"

Then, the sense he had made, the words he had said, became clear in another way. She asked him, "But, if you don't like bought women . . . why did you come up here to me?"

Thoughtfully, Turtle answered. "Well . . . because I know that if you could be bought, Ms. Ready wouldn't come to me. See . . . one thing, these ladies here . . . don't fool with me cause . . . I'm sposed to be bad luck, like I told you. But, sides that, she know I don't fool with them either, cause they can be bad luck, too! To me! So, if she told me . . . about you, then I knew you had to be different from the rest. And looka here, a pretty woman like you, and I get to meet her!"

Disbelief in her heart, amazement in her eyes, Luella asked Turtle with all sincerity in her yearning to know. "Do you . . . really . . . really . . . really think I am pretty?"

Very softly, Turtle answered, "I really, really . . . really do." Then he stood up and held out his hand to her. "Can I touch you?"

Timidly, bashfully, fearfully, Luella said, "Well . . . sure."

Turtle restrained hisself, moving unhurried to her, he sat on the bed beside her and reached out a hand to tentatively touch her hair and her face, speaking gently to her. "You feel just like a woman."

Softly and gratefully, Luella said, "I hope so." They were silent as he ran his hands over her arm, taking her hands in his. Luella didn't know what to say . . . or do. So she asked, "What we gonna do?"

"Everything we can!" came the excited answer. "Know what I'm gonna do?"

Extremely interested, Luella asked, "No. What are you gonna do?"

Turtle stood up from the bed, saying, "I'm gonna get us some champagne and . . . and some bar-b-que chicken! I'll be right back!" He left her side, then turned back to her, "I'm gonna get somethin special for you, too!"

Luella stood, anxious, "Don't go! You won't come back!" She took his hand and held it to her face, her eyes pleading, she said, "Don't go."

Turtle's heart like to just burst right there. Somebody was asking him NOT to go. He took his hand from her face and put his arms around her shoulders, pulled her to him and said, "I'm comin back. I might not get to my own funeral, but I sure am goin to get back here! How can I not come back to a woman like you? Just don't you go away."

He removed his arms from around her and stepped to the door, opening it. He said as he was leaving her, "Don't you go way, you hear?"

Luella moved quickly to the door, beside him, "Don't be long. Don't be long. Not just . . . just because . . . Not just for that. But I want you to come back. Really." Her last words were said sadly, "Really. Really."

Turtle began to have doubts of his own, his own past hurts forced him to say, "Look, Ms. Luella . . . I'll give you the money to pay your bill here and get your ticket . . . and you don't have to do nothin with me. You don't have to lie to me. I just am enjoying your company. You a real woman." He paused to look down the hall, then he looked back at Luella. "I know I ain't handsome. I know what I look like. It's just I ain't never been with no woman I could talk to, eat with, drink champagne with . . . like I read about! I read books and magazines, too, just like you do. I want to do that! I want to do all them things. But, you don't have to do nothin with me because I pay them things for you! And I am comin back! I might not never get nowhere else in my life, but I am gonna get back here."

As he left, Luella caught the door before it closed and

called softly to him, "Say, what is your real name. I don't like that Turtle name."

He turned completely around, but did not return to her. You could hear the pride in his voice as he answered her. "Sidney Wish Wayes."

She smiled at him and repeated, "Sidney Wish Wayes. I like that. From now on, you are Sidney to me . . . or Wish. I like that."

"I better go, now."

"You better come back."

They laughed together, again, and he was gone. She closed the door, repeating his name, softly. Then she went straight to the hazy mirror, asking it, "Is he lyin to me?!" For some reason the mirror was kinder this time, it answered, "You know, you do look kinda alright. You could try to do something with your hair though." So she took the wig off and brushed and brushed her hair until it was smooth and she tied it back with a string and pulled a few strands across her forehead to make bangs.

She went down the hall, rushing, and took another bath. Rushed back to her room and splattered the cologne over her body and put fresh lipstick on her lips and smiled. Then she went to sit in the chair by the window, looking for Sidney. "Lord, I must look like a picture frame to people, I be in this window so much."

The time seemed to pass so slowly. So slowly.

The sky was darkening. After another hour or so, Luella began to worry that Sidney had changed his mind about coming back. Her mother's words flooded into her mind. The golden halo that a promise had placed around her heart was banished by the doubts her mother's words and her past life had put there. Tears threatened to flow. She hung her head, and thought, "My happiness always turns into a pain." She sighed heavily and gave up another dream.

But, then, a knock sounded at her door. Her door. She didn't answer at first, because she was struck dumb. Then he said, "Luella? It's me! Sidney!" His happy heart felt a sudden fear. He thought, "Did she change her mind? Was she just foolin with me?" But the man in him bade him knock again and say softly, "Luella?"

Luella jumped up from her chair and, suddenly happy again, she opened the door. "You back!"

He was grinning as he came in with bags and a large package. He handed her a lovely bouquet of flowers. Her first gift of flowers. Luella took them directly to her nose, looking at him over the petals. The fragrance delighting her senses as well as thrilling her heart.

"Sure I'm back! . . . I ran all the way!" He set the bags down, opening them as he spoke. The first was a bottle of champagne. "Now . . . we gonna drink like kings and queens." The second bag held a bar-b-qued chicken, steaming hot. "And . . . we gonna eat like plain folks!"

Then he picked up the package, from the department store he had gone all the way downtown to purchase, and opened it. "And you gonna let me see how you look in the best shade of the night . . . twilight blue with the pretty pink roses embroidered on it!" He held up a beautiful, thin gossamer nightgown. Luella pressed her hand to her breast, speechless, and set down on the bed.

While she caressed the beautiful, soft nightgown, Sidney opened another bag, taking out two crystal glasses. Then, opening the champagne, he poured them full. "Have a little glass of champagne? Please?" He kneeled down to her. "And let's talk . . . and dream together."

Sidney's eyes were bright with happiness. This was the first time he had done this with a woman! His mind flew in all directions. "Let's even dance! Ain't nobody here to look at us or say nothin. This is the happiest time in my life . . . Ain't gonna be nothin to spoil it!" He saw the happy tears in her eyes. He set on the bed beside her and placed his arm around her as she turned to look into his eyes. He pursued his dream. "We have a few hours of a quiet, peaceful . . . lovin life, after all the sadness. We together!"

When they had finished the champagne in the glasses, he poured more. "Here . . . have a little more champagne." They sipped and said little small things, giggled, laughed and he hugged her a lot.

Then, for a moment, he looked into his glass where the champagne sparkled and bubbled and became serious. "When I was young . . . I didn't have to struggle, like I seen some people do, for the truth about life. I knew . . . that those of us with strange bodies, faces other people call ugly, people who just weren't pleasin to the eyes of the 'normal' people, we long and yearn for the cemetery. Just want to die and end all our misery. But, you know, I have found out, it ain't all good, like it seems, for nobody. Sometimes those people who look like they got everything? And look like they gonna win those games we was talkin about? Sometime they lose the love and happiness they really want. And need! It goes away from um."

He took another sip of champagne. "Nobody, right now, couldn't be no happier than me. We got as much chance as anybody has." He turned to look at her face, into her eyes.

"But, Luella, even if this is a dream . . . let me . . . please . . . let me dream til I die."

Then, they danced a little, slowly, to the music only they could hear. All Luella could say in the haze of the golden halo around her heart, clouding her sight, that had returned twice as strong, was "Ohhhhhhhhhh, Sidney."

Later, she stood up, picked up her new gown and, stepping to the door, said in a low, melodious, mellow voice. "I'll be right back in a minute."

Sidney watched her with starving eyes until she closed the door behind her. He looked proud. He looked happy. He stood, he had to, because of all the nervous energy pulsating inside of him. From love. He was a sensible, practical man, always showing good sense. But. He was in love.

When Luella returned, her shyness made her come in the room sideways through the door and hit the light switch that turned the light off from the ceiling. The only light left burning was the small lamp by the bed. She was not trying to be sexy, she was simply shy. She had never been seen in front of a man in only her nightgown before.

Sidney ohhhhhhhed and ahhhhhhhed, then took her by one hand and turned her around so he could see all of her. He pulled her into his arms. She fit just perfect. They fit in each other's arms perfectly. They moved, unhurried, savoring each new moment, toward the bed.

Then, a knock was heard at the door. They looked at the door, but neither one answered. The knock came again. They still didn't answer. Sidney smiled down at Luella, so she would not be alarmed. Finally, a voice was heard: the voice of the landlady.

Ms. Ready said, not too loudly, "Hey in there! It's gettin to be another day. You gonna owe me for another day."

The new lovers laughed softly at Ms. Ready, then Sidney answered loud enough for the landlady to hear. "Take your little pencil, Ms. Ready, and write on. Let her roll, Ms. Ready, just let the good times roll on and on, forever."

Ms. Ready didn't say anything else and they heard her walking away.

They were laughing, softly, at the very idea of themselves being happy . . . as they clasped each other tightly, holding on to the happiness and the moments.

Part VI

Luella had planned to leave as soon as she was able to obtain a bus ticket home, but after the first night with Sidney, she was delirious with her joy and Sidney was overwhelmed with his joy and happiness. Ms. Ready was happy, also, because she was paid even though she had to lower the price of the room back down to three dollars a night because Sidney knew better than five dollars.

On the third day later, as Sidney was coming in with more flowers and the bags which he brought every day, Ms. Ready asked him in a playful way, "Man, ain't you workin no more?" They laughed at her meaning.

As he passed her on the fourth day, with more flowers and new packages, she asked, "What y'all doin up there locked up in that room all the time? You gonna wear my room out! And she done already got every vase and jar to put them flowers in I had!" They laughed.

So, on the sixth day Sidney took Luella out. He had bought her three new nightgowns, one each day, and now he had bought her some daywear; two blouses, two skirts, some smart, comfortable shoes, one nice yellow cotton dress. She brushed and brushed her hair every day, tying it neatly back. The wig was thrown away.

They walked all around the city, even down by the water. They went to the parks they were allowed in and, once, to a picture show. But, by evening, they rushed back to their flower-filled room. She met Dora and her family. Dora liked her, as sisters do when they love their brother and want to see him happy, and Luella liked Dora. Luella petted Sidney's dog all the while when he showed her his part of the house. "I built all this myself!"

"Ohhhhhh, Sidney! You can do all this kinda work!"

They never talked of marriage. Each one wanted to, because they were in love. But each one still had doubts about their self. Each one thought the other might like them, but not enough to marry.

Luella thought, "He might like me enough to do all this, but he ain't gonna want to live with nobody like me for the rest of his life."

Sidney thought, "She bein awful nice to me, but ain't no way she gonna marry up with no hunchback man and worry bout what kind of children we gonna have."

So it was their time passed. Finally Luella just had to go home. "I have left my house and my pets with my Aunt Corrine, she's a neighbor, and I really do need to go back and see about em." His sister, Dora, had been taking care of his dog. Luella didn't want to go. Sidney didn't want her to go. But life was life.

At last, she just had to go home. Her last night with him they stayed in the room, eating carryout food as they set in bed listening to the music from his radio. They made love because it was their last night, but they would have made it anyway whether she was leaving or not. Then they fell asleep in their spoon position.

In the middle of the night he woke her up, saying, "You were cryin in your sleep. What's the matter, baby?"

She didn't answer, just moaned and turned around closer to him, and they just, naturally, slipped smoothly into making love again. They were both so emotional and anxious, Luella thought her eyes would just roll right out of her head from all the beautiful feelings he made her feel, and her ears might just fly off from all the beautiful, loving things he was saying as they shared their last loving. (I'm not gonna tell you what he said.) But, one time, Luella said, "Oh, Sidney, I'm so . . . wet . . . down there."

And Sidney answered, "Just drown me in your love, baby, drown me."

When they made love, Luella rubbed his back in her passion. All of his entire back. She made love to that hump in his back that he hated. He had not expected that touch. To say it thrilled him to the tip of his curling toes would, indeed, be an understatement.

The morning came and he left to get her ticket for the bus while she packed. Alone, she cried as she packed.

Ms. Ready knocked at the door, but didn't come in until Luella said, "Come in."

Since Luella was moving around the room gathering

things, Ms. Ready set down in the chair. "So . . . you gettin ready to leave us, Luella?"

Sadly, Luella answered, "Yes, mam, I am."

"Well, I hope your trip to Memphis turned out better than it looked like it would."

"Oh, Ms. Ready, I just don't know how to say 'thank you' for bringing Sidney to me, introducin us together, and all."

Ms. Ready laughed a little, "Don't thank me for the 'and all' stuff. You all did all that yourself!"

Embarrassed, Luella nodded her head as she turned away, smiling.

Then, Ms. Ready got serious, she was usually laughing one minute and being serious the next. "Turt—Sidney is a good man, good as they come. I like a workin man. So, now you know there is better men than that Silki fool brought you here. And, next time, you keep your own money. You not no fool if you holdin on to your own house and things, so don't nobody need to count and carry your money for you! You told me once you was a Christian woman, so I know you heard that the love of money is the roots of all evil. So you ought to know right off when you see somebody lovin money too much; your money. Somethin bound to go wrong. Bound to! Cause the Bible don't lie."

Luella agreed, naturally, because it was true. "You sure are right, Ms. Ready. You right about Sidney, too. He is a good man. A good man; honest and lovin."

"Close as you all was, did you talk about marryin?"

"Oh, Ms. Ready, no. Sidney didn't mind helpin me and all, but marryin me? I wouldn't spect him to ask me that."

"Lord, Lord, what fools people can sure be. Well, you all knows your own business. And I'm glad you leavin! Cause

Sidney bout to wear out my front steps and you all bout to wear this room out!"

Luella blushed, then they both laughed. Ms. Ready got up to leave her to her packing, saying, "You take care yourself and come see me when you come back."

Luella shook her head sadly, "Oh, I prob'ly never will get this far away from home again."

Ms. Ready left her with a "Humph!" and a "Honey, you'll be back! I been round the block a few times. I know you will be back!" Then she left.

All things done, they were finally standing in the bus station, in the colored section. Luella was shedding tears, without a sound, and Sidney kept pulling her to him and rubbing her back. He had handed her the last flower. A gardenia. She kept smelling it and smiling at him over the petals.

Over his shoulder she could see a few people staring at his back. She almost hated them, but she hugged him tighter and kissed him with a loud smack on his cheek.

After everything seemed to have been said and there was silence between them, Luella asked, "We prob'ly won't see each other again, huh?"

Sidney sighed and looked worried, "It's hard to tell about the future. You got a house there, I got a place here. And my work is here where people know me and what I can do." He sounded so despondent.

They both looked like little, lost, miserable orphans who didn't have a friend in the whole world.

Luella pushed Sidney away, saying, 'Don't wait with me no

more. I can't stand all the hurt from knowin I'm goin to be leavin you. Just go on away. I'll be alright."

But Sidney reached and pulled her back to him as he wondered if she was ashamed of him or something. "Oh, baby, I can't leave you til I just have to and that bus takin you on away from me. I got to keep my hand on you long as I can."

At last her bus call came over the loudspeaker. She dragged herself to the line. He stood beside her til they went through the doors to the outside loading area. He held her hand til she got to the steps of the bus and she began to step up. Then she got out of line and hugged and kissed him, one more time, quickly. Then Luella rushed up the few steps into the bus.

The driver started the motor when the last passenger was aboard and Sidney stepped back from the hot air caused by the bus engine. But Sidney did not leave. He walked to the bus exit, stood on the sidewalk and watched the bus for several blocks until it turned, out of sight at last.

Part VII

Luella reached her hometown in the early evening. She walked home very slowly, tired from the bus ride and all the emotional times she had been through. Not wanting to mess her new clothes up, she had worn her red dress home, which was really coming apart now. On the bus, she had taken the red shoes and cut out the places for the growing bunions and corns. She carried her suitcase and the large box with all her new nightgowns in it.

Luella was tired, worn and thoughtful. When she reached her house she went in the front gate and after climbing the few steps to the porch, she heaved a deep sigh and set down on the porch swing, dropping her box and suitcase on the floor. As was her wont, she talked to the Lord.

"Lord, I been a long way from my home. I went away to live a little . . . see a little life." She looked down, taking a long look at herself. "Life sure is hard on a body, ain't it, Lord?"

She set there awhile, silent, looking out to nowhere. "Did I live, Lord? Haven't I lived?" She nodded her head, yes. "I blive I did get to live a little. Oh, that Sidney, that Sidney. He made me live."

Luella took a deep breath and stood up, gathering her things together to carry them into the house. At that moment, Mattie came around the corner and saw her. Taking in the ripping dress and cut shoes. Mattie's heart became gladdened at what she thought was a sad sight. "Well! I see you done come back alone!"

Luella answered with a tired "Yes."

But Mattie was heartened. "Well! Where that big-time husband you was gonna bring back with you?!"

Luella looked in her purse for her door key, wanting to get away from gloating Mattie. "He ain't here."

Mattie crossed her arms across her breast. "Where the reason you ain't never gonna have to work again, like you said when you left?"

Luella opened her door, "I don't know, Mattie! Just go away now. Come tomorrow. No, don't come tomorrow, just go away now."

Mattie laughed gleefully, "Girl, you ain't shit now! Just like I warned you! Bet you broke, too!"

Luella turned back to her, "Mattie, I ain't got the strength today."

Mattie wouldn't stop. Laughing, she said, "I know you tired! I know you sore now too! That man musta left you quicker'n money leaves a fool!"

Luella was too tired and her happiness sat somewhere in her mind keeping her from getting as angry as she felt like getting. "He left. You satisfied?"

"It ain't my satisfaction you paid for! It was yours! And I sure bet you didn't get that either!"

"Why you bet so much on me and my life, Mattie?"

"I bet you got more'n you bargained for!"

Luella went into her house, saying, "You right! Good night!" Then she shut the door, leaving Mattie outside, hollering at her.

"You don't even know what time it is no more! I tole you! I tole you! Now you broke! And me, your friend, needs a new icebox to keep my babies' milk cold! But, no! You rather give it to a no-count man, stead of your friend! See what you think of your friends?! You ain't shit, Luella!"

Luella couldn't help but open her door again, even as tired as she was. "No, I ain't shit, but you are! Cause what I think of you is laying somewhere in a cow pasture! And I can sure see what my 'friend' thinks of me!" She shut her door again.

Mattie hollered again, "And the preacher want to see you!"

"He know where I live!" Luella hollered back.

"Everybody know that! Even Silki! But the preacher gonna put you out'a the church!"

Luella had to open the door to answer that. "You all ain't got nothin but hell in that church noway! Thank the preacher for me."

Mattie gasped and said, "OOHHHH! Blaspheme! We all be here in a coupla days from now . . . cause you ain't fit to be in our congregation!"

Luella said, "Thank you for the compliment! I'll be here when you come!" She shut the door for the final time and leaned her back against it. She looked around her little house and tightened her lips to keep from crying as she said out loud, "I'll be here . . . forever. Alone."

Some people can doubt even in the face of love. Sidney, finally, ended up thinking that Luella did all she did with him because she needed the money. Luella began to think Sidney did all he had done because Ms. Ready asked him to do it. Luella had never had any loving before so how could she know that it didn't always feel like Sidney had made her feel; that it took "love" to get a feeling that good. Sidney had had sex, quick sex, so he should have known that it took "love" to have what he and Luella had shared. But, his innate doubts kept him from fully realizing what they had had. Sometime it takes time.

Luella visited Aunt Corrine to let her know she was home (she already knew because she had heard all the hollering) and to pick up her pets. They talked, a little, about Luella's trip.

"I don't know where Silki went. But I met a real nice man name of Sidney. He was real nice to me, showed me around and things. He the main reason I was able to come home. He bought my bus ticket."

"Child, you don't know how lucky you are you don't know where Silki went. I don't want to hurt you, but I am glad he 'went.' That Sidney fellow sounds like a real nice man."

"He got a humpback."

"Sound like he has a good heart, too."

Luella smiled a beautiful smile at Corrine.

Everything returned to normal: Luella tending her garden, rubbing the cat, petting her dog, talking to her bird. She bought some goldfish. "I need a lot of living things around me."

The people from the church never came. Didn't put her out. Mattie had lied again. Luella started going back to church on Sundays with Aunt Corrine.

Aunt Corrine began to hear Luella crying at night. Again.

Corrine didn't want to hear Luella crying again. She liked the happiness on her wistful face when she talked about Sidney. So she decided to have a little talk with Luella, her friend, who was like a daughter to her. She invited her to dinner for just the two of them.

After they had eaten, talking and laughing without malice about the people they knew and their church, Corrine poured two glasses of brandy for them.

"Come on, sit over here where you can lean back comfortable. Don't worry about them dishes, I can get to them later."

So Luella joined her, smiling as she reached for her brandy. "This the kind of thing Sidney does."

Corrine took a small sip of her drink. "Your Sidney sounds like he is real nice to be around; his woman, I mean. Have you invited him here to visit you?"

"Oh, no, Aunt Corrine. He never will leave Memphis. And . . . I don't know if he meant for us to . . . to . . . think of me and him as a . . . together."

"From all you tell me, Luella, the man was very serious about you."

"Well . . . he was sure nice to me. But, you know, ain't no man gonna really . . . love me; the way I look . . . and all. He prob'ly bought me them clothes to cover me up so he could take me out!"

"I don't believe that, Luella. You already told me that you all made love before he bought the clothes."

"Well, yeah, but . . ."

"Listen, Luella, you need to know something about yourself. You are not a ugly woman, by a long shot! And you got such nice ways! Love is not just for who the world calls beautiful people. Sometimes they are the ones with the least love cause they never know what somebody is after: them or to show them off. And beauty is in the eye of the beholder."

Corrine had Luella's full attention.

"You are serious about your love that is inside you. That makes you a valuable person, a valuable woman, because it means when you love, you really love. And don't think of Silki, because he came in the NAME of love without any of its reality. And he couldn't see what you really were because he had NEVER seen and couldn't recognize it. The man who cheats on love cheats his own self. It may not cost him much, but he gets even less cause he don't know what it is he is missing."

Luella stopped smiling and nodded her head, listening intently.

"You have a good mind. You just don't put enough in it, maybe read books instead of magazines, but you are a practical, reasonable woman. Not a fool. And as for your looks, well, there are places in this world you'd be worshipped like a queen. But, what I mean to say is, men might choose a person for their looks, but the woman won't have much in that man, cause when the looks are gone, that man is gone. And truth be told, there are no perfectly beautiful women in the world. Men either. You have a heart. A real heart. And it sounds like Sidney has one too. You tell me he has a humpback, well that humpback didn't make you get away from him. You sittin round here pining for him. What makes you think he is not pining for you? You ARE lovable! What you all shared, to me, has real substance. There is something to it! Not just fever and beautiful empty dreams. If what you say about your sex and lovin, well, that's the meat of life, not just the smell of the meat on a empty table of life! And goodness, sweetness, gentleness and faithfulness and honesty are the gravy over that meat! And you got all that gravy! That man ain't dumb. He knows that. And the way you say he held you in his arms, every day and all through the night? Well, he wasn't thinking of nobody else, chile."

"Oh, do you really, really, really think so, Aunt Corrine?"

Corrine smiled softly at Luella. "I really, really do. Now you go on home and write that man a nice letter and invite him to come visit you. I would like to meet him, too."

Luella finished her brandy, blushed at her own thoughts and started to the door, turning at the last instant to ask Corrine, "Aunty, if you feel that way about love, well . . . you ain't old, you still look good and you don't have nobody. I know you could, cause at church . . ."

Corrine laughed softly, thought a moment and said, "Baby . . . I been married, raised my children and now, I have peace. I have a good home, I go where I want to go, when I want to go. I spend whatever money I think I can afford to spend. I have had love, a couple of times, I think. Love is good, but you have to have the strength to endure it. Cause your own thoughts can give you pain. I am feeling no pain in my life. I like it that way."

Luella smiled at her, with love and gratitude, and started out the door to the backyard fence with the broken slats. Corrine spoke to her from the back porch steps. "And another thing, you don't know what I have, love or not, do you? I'm doin alright for myself."

They laughed, together, as Luella went through the slats to her home. Happy for Aunt Corrine.

Corrine did not hear her cry, again, because Luella did not cry that night.

But she didn't write Sidney. Still afraid he did not really want her. Could not really want her.

It had been just over two months since Luella had returned home. Life had settled back in its normal routine for her. Work a few days a week, cook her meals, play with her pets and work in her yard growing her vegetables and flowers.

One morning, just after daybreak, because Luella had started not sleeping too good again, she came out of her house and started working in her garden. Just clearing out the weeds as she did her thinking.

Corrine was up early, also, because she liked the morning part of the day to sit on her porch and have her coffee as she listened to the birds. She hadn't reached the back porch yet and had looked out her front windows as was her usual way. This morning she saw a man, walking slowly up the street toward her corner of the block. She did not know him, so stayed looking out of the window until she might recognize who he was. He passed her house as he looked at Luella's house, hard. He got to the corner and turned to walk back, passing both houses again.

Corrine started to put the curtain back in its place when her eyes were drawn to the man's back; it had a hump on it. Her mouth dropped open as she wondered, "Is it him?! Is that Sidney?" She started to rush to the backyard and call over the fence to Luella. In mid-rush, she stopped and said out loud to herself, "Let that man do things his way. It ain't my business. I won't say nothin less he starts to leave the street."

Corrine sat down by her front window to have her coffee and watched as the man went back and forth, slowly, several times. Finally, he dared to come through Luella's front gate, but he didn't go to the door. He sidled around the side of the house, going toward the backyard. Corrine changed seats to the side of her house next to Luella's. She saw him see Luella and stop. He just stood there, looking embarrassed, peeking around the house at Luella. "Why, that's a nice-lookin man!" Corrine thought as she sipped her cooling coffee.

Luella had finished picking string beans from her vines and now, with a basket full, she sat on her back porch and began to shell them for her afternoon meal. She picked by rote, indifferently. She shelled the beans for a few minutes, as he watched, then began to talk to God out loud.

"Lord, would you kindly tell me what you plan to do with me?" She looks up to the sky. "I know I am not gonna be no Moses, no Rachel, no Abraham, nobody you really need. They still want to put me out the church sometimes, but you don't need to tell me, they can't put me out of heaven if you want me there."

She paused for a moment, hands stopped working. "Lord, I don't like it here no more too much. I have done seen too much of life." Her hands started shelling again.

Luella paused again, shook her head and smiled, "And I miss that little funny man of mine . . . Sidney." She chuckled softly, "He a whole lotta man, Lord. And he's kind and sweet. He's a good man. I don't know what you put in that hump, but I bet a whole lotta men need it! Ooohhh, yes, Lord!"

Corrine was practically dying to be out on her back porch so she could hear everything better because Luella was speaking more to herself, not loud at all. The hidden man's face was reacting to all Luella was saying and he didn't look unhappy.

Luella had stopped shelling again and the pleased look was gone. She looked sad. "But . . . what I'm sposed to do, Lord? Ain't you got nothin to tell me? Am I goin to be alone always?"

Corrine cracked her back door open and put her ear in place. The next sound surprised her as well as Luella.

Sidney answered Luella in a ghostly voice. "NOooo-ooooooooooooooooooo."

Luella dropped the beans all over the porch as she suddenly set up straight. In a wondrous, amazed voice she spoke. "Is that you, Lord? Answering me?"

The answer came, "YESsssssssssssssssssssssss."

Luella, knowing what she thought was impossible, began to guess something. "You mean, Lord, I ain't gonna have to be alone all my life?"

The answer came, "NOoooooooooooooooooooo."

Luella stood, putting her hands full of string beans on her hips. "Well, where my man be?"

"RIGHTttttttttttt HEREeeeeeerrrr." Sidney slowly stepped

out from the side of the house into the backyard. "THEEeeee LORDDDD SENTtttttt MEEEEEEEEEE TO YOUUUU-UUU, Luella!"

Luella jumped and ran off the porch, down the steps, her arms wide open, running to Sidney. "The Lord the smartest one in the whole world! My beautiful, wonderful Sidney! The Lord is good!"

Sidney laughed with such gladness in his heart. He held her and talked to her as he rocked her in his arms. "This is the new me, Luella, I can't find my old self since I met you and you left me. You cried in your sleep that last night, now I cry in my sleep. I wake myself up moanin! And I kept tellin myself I didn't have to be without you less you told me so.

"When you left me on that bus, I said, There she goes, my only woman. I'm watchin my baby go away! Every day I see that bus goin away, every night I see that bus goin away. And every thing I ever had, cept my dog, ain't no meanin in it to me no more. Not without you."

Luella put her head back and looked in his eyes, saying, "I'm losing my hair! I go round talkin to myself. My health is sufferin, sweetheart."

Sidney nodded, "I need those nights you were right beside me where I can feel your legs cross mine, and your breath in my face. I want to feel the heat from your body and, oh, baby, I can't say all the rest out here in a yard. But, my lovin is suf-ferin. I been livin just for this minute. Even hot as it is back home, I didn't feel no heat, no nothin; you was my sun, Luella, you are my sun. I don't know what I'll do if I have to live with-out you! Let's go in the house."

Aunt Corrine was just grinning all over herself as she sat listening on her back porch.

Luella nodded her happy head and said, "Now! And don't say house, this is HOME." As they walk toward the house, she hesitated, holding his arm, suddenly serious. "You going to stay? Here? With me?"

Sidney nodded his head and pulled her back into his arms, but continued heading for the "home."

Luella stopped him again, saying, "You know it's goin to be hard sometime out here in the country. Ain't like no city! It might be hard for you sometime, Sidney."

Seriously, Sidney answered, "I lived in the city for a long time. Never got nothin there to make me happy. It isn't where you are, it's who you are with that counts."

Luella began pulling him toward the house again. This time Sidney hesitated, saying, "You know . . . people are gonna call you a fool. For marryin a man like me. They gonna laugh at us."

They were at the bottom of the steps now, leading up to their little home. Luella put her hands on her hips and took a deep breath. "Only a fool laughs at happiness!! It would take a fool to call us foolish! We pay mind to God!! . . . not fools! Now, come on in this house." Luella grabbed Sidney by his arms and pulled him forward to the house. "You just come on home! We are gonna live! Come on HOME!"

Part VIII

You know, they got married and brought his dog home.

Mattie laughed at Luella, at first, but ended up jealous, envious and mad.

Aunt Corrine heard other things, but she never heard Luella cry again, that is until:

The first baby boy was born, named Happi Wish; the first thing Sidney did was examine his back. It was straight.

The second baby, a girl, was born, named Lovie Ann.

The third baby, a boy, was named T.L.C. Wish. His back was not so straight and Sidney looked sad. Luella took her baby from him, saying, "Give me my baby. That's my favorite one!"

I know it's been said a great many times, until it is almost a cliché. Sometimes it's true. "They lived happily ever after."

But . . . that is just what they did!

The Eagle Flies

Life, oh, life. Oh wonderful life. Oh pitiful life.

The sun is heading down at the same time it is coming up. A beginning and an end . . . in sight. Every moment in a life has within it the joy or pain of your thoughts, your experiences, all leading toward a future, your future. All leading to roads we cross, just like the crossing of the sun in the sky. Some paths leading to forks in the road, a path to choose toward a future.

Closely, look closely; think carefully, and long. One of those choices, roads, may lead to somewhere you want to be; or somewhere you never did want to be.

This is a story of a few people in a small neighborhood, as neighborhoods go, that are neither rich nor poor nor all middle class. Just everyday people trying to live every day. Each of these people are going to speak for themselfs in their own way. Not as a chorus, because they are individual neighbors; together, but apart.

One of them, Vinnie, was a nice-looking woman. Clean. Neat in her mind, which was sensible, and in her appearance. Her clothes were almost all from the secondhand stores, now, but she was always clean and neat. She did her own hair, once a week, and after the first few days of curls, she tied a turban or attractive kerchief around her head to keep her hair from showing when she hadn't had time or energy to fix it. She worked too hard at her jobs to be a night-person, and wasn't really interested in bars, nightclubs nor alcohol. She worked too hard. She had a healthy, but tired body. She was one of those women who just kept "going on."

She had taken the day off from all her jobs. She just didn't feel well at all. She sat in her living room looking out of a window at the sky full of light rain, thinking of her family, her life. Vinnie sat at this particular window often. Through that window she saw bright, shining days full of promise. Cloudy days and rainy days can be promising also, but Vinnie didn't think she had a promise, personally. Her chair and this window was her thinking place.

Today, as usual, she was thinking of her family and her life. Vinnie looked around the warm, worn room at signs of her life's work. A shabby, tired room. Her eyes moved over the pictures and mottos on the walls. HOME SWEET HOME, PEACE, THE GREATEST THING IS LOVE, GOD BLESS THIS HOME.

She turned back to the window and thought, "Oh, God, I'm so tired. So tired."

Her tired eyes caught a movement in the sky and she turned her face to see better, catching the sight of a beautiful young eagle-looking bird gliding through the air on wings of the wind, so smooth, so beautiful as it dove and swooped, curving with the wind. Its wings spread, open wide and grand, playing with the wind. She thought, "You ain't tired, Mister Eagle. But there ain't nothin round here for you less you after that layin hen of Wynona's. You musta come out them hills. Fly on, fly on away . . . and I wish you could take me with you."

It wasn't really what was outside the window that drew her, it was what was inside her feelings, her heart, that held her at the window looking at the trees, the bird and the distant hills and space. Just space. She watched the bird again, high up in the sky. "Are you a eagle . . . or a hawk? Just a big bird flyin, seein things in all that space." As she watched closer she could tell from the bird's flying it had been hurt. A wing slightly drooped, didn't seem as strong as the other wing. But it kept going, kept flying through the sphere. It swooped and swerved, dipped, dived, then soared again, it seemed, to the top of the sky.

Over time, Vinnie would begin to love the faulty-winged eagle-hawk-bird as she watched it fly through its life and her own life. She loved its strength, its power to keep flying, keep trying, even with a weakened wing.

Then her mind returned to thoughts of herself. "I been had a broken-wing life! And I been tryin to keep on goin. I had to."

Vinnie had been married eight years when her husband left. Just left. It wasn't a smooth, easy move, but she had slipped, somehow, into his place and found another part-time job in order to support her family. At that time, she had a son, Richard, eight years old, and a daughter, Delores, seven years old. She found three part-time jobs, two hours three times a week, cleaning up, doing domestic work to hedge her full-time job as a file clerk at a bank downtown.

Naturally they all had to learn to make do on less . . . much less. But she had taken care of her children, kept her house and herself together. "Lord, I'm so glad I made my husband start usin that sex protection after the second child." Because she already had had to work during both pregnancies. "Enough of this," she had said to herself. "He might not'a liked it, but he wasn't afraid of hisself gettin pregnant." He had stayed those first eight years, but had been gone now for fourteen years. "Fourteen long, haaard years of tryin to hold on to this house." She had worried him to death to buy the house. He hadn't wanted to. "That ole piddly little house?! Let's wait til we can do somthin better'n that!" he had said.

Vinnie spoke out loud to herself, "Fourteen hard years of payin bills, buyin food, buyin clothes; I don't care if they do mostly come from the secondhand shop. I was sewin, cookin, knittin. I learned everything I could to make somethin to put on my children's backs."

She looked down at her hands; calloused, dry, red and rough . . . working hands. Vinnie used lotions she bought out of the ten-cent trays in secondhand stores on her hands, but they were soon back, had to be, in water washing or cleaning and even being slashed by paper cuts. Her fingernails never got a chance to grow. "I love pretty hands. Like the hands of the ladies I see at the bank and the ladies I work for. Everybody but me. My daughter has pretty hands. Even my son has pretty man's hands."

Vinnie had raised her children to adults laying hard on them to study, study, study. "Get them good grades so you can go on to college. Be somethin! Be somebody someday! We ain't got no college money right now, but we'll make it."

All by herself.

Her son, Richard, had a paper route once but was fired when his boss got so many complaints about people not receiving their papers he began to check up on Richard. Finally he found Richard burning them in an old barrel used for trash. Vinnie wanted to argue with the boss, as she had been doing the past month or so, but she happened to be home and eyes don't lie. Least hers didn't. There wasn't much of anything else Richard, then twelve years old, could do, or wanted to do, except hang around girls and you don't get paid for that, at least he didn't. If he ran upon any spare change, he spent it before he got home or hid it away.

Richard did like one thing: music. He studied the drums at school and became pretty good at it. He knew his mother had no "extra" money, but he pleaded and begged his mother to buy him a set. She didn't have enough money for just all the food she would have liked to feed her children, much less for drums. But Richard wore her down until she went to the small music store and pleaded with the shyster-owner there to let her work filing his papers or cleaning his store on Saturday nights to pay for the drums. The shyster let her get almost finished begging as he kept saying "Maybe" for almost two weeks. Then when he saw she might find another way, another store, he told her "Okay" to both filing his papers,

papers he usually left for weeks, and cleaning the store on Saturday nights. Richard got his drums. Not any cheap set either, because Richard and the shyster had a lot in common; they understood each other.

Richard didn't get bored with his drums as he usually did with things. He practiced until sometimes Vinnie, on the little time she had off from work and needed to lie down for a moment and have some peace, would go into her closet, sit on the floor and press her hands to her ears, uselessly.

Vinnie saw to it that Richard graduated from high school. He left home almost immediately afterward. "I'm going to New York where musicians mean something! I'm gonna make it, Ma! Big!"

Still, every time he wrote home, he asked for money. Vinnie, who never seemed to get finished paying Mr. Shyster, just quit one day. Said, "It's been five years. I know you are paid off by now." Mr. Shyster didn't want to agree, but he knew Vinnie was a hard worker and an honest one. He wanted to keep her on so now she got paid a small sum for continuing the Saturday work. Vinnie just sent the money straight on to Richard to help him get on his twenty-two-going-on-twenty-three-year-old feet.

Delores had stayed out of their business. She didn't want to be asked to get any kind of job, part-time or otherwise. She just wanted to look good and get to college. She learned how to sew so she could have more fashionable things to wear her mother didn't have time to make. Just for herself. She stole money from her mother's hidden jar to buy lipsticks, body lotions, hair curlers and such. When she graduated from high school she had to wait a year for college money, until her mother diverted some money from other needs like keeping the house repaired.

Delores graduated and her grades were good enough so she was able to get a small scholarship from a small college near New York. "I'm going to college, Mama . . . and be a doctor . . . or a model. Maybe a fashion designer." She had good grades from school because she was serious as she thought about "getting out of this house and away from a mother who does domestic work and has a raggedy little bank job and is always broke." Tuition was still expensive though, and Vinnie had to keep working all of her jobs. She even thought she needed another part-timer, but there just was not enough time in the day. So she worked her jobs and still had nothing to show for it but money-order receipts stacked in an overflowing drawer.

Richard came home very seldom, maybe once a year or so. He brought his clothes to be repaired and put his mother in more debt for the latest coat or suit and shirts. "It's cold in New York, Ma, and I need something to keep me from freezing to death! C'mon, Maaaaaa." Ma always did.

On this morning Vinnie sat looking out of her window for the eagle, but it was not in sight. As she looked at the other smaller birds, the gleaming wet trees with rustling leaves and the near houses, she felt her soul was out there screaming in the rain. Sad and tired.

Her children had been gone off to make their lives several years, at this time. Four years for Richard in New York, three for Delores in college.

Vinnie rubbed her ragged hands over her knees and the skin snagged over the material. Now she looked at that old couch she had planned to replace once the children were gone. She listened a moment to her refrigerator as it moaned and groaned, begging for a rest in some junkyard. "Bless its heart," Vinnie mused. "It's been working fifteen years for me and who knows how long for somebody else before that." She smiled sadly, "Go on, Florence (that's the refrigerator's name), go on, moan. I understand."

Strange as it may seem, Vinnie felt lucky she had a family. She thought of her neighbors, Wynona and Josephine, who lived alone. "Least I got somebody of my own. I am not alone. Thank you, Jesus."

She looked out of the window just in time to see the small speck that was her eagle flying away toward the hills. "Lord, I'm tired though. I could just drop dead. What am I to do? Help my babies hurry up so they can help me and I can rest just a little? Maybe Delores will be a doctor, but I don't think so. She ain't so serious anymore about her studies. She writes more about her 'social' life. Maybe she will marry a doctor and have a baby and I can go live with them and take care my first grandbaby for em." Vinnie fell asleep praying and dreaming.

Next door, her friend Wynona was sitting up looking out her window also. But her thoughts were different. She was lonely. She didn't hear from any of her three children. Maybe on Christmas . . . or maybe on Mother's Day. Mostly she called them when their phone number wasn't changed because they had moved. Wynona also had two living sisters that she didn't hardly hear from. Sometimes for a year or two. Wynona was so lonely. Sometimes she cried when she prayed to God. Her little spirit was outside screaming in the rain.

Wynona was a woman with a heart full of love. She had a cat of her own but fed several of the hungry homeless cats in her neighborhood. She had two chickens she raised for eggs, but she never would kill them on a hungry day because she loved them too. She had a dog, old now, but a trusted friend. He slept beside her on her bed; warmth through the night. She hugged him often, and told him, "Bozo, if you was a man, I'd kiss you!" Everyone fussed at her about the dog's hairs everywhere, but she just told them, "Hell on that! That is my dog under all the dog hair! He's my friend. My best friend and I love him!" She said that to her church lady-friends when they came over for coffee or a beer.

Wynona went to church regularly. It was like having a family, since she couldn't keep up with her real family at any given time. She went to church and she bought lottery tickets every week. Husband dead, years now. Children moved away years now. At sixty years old she was alone with her church and her cat and dog, goldfish, chickens and lottery tickets every week. And her friend Vinnie.

Sometimes when she was just sitting, thinking, she thought, "Oh, yes. My friend Vinnie. Poor thing. She just working herself to death for them useless grown kids of hers. She don't even have a dog. Couldn't afford to feed it, I guess. Next time I catch a litter of kittens I'm gonna give her one. She need a friend inside her house. Somethin movin and breathin. Specially sides that ole man, Twink, that keep tryin to court her! Cause he need a home!" She mused on about Vinnie. "That Fred Evans who courted her was a good man. He just got tired of waitin. She say he thought she was a fool. But a woman, a mother, got to love her children."

Wynona shook her head in sadness for Vinnie as she

reached over under the picture of Jesus on the cross and pulled out her latest lottery tickets, turning them over and over in her hands as she spoke to them. "You gonna be the ones? You gonna be the ones what win for me? Change my life? Please, Lord Jesus, let these be the ones! You know I'm broke and need everything."

Fred Evans was a Real Estate man. This was a kind of small town, so houses didn't move too fast. Had himself a nice home and his hand in a few businesses with his friends; The Clean Cleaners for clothes and a small shop named "EAT" that sold fried fish and chicken with a salad on the side. He wasn't getting rich or anything, but he was doing alright. He had a good mind on him. Worked hard.

Fred liked Vinnie with her nice face, neat hair and strong little body. She had good, nice long legs, but it looked like her calves had tennis balls in them. She had muscles because she was always walking to some job or bus stop. Fred courted Vinnie when he could catch her.

Vinnie didn't want to have no truck with sex, protection or not, because she just didn't want no more accidental babies for her shoulders to bear and now . . . they got all these new diseases and things . . . But that might be why he was stuck on her more than any of the other women that were trying to get him; church women, waitresses and barflys. All after him! Well, he had a house and they could eat chicken or fish and get their clothes clean too! If they could get him. But he didn't fall for any of them. Leastways none nobody could see. But he was a man, so, you know, there was somebody somewhere. But it wasn't in Vinnie's face.

After a while, chasing her and not being able to catch her, he decided he wanted to marry her. But he didn't want to marry any extra baggage like hanger-on grown-up kids. He didn't like the way her children, grown children, treated her. He thought they used her, you might say. Vinnie and Fred argued about that a lot.

Fred would say, "That boy is grown . . . a man! Let's make him get a part-time job at least, wherever he is. He isn't in college! Let him work! He'll appreciate life more and appreciate you more, too. Why does he let you suffer like you do? Killin yourself! You a fool for your kids, Vinnie!"

Vinnie didn't want to hear that.

Then again, he would say, "Vinnie, baby, that daughter of yours is a good girl cause she is still in college, but she could get a part-time job and help herself some, too. She is young and strong and they have special jobs for college students. We can help her with her tuition for college, but all these extra expenses, extra things, they can both do without em. It will teach them to grow . . . be independent!"

But Vinnie didn't want to hear that either. She kept thinking, "But I'm a mother. A mother! Those are my children."

So.

One day he happened to lend some money to a man on a little Toyota that ran well. When Fred didn't get paid back according to the agreement, he thought of Vinnie, whom he really cared about, always being tired. He signed the pink slip over to Vinnie, saying, "Here. Ride to your jobs and give your feet a rest." With that he left off courting her . . . as close. Just stop by maybe once every week or two, or so. Some people are like that; if they give you something big enough they get mad at theirself and step back a ways for awhile.

Vinnie missed him. Now, Fred was mostly gone, there wasn't even that tiny little bit of romance in her life that makes a person welcome each new day. She would just be in that house, alone, with that stack of money-order receipts. Or sit by her window, looking for her eagle. That eagle always lifted up her heart a little. It seemed to know just where it was going and just what it was doing.

Wynona lived on one side of Vinnie and Josephine lived on the other side. Josephine's house was a little perkier, fresher, cleaner. Had a nice yard and garden that the owner, Josephine, worked in every day.

Josephine was a nice-looking forty-nine-year-old woman who had been married three times and had three divorces from which she had garnered enough money to end up buying her own home and a triplex she rented out and kept up. Oh, she was smart! She took care of herself!

She being nice-looking, there were gentlemen who came around to court her, but, somehow, they didn't seem to last long.

But Josephine said that didn't bother her. "I don't need these rocks comin over here to weigh me down. They just lookin for a slave and a house! I ain't cookin for no man, woman, chick or child. I got more sense than to marry me a job! Washin and cleanin up after somebody. No, Lord! I'm waitin for a rich man to come find me! Or a good strong man with two jobs or one real big job will do!"

Josephine dressed nice and kept her hair up and had professional manicures. She wore gloves in her garden and in her kitchen sink so her hands were nice with moderately long shapely nails.

She liked to entertain a little so she often gave ladies' luncheons and invited a few church members and other friends of hers, including Vinnie when she wasn't working, but seldom or never did she invite Wynona. "Them cats and that dog just follow her around. She full of animal hairs and cat hairs on my furniture just drive me crazy! And I don't need any extra work. If I wanted to clean up pet hair I'd have a pet of my own, but my pet wouldn't shed like that!"

The luncheon ladies would sit and talk gossip and admire Josephine's house (which was why she invited them) and the new dresses or hats Josephine had, she always brought out to display.

Josephine was a smart woman, always had been, and she let everyone know. "My mother didn't intend, and I don't intend to grow up to be nobody's fool!" Then she would describe what a fool some women could be for men, which instances included some of her friends sitting at that very table. She could go on and on about men and how well she knew them. "You ought to get rid of that man if he don't know how to treat a woman!"

All her friends were not really friends, but she served a good lunch and you could catch up on the latest gossip. But Josephine thought she had a wide circle of friends and acquaintances, which didn't matter anyway because all she really wanted was an audience. As Wynona mentioned to Vinnie, "So . . . she buys the food, prepares it and cleans up after they are all gone, with her smart self. I'm tellin you, ain't nobody gettin clean away in this world without it costin em somethin! She's workin right on anyway!"

Josephine never had seen the eagle flying near her house. She seldom looked up.

Vinnie has to be the one to tell you about this because she knows all of it.

"Well, everybody was busy doing their own lives when all of a sudden two or three things happened around the same time.

"First, a lady, no, a woman moved into the neighborhood right across the street from me. The woman, whose name turned out to be Betha, I think, lived with her mother or her mother lived with her, anyway, they were together. Betha had a boyfriend named Tom or Dick or something. She was loud and you could hear her saying Dick all the time so everybody thought that was his name.

"They drank and partied a lot over there so Betha was usually high off that liquor. Didn't take them but about fifteen minutes to move all their furniture in, but a few days later I saw them carry in a new phonograph player. A record player. Everybody in the neighborhood could hear that loud music all times of day and night. People shoutin out their blues and Betha screamin right along with em. Now, I love music, but there is a way to listen to it and keep it in your own house. We were all wonderin how to handle all the noise when something else became clear: when the music was turned off you could still hear all the screamin!

"You could hear her screamin at her mother when she wasn't screamin at Dick. She was just a screamin, loud woman. Her mother was about seventy or eighty years old and that loud music must have driven her crazy. I thought back to my son's drum-practicin and I knew what she was going through.

"Betha cussed her mother out somethin truly terrible too!

I mean, she called that poor old lady, her own mother, bitches, M.F.'s (you know), ho's and oh, all kinda bad, sick, dirty things! I would never dare talk like that to my mother, rest her soul. Never!

"Wynona would just cringe when she heard Betha screamin out bitches and all that other stuff at the old mother. She said, 'I rather my kids not be round me than talk to me like that.' Course her kids were not around Wynona very much at all anyway.

"Now, there was a little screened-in front porch that Betha brought the old mother out to sit in, rain or shine, wind and all. I would see her as I went back and forth to my jobs. Betha sat that old, sickly lady on a wooden chair that had most of the back wood-rest broken off. The old lady, her mother, leaned back, all day, on one board left on the sideback of that chair. I am not lyin! Was a old rickety table there and Betha shoved her mother's food plate on it and with a bent fork, no knife, and a cloudy glass of water or soda pop; that was her meal. Tryin to sit up on a broken rickety chair and eat off a rockin table. No dozin off to sleep in that chair. That old lady never did seem to complain though. Scared to, I guess! She just sat there starin way off through that screen round the tree or two in their yard and off into the sky. I bet she sees my eagle sometimes. I love that ole eagle, but I bet that bird is after Wynona's hens.

"Anyway, the old lady always had a nice, polite smile for you as you passed, even from across the street. It just made me and Wynona so sick and sad to see her treated like that, we felt like cryin. Josephine shook her head and said she was going to call the cops, no, the police. (Josephine is very proper in her speech.) But, no police ever came. Probably because

Josephine didn't call; I know she didn't want Betha getting mad at her!

"I finally started walkin over to that side of the street when I came home from work and I would say a few soft kind words to the old lady, whose name, she told me, was 'Mrs. Megalia Foster,' so I called her Mrs. Foster and smiled and talked to her for a few minutes, through the screen, cause I didn't want that big Betha comin out hollerin at me or the old lady. Chile, it was sad. I took to taking her a dish of dessert or a bowl of beans, rice and a big piece of buttered cornbread when I was cookin for myself between jobs and saw her out on the porch. Well I knew she would be out there because she just always was out there in all weather. Betha always came out then, smilin, and she would say, 'I'm gonna put this away for Mama for later.' I believe Betha ate it once it got inside the house, but I shouldn't be so mean to think like that because it was her mother. Once I started goin over there takin food, Wynona started doin it too.

"Josephine put her hand on her hip and told us, 'You all are fools! You better learn to stay out of other folks' bizness!'

"I don't know where I got the time from, but I looked around my house lookin for some chair that the old woman could sit on and rest her back. Wasn't nothin there, so, later on, I went down to the secondhand furniture store and bought her, bought her!, a cheap, good, stuffed comfortable chair. And I don't know where I scraped that money up from. Just looked through every little savin spot of mine and told the clerk why I was buyin the chair and we worked on the cost together. Plus, God is good.

"I was tryin to get it into my little car to take it to the old mother when Fred came along and so we met again. He was in his truck and he offered to carry it to her for me. He sometimes has a tender heart that will open for me.

"I got real nervous and fluttery when I saw Fred because I really like that man. More than like him. I love him. I miss him. I surely do. It has taken every ounce of strength I have to keep myself from callin him on his own phone he gave me. But, I'll tell you more about that later."

Wynona has to be the one to tell you this.

"When Fred drove up in his truck with that chair in the back of it, I was lookin out my window, as usual, cause I don't have nothin much to do once I clean over my house in the mornins. Anyway, they put it on the porch with Betha's smilin permission and sat Ms. Foster in it. The old mother just leaned back real slow as she smiled up at the people round her tryin to make her comfortable, but in that smile was a few tears. I was so glad to see Vinnie had done what she had done because Ms. Foster sat out there way late into the night sometime, two, three o'clock in the mornin hours. Don't ask me how I know, I just know! I sit in my window a lot.

"Once Vinnie asked Betha if she could take the old mother to church of a Sunday and Betha smiled at her (she smiled at everybody but her mother, it seemed) and said 'Yes.' After the church meetin, Vinnie took Ms. Foster for a ride. The old mother was just as happy as she could be sittin there in that car goin somewhere! As they rode, they talked and Vinnie asked her, 'Why does your daughter talk to you like she does?'

"Ms. Foster looked down into her lap as she folded that little raggedy handkerchief over and over again. She finally said, 'I don't know, chile. I didn't raise her that a way. I am a church-goin, when I can, woman. A God-lovin and -fearin woman. Always was. My mother was too. I worked all my life . . . all my life. From the fields when I was a young girl, to the kitchens when I was married. At the hospital, where I was workin when I got sick, I was workin. I never in my life talked like my chile do.'

"Ms. Foster was quiet a minute, then she said, 'Betha was named after my mother, who died eight months pregnant with her twelfth child while she was pullin sugarcane stalks. Bled to death fore they got help for her. My poor mama.' Ms. Foster took a deep breath, then said, 'Betha never did like school.' She unfolded the handkerchief again, then proceeded to fold it up again. 'I wanted her to get an educationer. Learn somethin. Do somethin . . . else. But . . . she hate school; she love boys better. I guess she never learned no new words to say cept them cuss words, so she just keep on sayin them old words she picked up in the streets and them juke joints.'

"The old mother began to cry silently then, tears rollin slowly over the hills and valleys of her worn face. Vinnie tried to drive the car and hug her at the same time, and couldn't, so she pulled the car over and held her. Then as she wiped her tears with that folded handkerchief, Ms. Foster says, 'I forgive her . . . cause she is mine. She all I got . . . cept a Security check . . . and she take that. I don't care.' Old mother Foster tried to pull herself together then, and sat up straight as she could. 'I don't care. I ain't long for this here earth nohow. Death is my friend. For a long time now. I waits for him. God is good . . . He'll make a end to that ole devil's work.'

"I don't know where she got the money from, she spends every dime she don't need for bills on her grown children, but Vinnie took old mother Foster to have a good meal. She say she got the old mother to laugh now and again. So Ms. Foster had a good time. THAT day anyway.

"Now, let me tell you, when Vinnie drove up to Betha's house and looked through that screen as she took Ms. Foster onto the porch, she saw that nice stuffed chair all torn and broken down. Betha and her boyfriend sat on it and had a fight on it, with it, all around it and all over it. If you tried to sit in it, it tilted backward almost to the floor. Now the old mother is back on her wooden chair with one backboard to lean on. Vinnie dragged herself home to cry cause there was no more money to spend on another chair that might end up the same way. She cried and she did some hard thinkin.

"Round that time, too, I had prayed and been talkin to God and bought them lottery tickets and one day . . . I WON! Fifty thousand dollars! Dollars! Lord, have mercy, Yes!"

Later, Josephine just put both her hands on her hips and said, "All she did was win back most of what she has already spent on them tickets! That money be gone soon too, back on some more tickets."

All Wynona's lonely years came down to nothing. First, Wynona told Vinnie about her winnings. Vinnie just sat down and looked stunned. Somebody won! She leaned back in her thinking chair by the window and just looked at Wynona's sparkling eyes. She shook her head, over and over again.

"Wynona! You can do so much! Some of all them things you been dreamin about! Get you your own house. Buy you a car. Buy you some decent clothes. A good stove. A good refrigerator. A . . . Girl, you don't need to never, ever worry again! You free!!"

Wynona just laughed and cried at the same time. Grinned and pressed that ticket that lay in her brassiere against her breast and lonely heart. "Oh! You know you been my best friend. I don't know what I would do sometime without knowin you are over here and close. I be so lonely sometime. I don't talk much about it, but I miss my family and people I know love me bein around me. I'm gonna go see my family! Get me some of that ole-fashion family love." Her face shone with her love. "Then I want me a house and a car. I'm gonna pay all my bills up and take me a trip to see my sisters and go to my mama's grave and put a tombstone and a BIG load of flowers on it, plant em! . . . and my daddy, too. I'm gonna help you too, Vinnie, cause you been nice to me. You are my friend. And I'm gonna get me a refrigerator and get you one just like it. But I'm sure gonna hate to move away from you. I'm gonna try to move out there in that nice area where Fred lives. It's a nice clean place where ain't nobody cussin they mama out; leastways not how you can hear em."

"I'm gonna, I'm gonna, I'm gonna," was Wynona's song and she sang it, hummed it, tapped it out with her feet when she was trying to stand still. She was happy.

Josephine mumbled to Vinnie and any other person she talked to about Wynona, "She need to try to get her a man and throw that dog and all them dirty pets away!" But she made a mistake when she told Vinnie, "I been seeing a big ole bird flying around here! I'm gonna get my gun and kill it! It's too big to be flying over my house! Vinnie told her, "I see you with a gun pointin at my eagle and I will report you to somebody who will do something about it! And if I don't see you with a gun and something happens to my eagle, I will still report you. That eagle isn't botherin you! You leave that bird alone!'"

Well, that's the way neighbors are sometime.

Vinnie can sure tell you this because she was looking out for Wynona.

"In the end, Wynona didn't have to buy no tickets to see her children or her sisters or any other distant relative she knew she had or didn't know she had, cause it wasn't but a week or so before every one of them was at her little rented house, crowding them weak walls out. She couldn't tell how word got around so fast, she had only told her children and her sisters. But word sure did fly. Just like that eagle, chile.

"Wynona's grown kids came home for the first time in two years or longer, huggin and kissin her and puttin in their bids. Beggin for just a 'little' help. Only one, a son, didn't ask. He seemed to just be happy for his mother. Then her two sisters were there, don't know how many years since she had seen them. They were huggin and kissin her, talkin bout their dead mother and what she would want Wynona to do for the 'family' and asking her for just a 'little' help. Her husband had been dead more than ten years, but his mother and brothers and sisters, nephews, nieces and somebody's grandchildren and great-grandchildren and all the way to cousins and near cousins, aunts and uncles were there. All of them! So glad to see a woman who had been there in that house so many years . . . alone. Without them.

"Wynona put them up in motels and hotels, and she had to pay! because they were her 'guests' and they couldn't afford it. So she paid. And paid. And paid. Well, they all had to eat, didn't they? They even said, 'First vacation I ever had, so I ain't cookin, honey!' I think Wynona was just overwhelmed and confused by all that attention and her mind wasn't workin any too properly.

"Yes, she sure did pay and pay. And gave, and loaned, and gave, and loaned. Each fond, loving relative left as they got 'some' of what they wanted. But it was never enough. I heard one as they left carryin their little torn-up luggage say to the other relative, 'Wynona is a stingy bitch and she ain't gonna know what to do with all that money noway! Prob'ly gonna end up givin it away to some fool she got hid somewhere! Never did see no man round here and I know she got one!' Then their voices faded away as they stumbled down the street with their bags and full bellies and the fresh extra cash Wynona had given them.

"Of course her grown children fought their relatives for the money. Not for Wynona, but for themselves. All but the same one, the son who had never asked for much and didn't have much. He didn't come home often because he thought he had nothing to bring. He didn't know his love would have been enough. He kept tryin to talk to her alone. 'Ma, let's go look at houses for you.' Or 'Ma, put some money away. Hide it.' But the other relatives who happened to hear him thought he had some hidden motive and kept comin between them. Then her other children began to lie on him and his 'secret plans.' Wynona was speechless. And gettin broke. Fifty thousand dollars is NOT that much money when you have twenty-five thousand relatives askin for some.

"Wynona came to my house wakin me up several mornins. I was always dead tired of always workin and still bein always broke. But she is my friend and needed to talk. She was a nervous wreck from her relatives and Betha screamin across the street. She couldn't half sleep because someone was always tappin her shoulder while she was tryin to sleep so they could whisper to her, alone, together.

"I was still half asleep, but I told her, 'Don't forget what you have been through. Seem to me you the only one who can really love you and see to your future. So you got to have sense enough to watch your money. So do it. Don't ask me, don't ask nobody. Don't you know what you need? What you want? You have been tellin me for twenty years! Now, do it. Think. That sure is what I been doin lately. I been lookin at your life and my own life. And my children. Think.' "

That is what Vinnie was doing: thinking. Just things running across her mind. Money. Finally Fred . . . and love. "Ain't no money in my life and there ain't no love in it either. I'm all the time worryin about money and bills and children. Grown children. My house is goin down. I'm goin down. I'm gettin old and there ain't no romance in my life. But I ain't old! I'm tired of supportin kids that don't never ask me how I'm doin. Don't ask me do I need anything. They never say, 'Mama, let one of them jobs go and just rest a little more. Do somethin for yourself.' "

Still, Vinnie went out and bought the money orders for

some new cymbals for Richard's drums; "I believe I can get this great job, Ma. I just need these new cymbals to make sure of it! I've got to be able to live, Ma."

She sent money for Delores to get a new cashmere sweater set. "I just have to have them, Ma, because I belong to this sorority and all the girls have one or even three sets. So there. See, I am not asking for two or three sets, just one set. I am the last girl to ever get anything, blah, blah, blah. I need a new coat, too. Coats are beige this year, Ma. I'll be the last one for that too, I guess. I will just have to go round in last year's black coat. I don't know how I can live on what you send me. It's very hard, Ma."

Vinnie sent the hard-earned money orders to Richard and Delores, but this time she wrote a little extra on her letter to each of them. Said, "You need to think about getting a job of your own for all these little extras you can't live without, because it's me that can hardly live." She was thinking hard now, about her own life.

In the meantime, one day when it was raining Betha sat her mother out on that screen porch on that rickety, one-board-back chair, just cursing her all the while. She gave the old mother a blackened banana and a dirty rinsed-out glass of water, just cussin all the while.

Wynona can sure tell you this.

"Now Betha was a big ole, strong woman. Husky like a man. And though everybody wanted to tell her off about the way she treated her mother, everybody was scared of her. But on this morning, letters to her children in her hand, Vinnie hesitated by her little car, then took a deep breath and walked across the street to Betha's house. Well, it was Ms. Foster's house because it was her check that paid the rent, but wasn't nobody gonna argue with Betha bout that.

"Vinnie stood outside speaking to Ms. Foster through the screen when Betha came out, smiling at Vinnie. Vinnie took another deep breath and asked her, said, 'Betha? How come you talk to your mother like you do?' Betha tilted her head as the smile became dimmer. Vinnie kept talkin to her, 'This is your mother. No matter what she might have done, she don't deserve to be all them names you call her. And she don't deserve to hear all those terrible, dirty words you say.'

"Betha stepped up to the screen door and opened it. Smile all gone now. Said, 'Ain't no G.D. nobody gonna tell me how to talk to my own mama! Not you, not nobody!'

"Every neighbor who was awake, their shades flew up with them lookin out, cause, you see, Betha's voice really carried.

"Vinnie didn't step back, just kept talkin, gently. 'Betha, your mother gave birth to you or you wouldn't be here. She loved you enough to raise you. Feed you. She bought and changed your diapers and clothes. Musta kept you from harm's way because here you are just as strong as you can be.'

"Betha raised her arm and opened the mouth that was in the middle of her terrible, angry-mad face.

"Vinnie raised her little hand up to stop her. Betha stopped! And Vinnie kept talkin, 'It hurts me, it hurts everybody, to hear you talk to her like you do, so I know it hurts your mother. And she is a old lady . . . so there is nothing she can do to you about it. That's why I thought I might mention it to you, what you are doin to your own mother.'

"Lord! As Betha stepped down the short steps toward

Vinnie, she shouted, 'Ain't nothin you can do bout it either, woman! So you best get on out my yard and MY bizness! This is MY mother! This is MY bizness!'

"Vinnie stood still a moment, then nodded as she turned to leave, saying, 'You're right. I just thought I had to say somethin and remind you she is your mother and we don't get but one. And yours ain't got long to be here on this earth. She is already sick and you are hurryin her on away from here. And when she is gone, God bless her, you are goin to miss her and wish for a chance to say somethin nice to her. And show her your love. Cause you do love her, you know. You have just done forgot.'

"Betha opened her mouth again, but nothin came out.

"Vinnie started walkin back across the street. I know she wanted to run, but she didn't speed up either. I would have flown, me. But Vinnie just went to her car, got in and drove on off to her daily slavery for her kids."

But, Vinnie was thinking. "I am a mother. Suppose, one day, I have to depend on my own children? I don't have no reason or proof to think I wouldn't be treated the same way Mrs. Foster is because I might be a burden and a bother to them. My life would be in their hands because I might be helpless to help my own self!"

She thought about Fred . . . because she didn't have any real life, even now, when her life was supposed to be in her own hands. She jumped in her little car, tossing the two envelopes containing the money orders onto the empty seat next to her, and passed on by the mailbox without looking at it. "I want to think about this some more." And she thought some more about Fred, too.

As it happened Fred showed a house or two that day to a newlywed couple and he was thinking about Vinnie also. About her gentleness and those round muscles in the calves of her legs. Her smile, her low laughter. Her lovin ways. He had heard about Vinnie and Betha and was frightened for, but proud of, Vinnie. That was the day he called the telephone company to arrange for a telephone for Vinnie in his name. "I will pay for the phone and pay her to make a few follow-up real estate calls for me from her house. That way I can keep up with her at the same time I'll pay her so she can quit one of those part-time jobs . . . and rest some." That is what he did.

Josephine, looking through her window at Fred coming and going a bit from Vinnie's house, said, "What is he doing always over there at her house? He is up to no good. But he won't get nothing because she don't have nothing."

Wynona was glad to see Fred around Vinnie a bit. "He a nice man and she needs one."

In the other meantime, Wynona was going around in circles. Distraught and confused. Her good son had had to leave to get back to his job so she had no true support she was kin to and could count on any longer. All the others still in her house just wanted her money.

"What am I gonna do?" she asked Vinnie.

"Tell em you're broke!" answered Vinnie.

"They won't blive me!"

Vinnie looked at Wynona like she was crazy and asked, "Who cares what they believe? It's your bizness."

Wynona's sisters each left with a couple of thousand dollars. "For Mama's sake," they said through their smiles. Her two other children left with five thousand dollars each. "For our future." But they complained she could have done more; "I need . . . I need . . . I need."

Vinnie was a little angry with her. "You need, too! Have you talked to anybody about that house you want?"

"No. Ain't had time."

"Take time! It's your life!"

Later Wynona did speak to Fred about finding her a house.

Josephine spoke to Vinnie about Wynona, too. "What's going on with that fool Wynona? She gonna give all that money away? She is a sure-nough fool!"

"This time, Mrs. Smart Josephine is almost right," thought Vinnie.

It wasn't but a day or two later that Vinnie came out of her house with Wynona, and Betha came out of her house at the same time. When Betha saw Vinnie she commenced to run across the street toward her. Vinnie froze in her tracks, thinking "Oh, shit!" But she stood her ground, didn't run back into her house or jump in her car, which is what she wanted to do.

She was scared though. Wynona just gasped and held her breath, thinking, "Lord, I have to help my friend. I guess we both gonna get whipped today."

When Betha got to Vinnie she raised both of her ham-bone arms and threw them around Vinnie and hugged her. Hugged her! Vinnie was surprised, astonished, relieved and grateful.

With a great big smile on her plump face, Betha said, "You was right! I love you! You a good woman! She is my mama and I sure do love her!" Then they hugged and all that. But it wasn't long before Betha had a fight with one of her boy-friends, Dick or somebody, and they broke that record player and Betha went back to cussing her mother again.

Vinnie mused over it. "But, well, what you gonna do about somebody's else's life? Maybe it just comes from being poor and not having nothing or just seeing everybody havin everything on television and you still always having nothing." Then she would sit in her window and look for her eagle. The eagle gave her something; she couldn't put it in words, but the eagle gave her something.

Finally, Wynona's last family got all they were going to get and they left with the words "I'm broke . . . I'm broke from comin down to your house here to see bout you!" ringing in Wynona's ears. Some who had arrived late and weren't close family didn't get anything. They left mumbling to each other, "Stingy dog! She too cheap and tight for me. She sure gonna have some bad luck from the way she act to me. And she need not call on me for help cause I ain't got no time for somebody won't help nobody. Specially her own blood!" They left belching with their full bellies and rested backs from their stay in a decent clean room at the motel where they had slept on clean sheets and used fresh towels Wynona had paid for. Don't tell me anything about some people. Just tell me what you gonna do about life and the way people are?

Wynona was so glad when the last relative was gone, her tears dried up and her teeth, the few good ones she had, shone again in her smile. That is when Vinnie told her, "One thing you could have done is get your teeth fixed."

Wynona smiled behind her hand. "I can still do that."

"How? You said you were broke. You have let your relatives talk you out of all that money and you may never get your hands on that kind of money again in a big chunk like that. Chile, you were blessed. And now ... all that money gone. And you still need a house. That one over there you living in is gonna fall down on you cause your landlord isn't going to never do no real fixin-up on it."

Wynona still sat smiling behind her hand. "Well ... I got a secret."

"What kind of secret?"

"I hid some of my money from me and everybody."

"Hid it? Where did you hide it in that little house full of your relatives?"

Wynona removed her hand in her excitement. "Well, you know my dog? Bozo? Well, he keeps a pile of dried-up doo-doo right just side of his doghouse. Everybody always was complainin bout the smell and the flies. Well, I don't smell it much cause I love him and I keep it cleaned up when I have time and don't have so much company. They was all complainin, but didn't nobody go out there to clean it up. I was always cookin them some food or goin to the store to buy it, or washin dishes and their clothes. My ole washin machine like to blew its rollers off! cause they want to wash every little thing stead of wait for a big load and they didn't want to mix up their clothes with the other relatives' germs. We washed nearly every day, well, I did, til I told them the machine was breakin down and they had to go to the launderette. They didn't want to spend their own money so some of them wore their clothes longer. My sisters rinsed theirs out in the tub."

"What's that got to do with your secret?" Vinnie smiled at her.

"Just that they always want to see my bankbook. I know they looked for it. I had to keep changin where I hid it. And I truly wanted them ALL to go and I know they ain't goin til I'm broke. So while I was actin like I was cleanin round my dog Bozo's house I had a big thought. Right away I told them I had to go to the store. I got a minute alone and dug down deep up under some things and got my bankbook and left like I was goin to the store, but instead I went to the bank. Didn't have but about thirty thousand dollars left and hadn't done nothin for myself, girl. Nothin! And I was plumb worn out from givin and doin things for them and I knew I might never see my sisters and children again if I didn't give em somethin."

Vinnie heard herself saying, "They are not children anymore. They are grown."

Wynona gave her a special look to remind her of her own kids. Then she went on speaking, "After I went to the store, cause I had to bring somethin home with me, I went to the bank and took all my money out cept for one thousand dollars cause I got to keep lottery-ticket-playin money."

Vinnie gasped as she thought of that money in the house with all Wynona's relatives.

Wynona spoke on, "Girl, I was so nervous you can't magine it nor blive it either. My knees shook and what few teeth I got rattled with twenty-nine thousand dollars in cash wrapped up in my apron stuck in a grocery bag hangin at the end of my arm. At first I thought of them people what snatch purses and I pulled that bag up to my chest and let my purse hang off my arm cause it was empty."

"Lord, have mercy, Wynona!"

Wynona smiled sadly as she continued. "When I got home I took some stuff out the grocery bag, waitin. I planned ahead and I had some spray and stuff I said I was gonna fix that dog-doogie pile with so they could breathe better, and I went out there with my grocery bag and sprays and my shovel and rake. I knew they wasn't watchin and they wouldn't come out cause I might ask for some help. I raked a spot and dug a right smart place down deep. It look like I was goin to bury that dog poop, but I buried that twenty-five thousand cash dollars instead. It was wrapped tight by then and I covered it with some of the freshest poop and some ole poop too and I knew that money was safe."

"Well! I'll be doggoned!"

Wynona laughed, "So was my money! Yes, I sure did! And I 'accidently' left my bankbook out after I finished givin my sisters a few thousand each: my kids already had theirs. After the rest of em saw that bankbook and tried to set their mouth to ask for some of that little one thousand dollars, I got mad. But I didn't say nothin . . . cause they my relatives and they family and I love em, but I decided then I would get sick and have to go to bed and be taken care of by them."

"Lord, have mercy! Please."

"So the next morning over the stove cookin some breakfast for them four or five what was still left, I just fell backwards onto the floor, holdin on to my chest where my heart is."

"Oh, Wynona. Poor dear."

"My children was gone, my sisters was packin. Them few holdin on carried me to my bed, feelin and pattin on me as they carried me, to see was I hidin any extra money on me. I was sad, mad and just through, but I let em cause I had the sweet smell of Bozo's poop on my mind. I don't know who called the doctor, but he went to actin like I need to go to the hospital; make him some money too, I guess. But I opened one eye and told him, 'Listen, Doctor, I'm just tired. You just order me some rest and quiet and twenty-four-hour care and I will pay you for this visit soon as everybody is gone and I can get up.' He caught on right quick and did what I tole him. And when you came over and everybody was talkin bout havin to leave and you said you would look out for me, they almost flew on way from here. You was very kind."

Vinnie laughed happily, "You were very smart! Now, I'm gonna call Fred and you go see if the worms are eatin that money. And it's gonna rain again, too. Go put it back in the bank for your own self's house and home, chile, and some teeth. Then maybe you can court again someday!"

They laughed and hugged. Friends.

Wynona went home to check her money.

In the beginning Josephine knew about the money and scoffed at Wynona. "She isn't gonna have that money long enough to buy a slop jar, which I know she needs! Lottery store gonna get it all back!" She ridiculed Wynona's relatives, too. "People always show up when they smell money! She a fool to let them in, cause all her family are poor as church rats and you know, they poor! The church gonna be after her, too! That fool won't have a dime in a week. I give her a week! Maybe! She don't ask my advice and I could tell her something because I am her friend. She ought to buy that house she been renting from me! Do something good for herself!"

When, at last, Josephine found out Wynona was looking at houses, she took herself over to Wynona's rented house. She told her, "You ought to hold on to that little money you got left. Why don't you fix this house up? I'll take it off the rent; even though you have cheap rent as it is. Just fix it up for yourself so you can live comfortable. You can live here til you die and never have to worry again. I wish you would get rid of that dog though . . . and them chickens. Shit everywhere! All over the yard!" That was not true, but Josephine was too smart for anyone to correct her.

Wynona just called Fred and said, "Hurry up, please!"

Fred found Wynona her house. It was a nice house with a small cottage in the rear that needed a little work. It was a little on the edge of town near the area where Fred lived. Clean neighborhood, trees growing along the street. She would be able to have a few chickens even, in a chicken house, of course, because there were eagles and hawks around coming from the hills. She put ten thousand dollars down and Fred gave her his commission fee for the closing costs, so she still had fifteen thousand left.

While the house went through escrow she got herself some new, fresh white teeth and that made her go to a beauty shop and get her hair done. She smiled all the time and everywhere. She bought a few new frocks, but not many. "I want to save my money for new furniture and a new refrigerator, chile. I might even think of somethin else I want!" Wynona grinned as she spoke.

It was the rainy season when Wynona moved. Vinnie, in her "thinking" window seat, looked out of her window, thinking of how lonesome it would be without Wynona next door. Then . . . she spied the eagle again swooping and diving, flying through the rain. Its wing seemed a little better. It flew faster, it seemed, and went further up toward the sky. Oh, God, how beautiful the eagle spiraled toward the sky with the clouds above it! It seemed to love its life, its body, its power to soar. She watched as the eagle soared easily and lightly as a feather until it flew out of sight.

After Josephine saw Fred coming and going to both Wynona's and Vinnie's houses, she went to visit Vinnie. "Girl, you let that man back in your life?! You sure are a fool! I thought you, at least, had some sense. He is too quiet. Quiet people are dangerous cause they fool you. He is doing something! I know men! They ain't no good. You were doing alright, already! Don't ask for trouble. He's gonna leave you again. You'll see!"

"He didn't leave me the first time, Josephine."

Josephine smirked, "I know everybody needs their pride, but he will leave you this time then, I bet. You are too easy to get. Men don't like women that come when they call."

"I didn't go when he called and he called for almost two years."

Josephine sat back and crossed her legs, said, "Well, you just take your time, girl. Because you are not getting any younger, you know. No sense making your last years—"

Vinnie interrupted her, "Thank you, Josephine. I know you mean well. But you know what they say about people who don't have nobody, tellin you about how to keep your somebody. So I'll just follow my own mind like I try to do on everything in my life. Sometime I'm wrong, I make mistakes, but at least they are my own mistakes."

Josephine took umbrage, "What you mean, 'somebody with nobody'? I got plenty men want me! You don't have the experience with men I have. I been married three times!"

"Alright, you're smart. But you are not smart enough to know what's in my mind."

"No. Some things are too small for me. Well, just don't say I didn't try to help you, that's all."

Vinnie smiled as she said, "You have done your best."

Soon after Wynona moved, Josephine started a small little affair with a gentleman visitor. It was just two dates long. The first time he asked her out to dinner and after she explained to him where she wanted to go, Delrichio (it was a very expensive place, but the food was delicious), they went. As they waited for their order to be served she said to him, "I know I am different from all the other . . . ladies you know, because I don't like anything cheap. I like the best of everything. You can ask my last husband, he will tell you: 'You never have to wonder what to get for Josephine, just simply get the best!' "

Then she blinked her eyelashes at him and said, with double meanings, "Everything I have is good!"

He did visit her again in her home, which was indeed filled with very good things, expensive things, too. This time after a dinner she cooked, she explained every dish she served to him and the kind of plates he was so fortunate to eat off of. They even had a "demitasse" in her living room with a fine fire burning in the fireplace. She told him all the things she wanted in a man and all the things she would not take from that man. Then she blinked her eyes at him again and said, "I am a woman though, and even I get lonely . . . sometimes. I miss the . . . comfort of a . . . man's strong shoulder. So, it is very, very possible I would marry again." She smiled seductively at him as she placed her hand on his knee. "I am smart enough to know when it is time to join my life with somebody again. The 'right' somebody." She picked up her demitasse and smiled at him over the fine rim of the cup.

The next week passed without a call from the gentleman, but she was a woman who did not call men. And she did not call him until after the next week passed. Well, there is nothing wrong with calling your man-friend, not at all, but if he does not call you back after the third call, you should know he must not want to talk to you, barring his being in a hospital or such.

But Josephine, being so smart, she began to call him every day for a month or so, sometimes four or five times a day. Finally, a woman answered. It could have been a daughter or a sister, but she hadn't let him talk about himself enough for her to know. So Josephine just gasped and hung up the phone.

Josephine was selfish, greedy and self-indulgent, but she

had her pride. She tucked her hurt feelings away, quickly, somewhere in her heart and laughingly pretended to herself he had never mattered anyway. "He is a fool. He does not know what he has missed."

Josephine thought the people in her neighborhood, and farther afield, looked up to her. That people looked to her for her wisdom and the good-sense advice she, unasked, volunteered to one and all. She thought that the church ladies, all the ladies, envied her clothes and style. She had never met anyone quite like who she felt she was. She was actually some form of sadist in that many people were hurt by her mouth in their business. Or she was a fool. She never ever questioned herself. She thought, "I have too much sense for some people! That's why they stay away from me! They don't want to hear the truth!" She ran potential friends away from herself all the time.

Josephine did have beautiful feminine hands and kept them professionally manicured. But even in the beauty of her hands she could not conceal the cruelty and greed and graspingness in her heart. It showed in the way she grasped, clutched and held things. She laughed the hardest at hurtful things spoken of others, particularly of women. Though her hatreds were not strong, they were fairly constant and full of green poisons. The eagle never swooped down low or flew long over her house and trees. Her spirit must have been outside cloudily surrounding her house.

In the times there had been some misery in the houses around hers, Josephine's spirit had been somewhat content. But, now that she thought her closest neighbors seemed on their way to some kind of future, her spirit was outside roaming in the rain. And the eagle would sail away from her screaming spirit.

While Wynona was going through her different little dreams on her way to moving away to her new house, Vinnie spent more time in her "thinking" chair, staring through the window watching for the eagle as her thoughts hung around her mind.

The thought of Betha and the way she treated her mother had stayed on Vinnie's mind for several weeks; even after Betha had hugged her. She thought of her own grown children. Richard could be on his own without her help except for emergencies. She would pay for Delores' college tuition and books until she graduated. "But can I count on them when I need them? When I am old and can no longer work like I do? They are all I have. I have given my life for them; as I should have because they are mine."

She thought of Fred, whom she loved though she thought she only thought of him because there was no other man in her life and there had been that one night. With him. She got weak in her knees when she remembered that night almost three years ago. "That good, good man. I have kept him out of my life because of my children."

Her mind turned, again, to memories of her relationship with Fred from the very beginning. She remembered seeing him around town for the last ten or twelve years. He always seemed somehow beyond her station in life; she was married and had two children, but she remembered noticing him as though from the corner of her eye and mind.

Fred had always been a mannerable man. Worked hard and was prosperous. They always said "Good morning" or "Good evening" as they passed each other. After her husband left, he began to say a few more pleasant things as they kept moving on about their business. Over the years, the extra words lengthened and they began to stop and move to the side of the sidewalk or aisle or whatever, his hand on her elbow, moving her out of the way of passersby. They talked longer. He made her laugh. And he made her wonder why he paid any attention to her at all.

Vinnie knew women, many women, liked him and would welcome his attention. "Well, this ain't nothin. He's just bein mannerly." Then, he asked her out to dinner. She had stuttered, startled, saying, "I . . . ah . . . I'll think about it," as she rushed away from him.

After that time, when she was going somewhere and saw him ahead in her path, she would wave at him and turn to go another way. Embarrassed for some reason she did not know. But Fred finally caught her and asked again, "When are you going to go to dinner with me, Ms. Escape Artist?" He wouldn't let her go until she answered him.

Vinnie laughed softly to herself, thinking back, "I know my eyes were wild because I was tryin to think of how my hair looked and why I had to put that ole hat on. Did it show where I had thrown that hem up on my coat and it had a button on it that did not match because I couldn't find the one that had come off. I knew I looked like a crazy woman."

But Fred had smiled down at her from his tall height with the pretty white gap teeth beneath the neat mustache. "I remember thinkin what smooth skin he had and wonderin if he shaved every day. Oh, and that whiff of men's cologne. All those things made me wonder: Why does he want to bother with me? I don't have a thing to wear! To dinner!? Is this man makin fun of me?" She shook her head. "No . . . he looked too sincere . . . and serious." Fred wouldn't let her arm go as he smiled down at her and said, "What's wrong? You think I'm goin to hurt you or make you pay the bill?" Then he laughed and it relaxed her. She liked his laugh.

Now Vinnie laughed at herself, "Oh, Lord, I said yes. I didn't know what I was gonna do. What was I gonna do? I must have been crazy. I turned to go away from him without sayin when we would go out, but he hollered out, 'Friday? Six o'clock! I'll be at your house on time. White folks' time!' I just nodded 'yes' and hurried on away from there. I was embarrassed and delighted, confused and wonderin what to wear, what to wear!"

Vinnie had been happy as she said, like a fool! A first date in eighteen years! Married at seventeen, a mother of one child at eighteen and then another child, and, now, eighteen years later. She had been thirty-seven years old acting like a fourteen-year-old on her first date.

But Vinnie was ready! She did it some way. A trip to the secondhand store; a dress she could wash, starch and iron herself. The brushing of her daughter's coat with a wet, stiff brush. Her daughter's old shoes shined. She was breathless and near tears from her frustration at preparing for a date she did not really want anyway (she told herself). But flowing beneath, around and over all her frustrations was an alive feeling that made her so happy, so happy, so happy!

When the time arrived, so did he. She watched his car pull up, grabbed her daughter's coat and started for the front door so she could be outside and he wouldn't have to come in.

Then she stopped herself, thinking, "This is my home. I don't need to pretend I'm any better off than I am. If it's good enough for me to live here, it's good enough for him to see." So she let him ring the bell and come in. She let him help her with her coat and let him close the door behind them.

As they stepped out on the porch she could now see, through his eyes, just all the things that needed doing. Painting, repairing, yard work. Vinnie looked skyward for her eagle, but she knew it would not be there, in the dark. She took a deep breath and just walked past all that work she never had time to do and Richard had seldom done and Delores was out of the question.

Fred opened his car door and helped her into his shiny, spick-and-span car. And they were off—to dinner. The restaurant was fancy and the food was good. When he brought her home, he asked for another date. "Next Friday?" They had talked so warmly, so comfortable and she had laughed so effortlessly and real, she said "yes" before she could stop to think. After he leaned over to kiss her on her forehead, she went into her house thinking, "What did I say 'yes' for? I have nothin to wear. Can't wear this dress again. This is all too much work!" But she slept warmly, pleased and full; a full, good night's sleep without even a dream.

Vinnie thought of Fred each day and night of the next week. At the end of the week came letters from her children and she had to push Fred out of her mind. Richard had written he needed some new thing and Delores wanted to go to the hairdresser; "For a change! It's been a whole month, Mama!" Their letters made her tired and depressed because she wanted to meet their needs, but each new need was like a new rock put in her arms to hold and balance along with the other heavier ones dealing with her jobs.

She did the same washing and ironing of the same outfit from the date last week. Fred picked her up looking at her with appreciative eyes again. He told her she looked wonderful, fresh and so good. They took a long drive this time to another very nice place. Fred even ordered wine with dinner.

As the evening ended he wanted to show her his home. She was thoughtful a moment, then said "alright" because he was a gentleman and mannerable.

It was a very nice house that held no telltale signs of a woman's hand in it. A very mannish living room and bedroom. Fred said, "A twice-a-week housekeeper kept the kitchen clean and stocked and all that." Vinnie smiled and turned to go back out his front door.

Fred took her arm, stopping her, as he said, "Don't worry, Vinnie. I'm not going to do anything to make you unhappy with me. I want to see you again . . . and again and again. I don't want to run you away from me. Foolishness is not my game." He started taking off her coat, gently. "So rest your coat and sit down anywhere you think you'll be comfortable, and I will fix us a drink and put some music on." She allowed herself to be led.

He put on some Bobby "Blue" Bland as he fixed the drinks and they even did a little slow dancing. Before the evening ended a little smooth Miles Davis and Billie Holiday. But by that time they had kissed, a little. Then Toni Braxton and Patti LaBelle, and the kissing got serious . . . real serious. None of it, honestly, was planned. Fred did not mean to misuse a dinner date with Vinnie, but . . .

Life and heart, body nor soul asks permission or makes appointments to come in or out to play . . . and they joined the party.

Suddenly the kiss their lips wouldn't let go of was stretched out on the couch. Clothes were up and some were down. It had been ten years or so since Vinnie had been in a man's arms. She tried to will her body to calm down, sit up straight and act like a lady. But her body answered, "Awwwwh, hell, why? Come on, plleassssse."

Fred almost helped her. He whispered, "Vinnie, will you love me if we do this? I don't want you to be disgusted with me." Vinnie, panties still on, was grateful for the moment allowing her to get back to her senses. She thought she was straightening her body to slip out from half under him as she raised her back and buttocks up to him and the poor man said, "Ohhh, Lord."

Then she tried to place her legs on the floor to help herself up and only one foot touched the floor, which left her in an open position and Fred groaned, "Mercy, mercy mercy." Then because everything was not in its proper place, he got up, picked her up and carried her into the bedroom and laid a whimpering Vinnie on the bed. He gently took her remaining clothes off, which she tried, a little, to hold on to because her underwear was not so good to see, and she didn't want to do this at the same time she did want to do it.

But his eyes were so full of love, he could not see, nor think of, any underwear he took off of her. He folded and set each worn piece aside, then undressed himself, never taking his eyes off her eyes. He slipped between the covers, pressing his body to hers as she pressed her body to his . . . then the music began. He strummed her body like a B. B. King guitar and she sang. And every time they reached the end of their song, they kissed and his hard strong body started a new piece of music and she always knew the song because she sang and sang and sang.

Finally, at last, she embraced him and said, "I just HAVE to go." He held her tightly, then helped her up, stroking her body as she moved away from him. They dressed and he'd stop to kiss her. They dressed some more, then kissed again. She combed her hair and he kissed her neck from behind her. He tied his tie, they kissed again til he threw his tie to the side. They put on their coats and kissed at the door as she opened it. They walked out to a misty, rainy, early morning. He took her home. They didn't talk. At her door he asked when he could see her again. She answered, "We can't do that no more. I didn't mean for all that to—"

He interrupted her, " 'All that??' " That's what you call it? I call it love. I love you."

"I . . . think I love you too, Fred. But this ain't what—"

He brushed her words away. "Then, I will see you tomorrow."

"Not to do that again, Fred. I can't do that again. Dinner, maybe. But not . . . that love." Then she had slipped through her door and closed it because she just didn't know what else to say. The next morning she blushed whenever she thought of what had happened, even all through the day.

She blushed when she saw him again. She agreed to go to dinner again, but she refused to go to his house. And it was killing him. He said, "I want to marry you. Is that what you want?"

"I have two kids, Fred."

"I love you, Vinnie. I will love your children." He didn't know them yet.

Vinnie smiled up to him. "Let's take time and see. I love you, too."

It was only natural that as he became more involved with Vinnie he would see the way her life was. They didn't have much time together because she was always rushing off to some job. Richard was a senior in high school, Delores was a junior at that time.

Fred began to offer suggestions. "Why doesn't Richard have a part-time job? I'll see what I can do for him. Then he can help hisself and you and save for his going off to college." He did find a job for Richard, but Richard didn't show up half the time and the friend that had hired him for Fred fired him, saying, "He just wants to listen to his music and pat his feet."

Another time, Fred said, "You better let that boy learn how to be a man, Vinnie. He is too old to have nothing to do! And he is planning on going to New York? With no money? But yours?"

Fred set up a small bookkeeping job for Delores, but she did very sloppy work, incorrect work, and she knew better. Just didn't want any job. To pay her for sloppy work was not right, to Fred, she had to build better work habits for the day she would have to support herself. He gave her a two-week notice to try to improve her work, she didn't, so he let her go.

These things weighed heavily on Vinnie and she couldn't bring herself to blame her children, so she resented Fred instead. By this time Richard had graduated and was gone to New York seeking out his future. Vinnie was working extra. Fred and Vinnie's time together grew less and less comfortable. And they weren't making love anyway, so Fred told her, "Maybe you have some thinking to do about your life."

She went back over the last argument she had had with Fred. It had started when he said, "Vinnie, you are getting older and I don't like to see you keep up all these jobs with NO help from either one of your grown children and no life of your own with me."

She had answered with a stiff lip, "I have a life. I have my children to think of."

"No," he had said, "they have you. That's good, too. But there is none left over for yourself, much less some for me. We are missing some of the best years of our life. If we were married . . . I'd take care of you. I'll pay college tuition as long as there are good grades and some effort to help themselves and—"

"Oh, leave me alone, Fred. I'm not goin to desert my children."

"Vinnie, we haven't even made love since that first time you let me hold you in my arms."

"I don't want any more babies."

Fred sighed, "I have protection and, Vinnie, I'd take care of my child."

"I don't trust 'protection' and I'm afraid of pills, pills, pills."

"Vinnie, you're afraid of life, in some way, and your children. Vinnie, it's good to love your children, God knows, but it would be good if they love you the same way back. Don't you know the greatest thing is to love someone and they love you back? Like I do? It hurts me to see you deprive yourself for . . . I can't take it much longer. It's been two years now. Two years. Lost . . . wasted. You could die without knowing rest, peace and love. I love you. I can't go on like this. I am a man. A grown man."

Vinnie had gazed despairingly around her little warm living room and then at the man she loved. Her heart yearned for him and for his love and the way he had held her body. Fred was thinking of her love, also. "How could she even forget that one night? And I have found out nobody can take her place."

Fred sighed, again, and picked up his hat, walked to her door and said, "I'm not getting any younger either and I'm not goin to let anybody steal my life from me. Especially, I won't just give it away. I want memories . . . with you. I want a home . . . with you. I want you. And if I can't have you, in peace . . . well, I'm not going to ask you again. And you are going to miss the best thing we could have . . . together. So . . . I'm gone, Vinnie."

He opened the door and stood there a minute waiting for her to say something, anything. Vinnie didn't know what to say, so she didn't say anything. He didn't slam her door as he left. He just stepped out and closed it softly behind him. She listened to his steps going down the stairs; not light or joyful as before, but heavy and tired. Then his car door slammed, she heard it all the way to the middle of her heart. Her nerves and feelings screamed aloud inside her body. But, finally, she didn't believe he was really gone for good. "He'll come back. Please, Jesus." That was when Vinnie's heart began screaming outside in the rain. Again.

But . . . Fred was gone. Though she saw him, now and

then, they just waved or even spoke briefly, but he didn't come back. Almost three years passed. Every day her heart screamed, dried and withered a little more. Richard never had started college and Delores was now in her second year at college.

Through almost three years, Vinnie was sad and bereft. Her heart grieving, her body calling, her mind saying, "Shhh-hhhhh." But she thought and thought, lived and breathed Fred, Fred, Fred. And she worked, worked, worked for her children. She always looked for her eagle, but saw it less and less. It was getting old, she thought to herself.

Now Vinnie was desperately, hurting-type lonely. Sad to the bottom of her little torn soul. Her body ached with its own memory of his love. They say time flies; in truth, time can seem to go by so slow, dragging slow, as it felt to Vinnie sometime. But, also, in Vinnie's mind, the years seemed to be fleeing from her; passing her by and taking her dreams with them. Even the possibilities seemed to be gone. Love was gone.

As she sat there this morning staring through the window at the rain, looking for the eagle, for her heart's reasons, she could almost see her own soul, still outside moaning in the rain.

Since the ordeal with Betha, Vinnie had thought in a different way about her children. She was leaning strongly toward Fred's suggestions, his philosophy of children, grown children.

Then when Wynona's money had been won Vinnie thought of how everyone came to get something. Only her son had not begged. He took his gift of money and went back to his job. His job. Also, when Wynona moved to her new house, only her son had written her: "Mama, I am so glad you will be happier." But he did not come to help. He was busy with his job. His life.

Vinnie thought to herself, again, "Everybody is busy about their own life. Everybody but me."

Wynona was so happy the day she moved. Fred had introduced her to a few workmen who painted, tiled and repaired things in her "new" house. Eduardo, a Hispanic fellow, was going to use his truck to move her. Eduardo didn't pass up any money because he had two children he was raising alone since his wife had died. He was an older, good-looking Latin man.

Wynona hadn't had a man-friend since when. She thought she was too old for "romance" and things like that. At the same time, she thought, "Vinnie was a fool for lettin that Fred man go." She even told Vinnie, "Girl, I always thought you had some sense! But, now, I don't know. And you done told me bout that night of lovin you had with him. Chile, if I had that chanct, I'd take it . . . old and ugly as I may be."

So she admired Eduardo and was glad he also knew how to do things around a house because, now, it was her own property and she would have to see to keeping it up to par. Eduardo helped her move by hauling the few things she had to carry over, because she was going to buy mostly new things. "All my things are mostly old, broken and tired. Like me." She laughed as she said that to Eduardo, flirting a bit and thinking, "I hope you know you are a little old and tired, too."

Eduardo kept coming around to check on her and to help

her in all the little ways a man is necessary around a house. Came to be the time when he hauled a cord of wood for her little fireplace, then carried some in and built a fire for her which they sat in front of, and she served him a glass of wine. Sometimes she cooked a meal for him. Didn't tell him about her money; no need to.

Another time he brought his teenage children over to meet her, a boy seventeen, Frederico, and a girl fifteen, Maria. Both were well-behaved, mannerable and sad. They missed their mother. Their mother's parents were in Mexico and Eduardo's father lived near, but was too old to handle two healthy youngsters and, besides, they were almost grown. Eduardo had wanted to raise them hisself. Wynona loved youngsters, still . . . But she was lonely in her new house. She had no new friends yet.

However, Wynona, with a little money and some new clothes, a fresh hairstyle, walked and thought with more assurance and self-confidence. She became more attractive; older but looking good. She was attractive to Eduardo, among a few others. Very few others, but how many do you need?

She became like a foster-mother-friend to Eduardo's children. They loved her because of her warm personality, warm home, homemade cakes, pies and dinners. She talked to them about life, education and attitude. Just plain ole common sense. Eduardo wanted to pay her but she wouldn't accept any money. She told him, "Just bring some groceries and I can cook a hot meal for all of you a couple of times a week, cause I may not be home every day. You are all welcome, you know, I like your little family." She didn't want to tie herself up in something that was not her life. She had already raised her children. Living, was on her mind now.

One day Vinnie visited her and as she was leaving said to Wynona, "Looks like you are courtin pretty steady there, girl!"

Wynona answered, "Don't be crazy. I'm too old to be courtin!"

But Vinnie laughed at her. "It ain't over til it's over!"

Wynona laughed back at her. "That's what you ought to tell yourself bout that Fred man! Why you want to keep hurtin yourself?!"

After a few weeks Josephine "happened" to come by to see Wynona's house while Eduardo and the children were there. She made a special trip back when he wouldn't be there. She told Wynona, "You are a fool! You just got through raising your own! These are some other woman's kids! That man is looking for somebody to use and you just falling right on in place! And who you tryin to look good for? Girl, you better try holding on to that little piece of money you got left, if you got any left."

Wynona retorted, "I may not be as smart as other people think they are, but I blive I know what to do about my own life!"

With all the things that had happened in Wynona's family and still hearing Betha cursing her mother, many things ran through Vinnie's mind when she sat in her thinking chair. She wondered more and more how her own children would be with her in her time of need. She decided to make a test: she would tell them she was sick. She picked up her phone, the same one Fred paid for, and made the calls. She had to call several numbers for Richard but was finally able to leave a message, and she left a message for Delores.

The next day Delores called and said, "Oh, Mama, if I leave school now, I'll lose so much time. And I have an entire event to organize and it's an honor to have been chosen to head it. Can you hold on for a month or two? Please, Mama! And don't die! Please! See a doctor, have you seen a doctor? Call me back and let me know what he says. Okay? I got to go now, Ma, there is a line here."

Richard called three days later, asking, "Sick? Mama, I'm in the middle of a lot of important things. Jobs, Mama, important jobs! See what Dee says and let me know. How sick are you? If you are real sick and maybe dying, oh Lord, maybe I can wait and take care of my business later. I'll check back at this number later to see if you have been able to reach Delores and call to let me know. Call me, now, you hear?"

Vinnie put the phone receiver down slowly, slowly after these calls from her children whom she had worked so hard for, sacrificed so much for. She moved slowly, slowly to her thinking chair, eased herself down into it and cried. It felt like the pain was coming from the bottom of her feet to some sharp pitiful point in her breast. She didn't look out of the window, she looked into her life.

She sat there as the day slowly darkened until she couldn't have seen out of the window even if she had wanted to. It was black night outside. She was dejected, rejected, tired, sad and emotionally desperate. And in love with a man who had proposed his love to her which she had refused. She had refused his proposal, his suggestions, his shared happiness, his loving, and for these last three years had been alone. Talking only to men who worked around her. Not dating. Vinnie laughed a deep jerky laughter in ridicule of herself.

She thought of how her house was going down, steadily decaying little by little all around her. She couldn't keep up with the house and her children's needs too. Her clothes were nearly rags even if clean. She wore stockings with little runs, shopped at goodwill stores, ate sparingly (which kept her slim, but never full).

It had started to rain and she looked out the window at the blackness and sound of water pellets hitting the glass, thinking of having to depend on her two children and she did not believe, now, she could depend on them. She didn't want to live with them, have them take care of her financially, but she wanted to count on them coming to see about her if she was sick.

She thought of the old mother, Ms. Foster, across the street being screamed at daily and who knows how she was fed. She thought of Wynona and her relatives who were there with the money and gone when it was gone.

Profound emotions are often silent, but they have words. She thought out loud, "I am almost forty years old now. For a dream that may never be, I am losing my chance at happiness. But, I made myself a victim. I don't hate my children; they are still my children. But, now, I will help them and live my life too."

Vinnie slept fitfully that night and woke up earlier than usual for her bank job. With the extra time she decided to sit right down and write her twenty-two-year-old son and her going-on-twenty-one-year-old daughter. She explained to them that they must cut down on their "wants" and get them-selves part-time jobs because she would not be doing as she had done for so many years. She told them she was tired and things must change. College fees would be coming, with good grades, but "extras" would cease. "I'm going to make a life for myself and I am starting today." She closed by sending them all her love as their mother. Vinnie signed, sealed and mailed the letters on her way to work, and of a sudden, her step was lighter and her back straighter . . . though her heart felt a bit heavy in her breast.

She continued thinking about her life all the day and Fred became more and more a part of the new life she dreamed of now. When she reached home that evening she made a cup of tea and went to sit in her thinking chair. The day had cleared of rain, leaving only a misty light fog in the air and around the trees.

She spied her eagle far off in the distance, high in the sky, only this time there was a tiny speck following the bird. As it drew closer to Vinnie's vision she could see that it was another smaller eagle. A young version of, obviously, its mother. The mother dipped and turned a bit, slowly, so her child, the young bird, could follow her easily. The smaller bird followed its mother with quick flapping wings, fighting hard to do everything the way she did. When the young bird fell behind in its efforts, the large eagle flew back to it and dipped and glided around it until it had regained its breath and direction, then they were off on the lesson again.

The mother eagle kept the young eagle at its lessons for more than an hour. She took no pity on her young, for she knew its life depended on its knowledge of the air and of its own power because they had enemies: man. The young eagle struggled, flapping, eagerly following the mother eagle. When its wings were stronger and it flew with a little surer sense of direction and the wind, the mother eagle headed back toward the hills and their home with her child steadily following her tracks in the air. It was a beautiful sight to see. Vinnie was mesmerized.

After her warmed-up dinner, which she ate without thinking about the food because she was still thinking of her life, she went to the telephone that Fred paid for and called him. She prayed as his phone rang, "Please don't let it be too late. Oh, Fred, don't let me go. I'll be lost. My world is empty. Please still love me."

Fred had been fooling around in these three years, but Vinnie was never out of his mind and heart. It was never as good, never the same with other women. And he knew where Vinnie was almost at all times. He knew what she had been doing. He periodically stopped by Wynona's and she told him of all he couldn't see, that she might know. But she never told him Vinnie hankered after him. He was giving up on Vinnie a little more each day.

When he answered the phone he sounded calm and professional, but his was a heavy sound, the lightness of life was not in his voice. In fact, he didn't even say "hello," he said, "Yes?"

Vinnie hesitated a short minute, then said, "Fred?"

His voice changed in an instant. "Vinnie? Hello, Vinnie?"

She took a deep breath and plunged in, "Yes, this is Vinnie and . . . I would like to invite you to . . . a dinner. Please."

"A 'group' dinner?" he asked.

"No. Just you . . . and me."

His heart beat an extra beat. "When?"

"Well . . . when you have the time. I know you are a busy man."

"I can come now."

Those words relaxed Vinnie, she laughed nervously though. "Well, oh, Fred, I'm not ready right now. I have to cook it."

He laughed softly back to her, "I'm ready. When?"

"Well, how about Friday? Six P.M.?"

"Friday? This is Tuesday!"

"I know, but I want it to be nice."

Fred frowned, "Why, Vinnie? I mean, why are you inviting me to dinner? What is this about?"

Vinnie turned her face toward her thinking chair. "Well, I'll . . . I'll tell you then . . . if you have time."

"Alright, Vinnie. Friday at six o'clock."

Vinnie didn't want to let his voice go, let him go and let the emptiness return. "Unless you have a . . . date."

"I said I'll be there."

Vinnie held on to the voice a little longer. "Fred . . . are you still mad at me?"

"I never was mad, Vinnie. I was . . . tired. It's been almost three years."

"I know, Fred, I know. I miss you. I mean . . . I miss talkin to you."

"Talking?"

Vinnie, even alone, blushed. "I'll have everything, dinner, ready Friday. Six o'clock."

Now, Fred didn't want to let her voice go, wanted to hold on a little longer. "Your man gonna let you have dinner with another man, alone?"

Vinnie had to laugh softly, "Oh, yes. Men are just waitin outside in line to have dinner with me. Is your lady gonna let you come alone, over here, I mean."

There was humor in his voice as he said, "I'll see if I can't make all of em understand that we are just old friends."

"Old friends?"

Humor gone, Fred said, "What else are we, Vinnie?"

"You're right, Fred. And good old friends are hard to find."

"That's real!"

"Well, see you Friday, Fred."

"Still giving me Fridays, Vinnie?"

"We can make it . . . next week."

"No, no, Vinnie. This Friday is fine. I'll see you then."

They said their good-byes and Fred leaned back in his squeaky leather armchair while Vinnie stood there looking at the phone trying to see Fred in a voice memory. These two people! His whole day changed, all of a sudden the day looked good. But not too good. "What does she want to talk to me about? Is she marrying somebody else?" Then his day went down, a little.

All the rest of the week Vinnie walked on air and hot coals at the same time. She didn't know what to cook, how to serve it to make it special, what to wear, what to nothing! She had three days to plan and get it all together. "And my hair! My fingernails, my everything! What tablecloth? My dishes. Ohhhhhh!"

Then she sat down and played his voice over again in her mind. Over and over again. She found it so hard to realize he was actually coming to her house this Friday. He wasn't married . . . yet! She thought of that first and last night at his house; his kisses, the way he held her, his smile, his voice. Her body trembled from the emotions she felt. It was not a sexual emotion. It was a feeling of love. Three years stronger. Strong enough for a lifetime. But, was his love still strong for her? Her heart was still outside flailing in the misty fog.

Well, you know all the things she did getting ready for that Friday. That Friday. Friday. She took a day off from work! First time ever! She spent the day at the secondhand stores. Vinnie found a real nice damask tablecloth, which when washed and gently starched looked rather grand as it fell in soft folds around her kitchen table turned dining room table. The two tarnished, slightly cracked candlesticks, cleaned and polished, looked elegant since there would be only candlelight shining on them. They, finally, created a lovely, rosy glow over everything. She bought two place settings of delicate china and two settings of matched silverware that winked brightly in the glow of the many candles she had placed around the room.

"I have no fireplace, so these burnin candles will have to do."

She didn't have much money left, but she divided it between food and flowers. She bought tulips to put in the slightly chipped crystal vase sitting in the middle of the table between the gleaming candlesticks, candlelight flickering over the delicately colored, beautiful flower petals. Now!

The house, of course, was clean as clean can be. And she had bought a black wool dress which showed her long, lean legs beneath the knee-length hem. A string of imitation pearls, good as new, from the secondhand store would be around her neck. She could not afford a pair of pretty new shoes. She happened to pass an Asian store with Chinese slippers in the window at a very low price. She bought a black pair of backless slippers that were velvet and had no design on them. "They're delicately pretty and would also be comfortable to serve in, runnin back and forth to the kitchen," she thought. She was going to look lovely, even beautiful, because there was so much life and beauty in her eyes.

Friday, she was bathed, deodorized, powdered, lotioned, cologned and dressed at 5:00 o'clock P.M. She had just checked the food. A whole fresh fish was waiting to be placed in the broiler. She lifted the double-boiler top that held the mashed potatoes sprinkled with parsley. String beans with slivered almonds (asparagus were priced too high). Fresh baked bread, the chilled butter was in the refrigerator. A fresh green salad waited to be tossed and a lemon meringue pie, homemade, sat atop the stove with golden-brown spires atop the meringue. Iced tea, iced beer or iced water were the only choices she had.

At five-thirty o'clock, Vinnie walked round and round the dining table and room, looking over her evening setting, thinking, "Why, this is beautiful! Why don't I do things like this for myself more often? Why should I wait to do it for somebody else?" Then she sat by her window, looking for her eagle. Outside, her soul was hovering near the window, waiting to come in.

At the correct time she heard a car pull up to her curb and knew it was him. She sat still and waited until he rang the bell. Then, for some inexplicable reason she felt anger in her heart. Brushing the very thought aside, she took a deep breath . . . and went to the door.

Thinking about, silently praying for, her future.

Fred, bright and smiling, stood at the door dressed in his finest. He came in with his eyes lighting up at the sight of the candles and the lovely dinner set up, the smell of good food cooking. And, then, Vinnie, the loveliest sight of all to him. He sighed, shook his head in wonder and thought, "Vinnie." He reached for her to hug her and she stepped into his arms and right back out again.

"Hello, Fred. My, you look well. Let me take your hat and coat."

He moved automatically, she was going so smooth and fast. Then he realized, knowing her, she must be nervous because of his presence.

"Now you just have a seat and I'll check on my dinner and get you a glass of iced tea or a beer?"

He smiled as he chose a chair close to her. "Well, give me a minute to look at you and say 'hello.' You are looking well and very good! And very beautiful."

Nervous, pleased and self-conscious, Vinnie went to hang up his things. A radio played softly as she came back with a glass of chilled beer. He held an arm out toward her, but she took his hand, then set down beside him. She petted his hand and began to make small talk about his work and health. He relaxed into her mood, thinking, "If this is the way she wants to do it . . . alright. I'll wait until later to kiss my woman like I want to."

In a moment, Vinnie went back to the kitchen to check on the food. All the thinking of her love for Fred as she had gone about the business of preparing for this dinner had ended. Now, she was full of confusion and even anger. She still loved Fred, but less. Her mind was not clear why.

As Fred waited, feeling very at ease and pleasant sipping his beer in the softly lighted living room combined dining room tonight, Vinnie was in the kitchen thinking.

Her loneliness warred with her anger at Fred for being able to walk away from her for almost three years, all over some money. "I was the one workin for my children . . . not him. I don't understand if he could love me, he could let that stop our plans. I wish I had forgotten him. I wish I had never found out about his thrill for me. Our love musta not been meant to be. He sure ain't been lookin back or thinkin about me."

She turned down fires and stirred a pot or two. "Why do I still love him? He didn't do nothin but make my life more empty than it was before. And the nights I spent layin in that bed without sleep or cryin myself to sleep! Prayin! Prayin for that man! And now I have invited that man to dinner and spent all this money. For him! I sure must be a fool!" She stood thinking a moment, then answered her own question. "Cause I'm alone . . . that's why. Alone. Even the eagle ain't there every day." After another moment, she put a smile on her face and returned to Fred, who happened to be looking alone himself.

And so the dinner went. She served him and he truly enjoyed the food over the small talk. Then things were smoothly cleared away and he sat on the sofa again, happy, full and smiling. When she sat beside him, at last, she took his hand in her own and her entire first rehearsed speech had disappeared and another, unrehearsed, was in its place.

Fred smiled, very relaxed now, with her voluntarily placing her hand in his, and said, "Come on, baby, tell daddy. Well, tell me, if you ain't sure I'm your daddy . . . cause I am, you know. Come on, tell me. What did you want to talk about? I'm ready to hear you, cause I want to get to more important things because, you know, I love you."

Vinnie sat back in the corner of the sofa, pulled her legs up on their sides under her and tucked her dress around them. She smiled a small smile. She wasn't too sure she was doing the right thing because she did love him. She took a deep breath and started, "Well, the first thing is I want to give you your telephone back. I have bought one of my own and put it in my name."

"Oh, Vinnie, you didn't have to spend your money like that. I know you are trying to help your kids."

"My . . . children are now on their own . . . except for Delores' college tuition and she is in her last year. She is getting a part-time job through her college."

Fred leaned back and smiled, satisfied with Vinnie.

She looked toward her thinking chair, then turned back to Fred. "Several things have happened around me that made me do some thinkin and I have taken your advice and quit workin myself to death and, also, so I could have some money for myself; my life. I didn't quit all my jobs, but I have more time and more money . . . for me."

Fred softly laughed, pleased. "Well, I'll be damned. That's good, baby. I'm glad, cause I didn't want you to live like that. I wanted you to live for yourself a little."

"Yes. Well, now I do. And since my mind kept thinkin after all that was settled, I decided I don't want you to pay for my phone anymore either." She sighed and smoothed her skirt over her legs. "My son is on his own now, and when my daughter graduates, soon now, she will be able to get a good job."

Fred nodded and encouraged her with little sounds of approval.

Vinnie continued, "I am . . . still kinda young, only near forty . . . and I hope someday to marry again. And to do that I have to go out more . . . meet people. And I didn't want other people, when I meet them, to call me on your telephone. That wouldn't be nice. So! I got my own."

Fred looked as though he had been struck by lightning. He managed to cover that first dumb look on his face, but he looked at Vinnie as if he thought she must be crazy.

Vinnie continued, "So I thought I would fix you a nice dinner to thank you for all the nice things you have done for me . . . and give you back your telephone."

Fred stammered a bit, "You mean . . . you are putting me out of your life? You know I already love you!"

Vinnie shook her head slowly while looking into Fred's eyes. "No, I don't know that. I know you SAY you love me. And I can't put you OUT of my life. You already left my life by your own choice . . . not mine."

"Well, you know I left because I wanted us to be able to have a good full life and not be burdened with unnecessary things."

"My children."

Fred blustered a bit, "Vinnie, you know I was right. You just said so. You've made changes yourself. That boy needed to assume some responsibility for hisself. And your daughter needed to stop leaning on you so hard. You were burdened under that load. It hurt me to see you workin all those jobs and running back and forth all the time tryin to be on time for em! You didn't have any clothes for yourself because your daughter demanded so much! Things needed fixin around this house. I wanted us to have a full life . . . not a drudge."

Vinnie nodded. "That's all true. And you loved me enough to leave me in all that? Alone?"

"I wanted you to wake up and live . . . for yourself."

"Well . . . you were nice, Fred. You left me in all that . . . for my own good. And you left me one convenience: a telephone . . . so I could call YOU."

"Surely you used it for other things . . . your children."

"Oh, the phone was very convenient for emergencies. But, now, I don't need it anymore. Your plan 'to help me' seems to have worked and I had a telephone in the middle of all my other problems. Now you can have it back because I may not be callin you."

Fred turned his body toward Vinnie and took her hand from her lap. "Vinnie, don't talk crazy. I didn't wait all this time for you to put me out of your life. I'm the one who wanted you to HAVE a life."

"Fred, you waited til I went through all of it by myself." She smiled that small smile. "I don't know how to thank you for leavin me in my mess and waitin until life is easier for me so you could come back in it when it is easier for you."

Fred was urgent, "But I was right! Look, you are doing better, look better. I know you feel more rested and better."

Vinnie was gentle, but firm. She knew she better be because for some reason she did not even know how to articulate it to herself. She knew she wanted a different relationship with Fred, a stronger, better one. The anger in her heart was real, even though she knew she loved him. "But I have only me to thank for that. You were right! But . . . how do I know what I would have to go through the next time you think you are right and, one time, you may not be right and I will have to change something I want to do or you will step away from me again?"

"Vinnie, I love you."

"Fred, dear, you say that."

"I mean that. You were always in my mind."

Vinnie looked, pointedly, around the room. "Well, I don't have anything to show for your love except a telephone and I'm going to give that back. The car is old now, but I could buy it from you for what you loaned on it."

Fred looked surprised, "You mean I should have given you money to help you burden us?"

Vinnie looked directly into Fred's eyes. "There are other things to give. Love, comfort, support, a day off, a weekend off, music, laughter, togetherness."

"I want to give you all those things, Vinnie." He reached for her.

She didn't move, to him or from him. "When I need them? Or when it is right in your mind? And convenient?"

"Vinnie, you are doing me wrong now."

"I'm not doin you anything, Fred. I still have a phone, same number. You can call me . . . if you like."

Fred looked at Vinnie a long time. She only half smiled, not in anger anymore, nor revenge or malice. Even her heart was hurting because she loved him. But, she thought, "He better learn my mind before I give him my heart to hold and keep and he sets it down somewhere, when it is convenient. When I become inconvenient."

When she closed the door behind Fred, she listened to the slow, heavy footsteps going down the stairs to his car. Again. She could see through the window as he reached his car; he held his head up and shook his shoulders as if he was shaking something off, got in, sat a few moments, then slowly drove away.

Vinnie sat down in her thinking chair and prayed, "God, don't let me make a mess of what's left of my life, please."

Vinnie joined a whist club, but went to take a class in bridge so she would have a different group of friends to choose from. She began to go out occasionally with a few of her girlfriends from her bank job. She did meet a few fellows and she went out with one or two of them, occasionally. She felt like making love, but she didn't feel like making love to them.

She was able to get a charge account and she bought a few good basic clothes, but she loved shopping at the secondhand store. Vinnie watched her budget; there were things she wanted to do with her house to make it more comfortable and safe for herself. She thought of going to night school to learn something that would give her more pay and security . . . for herself.

Often her new phone rang at night, but when she picked it up, no one said a word. And there were times just looking out of her front window that she thought she recognized Fred's car passing; always in the darkness of night.

Every once in a while, Vinnie saw her eagles. Mother and child. The young eagle was strong and sturdy now. It flew ahead of its mother sometimes as they played in and with the air. The mother eagle was getting old, but she was yet strong. Not as strong as of old, but still strong. The mother eagle always led the way back to their home as the young eagle would fly and glide, soaring as it trailed behind her. Vinnie was always filled with beauty and love as she watched life in the sky.

Eventually Vinnie met one gentleman she liked. Steve. Steve worked as a roofer, but was very nice and he liked to dance. He was a little plump, but light on his feet. They started going out every Saturday night. His only problem, to her, is he thought a date meant ending the evening in her bed. She didn't want that and told him it would take more time for her to get to that. He accepted that, for the moment, because he just knew that he would, finally, get what he wanted from her because all women pretended not to give in too easily. Besides, he liked to dance. Too, she was a nice-lookin woman who lived alone in her own house. He had a little time to put into this. "Who knows what might happen," he thought to himself. Vinnie was tiring of him because he never stopped asking, hinting and touching too much. She wanted to make love, not sex.

One Saturday night she didn't feel so much like dancing so he came over to play cards: gin rummy. While he was there, her phone rang over and over again, but when she picked it up, no one said a word. Steve commented on it, but since it was none of his business, she didn't say anything, just shrugged her shoulders.

The next morning, Sunday, it rang again, early. When she said "Hello," Fred answered, "Hello, Vinnie?"

"Yes?" Her heart skipped a tiny little beat.

"This is Fred."

"Hello, Fred," said in a very pleasant voice.

"I see you are dating, at least, I heard about it."

"Yes, Fred, I am."

"Well . . . I'm calling to see if I might have a date with you. A little dinner? And dancing? Unless you have a man . . . now and he won't want you to."

Vinnie smiled. "No, no. I'm a free woman . . . Fred."

"Well, Free Woman, may I have a date this Saturday evening?"

"Not Friday anymore?"

"Well, we can go out Friday and Saturday if you want to. I want to talk to you."

Vinnie looked at her clock, she was thinking of church, then leaned back into her pillow. She wanted to see him sooner than Saturday. "Friday is better. For dinner only, though. I'm kinda tired."

Fred's voice hardened a little, "Yes, I guess all that dancing lately can wear you down."

"I also work."

Fred let a long sigh escape, "Well, if Friday is alright, that's good. Still, I would like Saturday, too."

Vinnie smiled, saying, "Well, let's talk about Saturday on Friday."

Fred was silent for a moment, then, "Alright, Vinnie. Six o'clock?"

"Six o'clock."

After she hung up the phone Vinnie's heart was glad, happy, however not too happy because she loved him, but he was still Fred.

That Friday, he picked her up and they took that long drive to the restaurant and the dinner was, as usual with him, good. She had been reading a few new things about etiquette and this time she was not so nervous. She relaxed more and had a better time with him.

He drove slowly back to her house. As he parked, he asked, "I know it's late, but can I come in for a minute? To talk?"

"Of course, Fred, you know I enjoy your company."

Inside her house, Vinnie turned the radio on . . . softly.

As Fred removed his coat he said, "Put on some records,

some romantic records. Your son didn't take his record player with him, did he?"

Vinnie laughed gently, "You have fed me so well, I'm just too full to fool with anything. We're just gonna talk anyway."

Fred sighed and sat back on the sofa, then took another deep breath. Said, "Vinnie? Girl, woman, my life is more empty every day. I got most things I want, but these years you been out of my life, my life ain't nothing and I don't have no desire but one and that's you."

Vinnie, sitting beside him, looked down at her hands in her lap.

Fred reached for one of her hands and said, "I thought I was right. And I was, but I wasn't alllll right. But, I don't think you are all right either. I was kinda blinded by my own self. I could have done more . . . but I didn't think it would take you this long . . . if you loved me. I see the error in my ways now. With your help. And . . . and . . . well, there is no other way to say it. I just love you. I still want to marry you. You stay in my mind, between me and anybody else. Ain't nobody for me but you. And we can do things your way too. Together. I'm not right all the time; I see now. I mean . . . I can be right, but there is a right way to do things."

He took a deep breath because he had said quite a bit and she was still looking at her hand in his. "Vinnie? Do you . . . love that man you been going out steady with?"

Wasn't any sense in lying. "No, I don't."

Fred breathed half a sigh of relief. "You make love to him? Or anyone else . . . at all?"

"I shouldn't answer that, but no. Though I am sure you do. I have some dreams of my own for my future."

Fred held her hand tighter. "Well what do you think? Can we get back together?"

Vinnie thought carefully. She loved this man. He was a good man. But, the main thing was, this was her life and she wanted her remaining years to try to be good ones with a man or good years without one; whichever was best for her. Her. "Well . . . Fred . . . We can start over . . . if you like . . . and see where we get to this time."

His happiness bubbled so that he laughed out loud without intending to. "Oh, we are going all the way, this time. I don't want to lose you. Ahhh . . . Can I kiss you?"

"I don't kiss on my first date." Vinnie smiled.

"Just a 'hello' kiss?"

"Well . . . one."

Fred, smiling, "Then come on over here in my arms."

"Meet you halfway?"

"Let's each come as far as they want to, together."

They both moved toward each other and Fred held that one kiss for as long as he could, until they both needed to breathe. Vinnie kept it to the one kiss though it took all her strength because her body was hungry and she loved him, too. But, she thought, "This has got to be for real and it has to be right or it ain't gonna be nothin. I don't trust myself with my heart beatin like it is now."

The kiss held more than a promise.

Josephine, seeing Fred's car at Vinnie's so often, made it her business to let Vinnie know, "I hope you are not letting that man back in your life again! He won't do you right this time either! You need to learn about men! You a fool for that man! He calls and you go running! That is not the way to get a man!"

Wynona, of course, knew what was happening to both Fred and Vinnie because each of them told her how they felt. Wynona, never having listened to Josephine anyway, laughed with her brand of huge delight when she was told. To Vinnie she said, "Girl, I know you smart! But don't take too many of them chances cause he is a good man. I done told you that!"

In a month Vinnie was wearing an engagement ring. A small wedding was even planned for two weeks later.

One talk they had before the wedding, Fred said, "We'll sell your house and you live in my house until we get a larger one for us."

Vinnie answered, smiling, "No, dear. I don't think so. I'll just fix this one up and rent it out. That way the income can help us and if either one of us ever gets blinded by our 'own' ways, I'll always have a home of my own."

"Ahhhhh, Vinnie, let's not talk about that kind of stuff."

"But, you taught me, Fred, and you are right. We will stay together, always, but I may want to do something else with the house. No rush to sell. Let's just concentrate on being together."

Fred nodded his head, slowly. "Yes, let's just be together."

Another promising kiss.

Then, one day the wedding was over. Vinnie's things were packed and ready. Eduardo came to move her things out of her house. Vinnie watched the workingmen as they moved her things from her past to her future.

When the house was empty, Vinnie stood by her favorite window where her thinking chair used to be. It was another drizzly, misty day. As she looked out she saw those moving specks, way, way up in the sky. She stood still, watching them for a long time as the eagles came closer and closer. They flew so gracefully, so beautifully; gliding, swooping, turning in that wondrous arc, flying up one minute, descending effortlessly the next minute, with the wind flowing over and under their wings. The birds seemed to circle above her house, even though they were high in the sky; then when they flew above Josephine's house, the eagles seemed to arch their backs, one at a time, youth following mother, they would fly straight up . . . then off . . . then away.

Vinnie pressed her hand to the window and said, "I will really miss you, my eagle birds. I do not know where you keep your nest, your home and whatever is in it. You are untouchable in that sky. You seem to be so free. Please, stay awake to dangers. And know that some of my spirit is always with you." She sighed. "But this is my house and I am going to keep it in case I need it or my children need it. I will come back. To work on my yard and look in on old Mother Foster and I will look for you. Always, I will look for you. You are very beautiful . . . and I love you. I wish you would follow me to my new home and let me keep seeing your beauty. Try. Take care of yourselves. And I'll try to take care of myself. I am in Love . . . you know."

The eagles were flying away, soaring, their wings seemed to wave "good-bye" to her. Vinnie picked up her purse, looked around the room, then, walking back to her thinking window, placed both her hands on it as she watched them.

Her spirit had come into her, was no longer outside screaming through the days and nights.

Then . . . with a smile that came from her warm and happy heart, she turned to her old front door. When she closed the door behind her, in a manner of speaking, she flew, soaring away too.

The Lost and the Found

Now . . . I am not an old woman, nor a young woman neither. I'm not too smart, but I'm not too dumb either. And I don't go round tendin to other folks' business, like watchin everybody every day. And long as I been livin I ain't seen nothin more pitiful than a fool! Lessen its death. I got sense enough to know where I been, so sometimes I can tell where somebody else is goin. One of the things I seen is women proud to think they are beautiful, men proud of the same thing, but men add the pride of making babies. Chile, it's a dangerous world out there! Just chuck full of fools. And you can blive that! Yes mam!

I live in a little town that is so small, half of it is in the country. Oh, it's big enough to have some bars and food places for young folks to have a drink and dance if they want to. And it got three churches which I ain't sure God knows about, but I ain't no judge. No mam. I go back and forth to all of them . . . looking for the spirit of truth. Then I talk to God all by myself so He will not get my intentions mixed up with nobody else's.

But, the thing about fools is some of em think they havin fun makin fools of everybody else and the biggest fool of all is them! It's all kind of fools, you know: the fools they make and the fools they are their own self.

I'm old enough for things in my life to mostly all be behind me now. I live alone and I don't have too much to do, so you know you just do have time to sit out on your porch or in your window and watch the world as it tries to pass by, stumblin, walkin or runnin, even sometimes staggerin, along the way. So I just accidently see things in the day and in the night cause I don't seem to sleep good much as I used to. I was younger then and I guess I was just tired enough tryin to survive, to sleep longer. Now, my life ain't full of so much . . . stuff, so I guess I don't need so much rest. Even sinning is a job. Yes mam!

I'm a friendly person, so I got friends that stop by, now and again. They sit on my red porch swing and talk. I like that swing cause folks get comfortable in it and just talk and talk, chile.

You may call me Mrs. Everly. I got a first name, but you don't need it. You can come on by and sit and talk sometime.

The reason I'm talkin like this is because I got a friend of mine in my mind. She is a young girl, but she is a woman, cause she got two children, sons. She made some mistakes cause she got them kids and she ain't never been married . . . yet. He, the father of them babies, always promisin her though. Men usually make them kinda promises. Keepin em is somethin else. Yes mam. Promises are free. You can make em all day if you want to! Keepin em, sometimes, takes a heap more time.

Now, I know it's new times we livin in, they say. Modern. You know what I mean; livin with somebody you ain't married to, or havin babies for em and you still ain't married to em. They gettin what they want, but usually you ain't! Times may be new, but human beings ain't and they will do what you let em do or what you make em do. Yes MAM!

Somebody need to tell them women if a man want you, they will marry you! That's true! If they don't want you, just want your body for a good time, then, seem to me, you can't leave them alone fast enough. When I was growin up, I knew for my own self, if you didn't love me enough to marry me, respect me, I couldn't love you enough to let you use my body . . . too much, and certainly not put no baby in it! No mam. I owed my possible baby more than that and I sure owed myself more! I did not intend to go down the street draggin no tears runnin down my face and babies holdin on to my dress tail and a bag of dirty diapers in my arms! while the daddy is somewhere else tryin to make another one. No sir!

But, can't nobody run life like they want to every time. A little bit always gets away from you.

I'm thinkin of that nice young woman I was tellin you about; her name is Irene. Irene is a friend of mine, too. I try to help her when I can. She lives up the road there, in the country part of this town. I can see the house from here on my porch. Now, that boy-man who made them babies, they call him "Cool" cause he cool. Makes me want to laugh, but it is too pitiful. He got Irene and she been waitin on him to marry her for bout nine years. She love him, she say. He SAY he loves her, too.

I have to stop and tell you this little thing. I have a nephew name of Joe who has a little bar and cafe just a little ways up towards town and Joe loves that red swing of mine and sittin talkin to me. He say it rests his mind. I don't never go to his bar cept for the times his cook don't come in, then I go up there and cook for him. It do me good. A little exercise, you know. Plus, you see some STUFF goin on in there! People's business and all. Joe told me Cool loves all women. That mostly he comes in lookin for some "action." See? I told you! I hear... they say... women give him presents; gifts and money, clothes and just whatever he need... That's what THEY say...

So that's why Cool be at them bars all the time, when he ain't hidin from somebody. And Joe is why I hear bout what might be going on sometimes.

Every once in a while, at night when I can't sleep and be sittin at my window, I see Cool walkin down this road front of my house and I know he headin for Irene. She cook him something nice and, the boys are sleep, so he make some quick sex to her and get some safe sleep he sure must need, then he gone again, til next time he need some food or safe sleep. But, I got to tell the truth about him; he looooves his sons! They are his pride and joy. He don't give em much, he lets Irene do all the gettin and givin, but he brags about them all the time. When anyone questions his manhood, he throw them kids up in their face and pounds on his chest. Just like a fool. He act like it was something hard to do, like everything on earth ain't makin babies all the time. Or wouldn't the earth be empty? So what kind of man do it make you just cause you made a baby?! Jesus help me!

Irene don't give him no money, though. Can't. She ain't got none to give. She bout thirty years old now, Cool is bout thirty-six or -seven. Irene works domestic, so she can carry her sons with her when they not in school. You already know she don't make much, but all she makes go into those sons of hers.

There is an older man, Russell, Russell Summer, who owns that house she rents. Russell bout forty-five years old or so. He is the nicest, kindest, man! He go check on her pretty regular, cause he got to keep that house up. But I don't think he is tryin to court her. I don't see nobody else going to Irene's house like they courtin her, either. She just waitin. Working and waitin for Cool, Mr. Main Man, to get a real job and marry her. Poor chile.

Irene visits me and we talk, sometimes, cause when life gets too full of sh—stuff, you got to let some of it out and I am her friend cause all women are my sisters, specially the sad ones.

I got two friends much closer to my age. Rether, bout sixty-five years old. She use'ta always like to be in some juke joint or bar. She thought she was a "swinger," as they say now. She like to say that too. Rether had different men, lot of em, in her life. She alone now. But you can see every drink she ever had and all them lines that was slapped and knocked into her face. They ain't no love lines either, they lyin lines. Rether even got nerve to think she still look good, too! Now, I know women can look good at sixty-five, even seventy-five years of age, but Rether ain't one of them! Them older lookin-good women took better care of their self! See, lipstick and powder don't cover up bitterness and old pain and selfishness. They the things that make you look old. She likes to think she still looks like she use'ta, and I don't worry her none about it, cause what she got left . . . but dreams?

Rether got a niece named LaTanya. LaTanya! They call her Tan-Tan. She only bout forty-four, forty-five years old. Combination waitress and sell a little bit of herself sometime, but still she be broke all the time. Hear tell even she likes that ole Cool.

My other friend is Agatha. Don't know where her mother went to come up with that name, but she sure did and Agatha got it. And you have to call her "Agatha" cause she does not like to be called "Aggie." She bout sixty-seven now. She always was what some people call a prude, but she was always neat and I have to say she musta been wise cause she had two husbands and kept em. The first one died, then she got the second one. She's a good person, keeps a clean body and a clean house. They left her with a nice house ALL her own, not the bank's, and it is full of very nice things. She drives her own car. Rether ain't got one.

But, Agatha is nosy. Very nosy. (Not like me.) I have the print of her behind in my red swing over the years. That print is only pink now. So . . . such as they are, they are my friends and it's hard to fine good friends, chile.

Well, anyway, I knew em when they started, Cool and Irene, bout ten years ago. I have watched the years go by, leavin shadows on Irene's face, and don't never see no shadows on Cool's face. Course, I mostly see him at night when you can't see shadows too good noway, but from all I hear, a shadow ain't got no place to stop in his brain long enough to reach his face.

Now, I ain't too old to remember how it is being in love, cause I had three husbands and two of em didn't die. I loved em all! So I know bout love. Heck, one of em, when he made love to me? Could make me speak something sound like Spanish. Couple times I think I even spoke some Chinese. I'm just tryin to tell you, I know somethin about love. And I love that little Irene cause she try so hard. And when she come to see me, tears runnin down her pretty little face, it just bout like to kill me inside my heart.

She has cried a lot, right there in that red swing with me sittin next to her, holdin her, tryin to soothe her grief. I tell her to find somebody else. I KNOW somebody that is a good man would sure want her! I tell her plenty things, like there are twenty million men look as good and better than he does, and at least half of them would want her. I don't know if she takes my words to heart or not, but I ain't givin up! I talk to her about pure-dee, down-right, do-right life. I don't want her to keep bein no fool for nobody. Specially not be a fool FOR a fool. No sir.

See, I know she is poor; "necessity" poor. She gets all the things her children need, but she don't get nothing she wants. Now, I know, also, a woman like to look good for the man she wants to marry her. More'n a couple times I went and bought pretty material. Oh, I can sew, chile, I mean, I can sew! Anything! I sew for her sons, too. And I made her nice pretty dresses for her to wear to church and when she knows Cool would be comin to see her. I don't have to like him, but, since she loves him, I want her to be happy. I want him to see what a pretty woman he had. But that damn fool couldn't see them dresses for takin em off of her and castin them out the way. He can't see nobody but hisself!

Well, what you gonna do? Least I know he loves them two boys. Joe, my nephew, say he always braggin about them boys! ALLLL the time. See, I know what it is; those boys, sons, make his manhood. Yes sir! They are all he has to show for it. You can't count these women who be runnin after him to be nothin cause they would be runnin after somebody else if he wasn't there. No, they don't count for much. Cause if you have to run after somebody, they must not want you, cause people run towards somethin they want, not away from it. And my gramma told me a man is a hunter, you know; you better let him do the huntin! Yes mam.

Don't too many people like a fool, but another fool! I sure hate to think Irene is a fool, or goin to stay the one she is for Cool. She is such a nice person, sweet . . . and a good mother. I mean!

Now, you know what? It's too bad she ain't old enough for that Mr. Summer. His wife passed on bout ten years ago and he ain't picked nobody else yet. Ole Rether tried, but she too old for that man, he bein only in his forties. He got a nice house and other property too! Besides the one Irene lives in. Got a good steady job cause he works for hisself. Painting contractor. That's how he got some of his property; bought a few of them old houses and fixed em up. Yes mam, he is one of the good men. I told Irene he is the kind she needs cause you can love a man like that. Safe love. SafER anyway.

People think "safe love" must be boring. Not full of surprises like that challengin love Rether always wanted. Sometimes anything can be boring. But Rether's "challengin love" ran over her like a tractor, her face and her life too, I think. Whereas Agatha's safer love left her face, body and life intact. She still had a future when he was gone.

Now I don't mean you're not goin to have any trouble with a man, or woman, who gives you "safe love" cause you can only tell what has happened the last minute; you don't know nothin bout what's gonna happen the next minute! And you don't know nothin bout what nobody is gonna do until they are dead. But, everybody knows, some people are more careful with their life than other people. Have more chance at happiness and peace. That's what I mean.

Mr. Summer did some work for Agatha and she said he talked about Irene a little. Say he sure does like her and wish she would do better for herself and the boys. He love them boys, but I know he got better sense than to love another man's woman. And it is good of Mr. Summer to pick the boys up and carry them to church on Sunday cause Cool sure ain't gonna do it. Irene goes when she ain't too tired. Chile, that church too slow and quiet for Cool, but Irene, tryin to smile, says he likes to see her boys go. He really likes somethin good belongin to him. Phooey!

But I have come to find out, there was a lot of things I did not know, chile. Me! Sittin up here talkin bout other people bein fools and here I am some kind of fool myself, thinkin I could know into somebody else's life. And judge, even! God is right, honey, don't think you know so much you can judge nobody.

Oh, ain't life somethin?! Lord, every day I wonder at it! Then I look up and I have found somethin else that makes me marvel at it again. But, that's life and ain't it good?

Listen at me, sittin up here talkin you to pieces and you

ain't said nothin. But ain't I right? Trials and tribulations teach you all kinds of things? Now, what have you learned? Are you one of them fools? I have to laugh at myself cause listen at me askin you that!

I remember my nephew, Joe, tellin me how Cool be in the bar braggin, sayin, "I got me TWO, not one boy, but two boys! BOYS! Show you I'm a man." Yes, that's how he talks. Say, "And if don't nobody else ever love me again, which ain't likely, I know that woman, my boys' mama, do! Yeah, I am a man! Done proved it!" That's how he keeps them other men from goin after her.

Well, anyway, I watched things with Irene and Cool, not particular from everything else I watch, but she was just down the road from me. I have watched them boys grow up. They bout seven and nine years old now. My, my, time flies don't it? Irene was always so down-feelin cause Cool wasn't marryin her. She seem to be doing better now, done got used to the facts. Prob'ly cause she don't see him for long stretches. But, then he be back tippin down that road again to see her and check his hold on her. She let him in, feed him them children's food, let him love up on her and let him rest. Then he be gone again.

Last year or two Irene say she don't let him love up on her much no more. Say she was thinkin she might get pregnant again and she don't want that. Say she got just the right-size family to have to raise. But Cool still watchin her to see that nobody else don't come around her!

In fact, come to think of it, a long time has done passed and Cool ain't been too close round her. I know he ain't too far off though. But, chile, Irene don't look too sad too much no more. I guess she don't have time, workin them two jobs she got. She, sometimes, let Mr. Summer keep her sons cause they couldn't always go to work with her some days.

Mr. Summer be so happy to keep them boys cause he has no children of his own. His wife, what died, was sickly almost ever since they been married, but he never forsaked his wife. When she died, bout ten years ago, poor little thing, 2,900 women came after him. I mean they was bearin down on him; even come from out of town! They bring food, offer to wash his clothes, clean his house, all like that. But not one of them got a foot stuck in that house yet. After he was done grievin, bout a year, he kept company with a few of em for a time, then he just got quiet and seem to resign hisself to bein alone, goin to church, workin his houses. Wasn't gonna sing no more love songs, chile. That's sad, ain't it? A good man, too! I guess that's why he takes up time with Irene's sons. That's good, cause I know they love him for all his kindness to em. I know he needs their love too, cause everybody needs some love.

You know, he comes over here and sits in that swing and talks to me, too. Yes sir. During that time, right after all them women was bout finished huntin after him, he was feelin low and come by here cause he knows I liked and respected his wife and did little things for her and him, too. We could always talk, like good friends, cause he knows I don't repeat things I hear. No mam. You will never hear me repeat nothin I hear! So we talked about his life.

He said, with his eyes just as straight and clear, most of the sadness gone, "I want . . . a woman . . . a woman . . . I can call my own. When she calls somebody, it's me she calls . . . and thinks of. She don't need to be no great beauty, cause I'm not much to look at myself. And she don't need to wear all them fancy clothes, less she just want to. I like pretty hair, but she don't have to have hair hangin all down her back. I want that woman . . . to come home to . . . to love and care for, take care of. I want to eat her food and sleep in her bed, our bed. I'm not a woman-chasin man, Mrs. Everly, I am just a one woman's man. I want one good woman to spend the rest of my life with. I don't want to grow old, (he laughed softly) older, alone.

"Me and my last wife, bless her soul, we didn't have no kids cause it would have killed her, sooner. I wanted a family, but I wouldn't leave the wife I had. Not cause I'm such a good man, but cause I wouldn't want nobody to do that to me . . . and I loved her. She was always the sweetest little thing you ever saw. Better than many a woman in this world with good health. Only . . . she was sick. I still love her in my memories. I never been sorry I married my Elizabeth. And I am gonna be mighty careful the next time I get married, if there is a next time. I don't know. Time's passin. I'm gettin . . . older."

With a wave of my hand, I told him, "Chile, you ain't old, and you look good. Some women I know would try to pull you out your coffin. Dig you out your grave. And you got property, too? Humph, honey!"

He laughed, like I wanted him to, so he could take that needin look off his face. He waved his hand back at me, said with a smile, "Mrs. Everly, I don't want nobody who wants me for my 'property' and all. Hell, anybody can buy a house. No mam. I know about love, Mrs. Everly. I know a great deal about love . . . and that is what I want." See, he could tell me the truth cause I prob'ly wanted the same things he did. Almost.

So we talked a bit more, then he had to go on bout his business. I sat and swung in that ole porch swing for a long while. Just thinkin bout love . . . and life . . . passin some people by.

Later, that evening, I looked up and caught a glimpse of Irene, way down the road, knew it was her cause I made that yellow blouse she had on, a couple of years ago. She came out her house walkin Mr. Summer back to his car, so he musta stopped there. Made me think of Cool, who had what Mr. Summer wanted and didn't have sense enough to know a good woman from a hole . . . in the ground!

Well, I've watched em all bout ten years now and Irene is bout thirty years old now. Gettin older and them sons are, too. Times is gettin harder and things more expensive. Damn that Cool. Them kids needed a mother AND a father!

Then other things happened round me and I put Irene out of my mind for awhile. It's awful sad for me to always be thinkin about. And I got my own life to run. I need to laugh and be happy once in a while.

That's why, round that time, when my nephew, Joe, called and asked me to come in and give him a hand because his cook had the flu (or a hangover!), I said yes cause it gets lonesome and borin just sittin on this porch all the time. That bar is somethin interesting to do and I can use the money he is gonna pay me, too! Sure can. And I don't have to eat my dinner alone them days neither. Yes mam.

I love my nephew, Joe, cause he is a good man. He takes care of his family. Lord yes. He's bout forty-three years old now, and I know he gets tired with them long hours and some of them people that come in his little second-class bar in that second-class neighborhood. It ain't the best, but it ain't the worst. It's small, only eight or nine barstools and two or three little tables in there. Most what's in there are the usual beer and liquor signs all lit up, and it's a good thing cause its kinda dark in there, cept in the kitchen where I work. But I love to go over there cause it's like lookin at a real good picture show! Sometimes.

Well, it was about twelve o'clock in the afternoon when he called me, so I got ready and went down there after I shopped for a few things I knew I would need. Coming out the bright sunlight, it was extra dim in that bar, but first thing I saw was Cool leanin up against the bar, laughin and talkin, drinking a beer. Joe tryin to catch up on all the busy work to be ready for the evenin crowd. I went on back to the kitchen after we all spoke and Joe thanked me for comin.

I started gettin my things ready to fix two kinds of orders. I ain't cookin all day in this kitchen cause it ain't never really clean like my own is. They can have "this" or "that" and that's all.

After I got things to going and was through makin my little noise, naturally I paid more attention to what I was hearin from the bar part. First thing I hear is Cool sayin, "Yeah, man, I lost big money in that crap game the other night, but I caught up on things last night!" Can you magine that?! He's spendin his money gambling!

Joe has a low-soundin voice, but I heard him say, "You sure finally got lucky, man."

Cool, so smart, said, "Well . . . you gotta stick with things, man!"

Joe put up some glasses (I heard em clinkin) and said, "Sometimes . . . sometimes not! I don't like them games, cause somebody always get mad or somethin and then somebody gets hurt."

Cool must have pulled out a gun when he said, "This here

keep me from gettin in too much trouble! I ain't never had to use it, but I let everybody know I got it!"

Joe sounded nervous when he said, "Man! Put that thing away! I don't like them things! Only a fool carry a gun! Put that damn thing away! Take it out'a here even!"

Well, I just come out that kitchen's half-a-door and moved closer to em. I still stayed in the darkness cause this is Joe's business and I know he knows how to run it, but if Cool didn't put that gun away or take it out, I'da taken it from him and whopped him cross his good-lookin, stupid head with it.

Cool said, as he put the gun away, "Cool it, man. I ain't crazy. I always know what I'm doin! And that's all you have to do. Know what you doin! If you can't tell a snake from a worm . . . you betta stay out the jungle!" He laughed at his own joke, alone, cause me and Joe wasn't laughin.

Joe commence to wipin his bar glasses again, said, "You got a point there. But you got to go a long way on this here earth to get out the jungle." Joe put them glasses away as he said, "But you know what? I don't see how you fellows have enough money to gamble with, drink with, still eat and sleep somewhere . . . and dressin clean."

Cool laughed that ole prideful laugh some men have, "Ain't nothin to it!"

Joe shook his head, "Well, it beats me. I have to work."

Cool explained, "Reason ain't nothin to it cause half the time most of these jokers owe everybody! But I don't! I do a little work sometime though. Can't tell that lie some of them tell and say I don't!"

Now Joe laughed, sayin, "I know you work sometime! I

know you HAVE to cause don't nobody want to lend you nothin no more. You don't pay back."

"That's a lie!" Cool sat his beer bottle down, hard.

But Joe didn't get excited. "Man, this is me . . . I been here. I know what's happenin!"

"You don't know everything!"

Joe decided to cool things down. "At least, you ain't tryin to pimp none." He laughed as he said, "Too much."

Cool shook his head. "Uh-huh, that's a fool's game."

Joe didn't leave well enough alone, "Course you prob'ly can't nohow."

Cool laughed and said, "Brother . . . I can do whatever I want to do!"

Joe poked fun at Cool with a little grunt. "Huh!"

Cool said, "Damn right! Pimpin just ain't my game."

Joe held his arms out wide, said pleasantly, "That's what I was sayin . . . it ain't your game."

Cool picked up his new bottle of beer. "Ain't cause women don't love me! I ain't never had no trouble with women! You know that!"

Joe sighed, sayin, "Everybody always think I know so much."

Cool laughed lightly, "Cause you say you do. But you know somethin else, man? I love women. All of em!"

"I see you tryin to, anyway."

Cool spread his arms, said, "Man, I saw a woman the other day and I wanted to jump out'a the car and make love to her right on the sidewalk! Make her feel better than she ever felt in her life . . . But, I was cool. Got too many women now I can't get rid of."

"Yeah, bad luck just follows you around."

Cool laughed, "That's cause I am a strong man. I ain't weak! Women don't like weak men! And I got a strong, smooth, good, hard body!"

Joe just looked at him, "It's sposed to be a good thing if you love yourself."

"Well, I sure do! And women do, too. They good to me too!" Cool laughed proudly. "They . . . some of em, give me money and plenty presents." I looked at him as he smoothed his hair with one hand and I could have gone out there and bapped him upside his head, gun or not!

But Joe knows his business. He said, "That's kinda sad, man, takin a poor woman's money. Prob'ly welfare money sometimes."

Cool leaned over the bar, confidentially, said, "They ain't all poor! I got one . . . you know that lady with the . . . no, I better not mention her name . . . she too well known." Cool took off his little stingy-brim hat and held it up, saying, "You see this sharp hat?" He didn't wait for an answer. "She just gave me this fine hat! It's brand new! This my good-luck hat. My luck is gonna change! From now on, with this hat, my luck gonna be so good I almost won't be able to stand it!" He laughed happily.

Joe grunted. "Huh!"

"She gives me all kinds of things, man. I got more shirts and suits . . . and that good men's cologne! I got plenty of that!"

Joe started wipin off the bar. Said, "Well, I must be doin something wrong."

Cool laughed softly, "Hell, all you got to do is tell em how pretty they are. They ALL want to hear that. Even the real down-home, plug-ugly ones. Now that ain't hard for me cause I love all of em! But I know them. I know women! I don't let them get ahead of me!"

Joe scratched his ear (I can see everything) and said, "You know, them women can wear you out, man."

"Yeah, man. You right! Sometime I wish I was four men, then I could spread myself out more. Travel all over the state and make more women happy."

Joe must of thought I could hear them. "Man, I think you think about screwing too much . . . if you need to be four men."

"It's all in what you can handle! Right now, I can handle things two times a day . . . some days."

Joe scoffed at him, "Seem like a man with your tastes can be kinda ruled by women . . . if women are all he thinks of."

Cool laughed, "Nope . . . ain't true! Sometimes I don't fool with none at all. No . . . I know I have to rest my body sometimes . . . a day or two."

"No shit?"

"No shit! That's why I like married women. They can't always get out, and they got someone else to take up the slack. I don't even really care if a woman I got has somebody else sometime cause I'm pretty busy myself and can't always get to em! . . . in time. You know what I mean?"

Cool took another long drink and I wished I had one too, cause it was gettin hot back where I was, from things bakin in the oven, but I couldn't leave from where I was cause I would miss hearin this man who thought he was a man, bein what he really, truly was; an empty, hollow, ignorant person who didn't know nothin bout life. I wished Irene could hear him. I wished that woman who gave him his lucky hat could hear him.

Then after that little silence, when they both seemed to be thinkin, Joe asked Cool. "What's happenin with that nice little woman you been foolin with for years? Irene? Wasn't that her name?"

Cool's laughter was still hangin round in the air, but now he sounded bored, "Yeah."

I was back there prayin that Joe would not stop askin questions. He didn't stop. "Irene Tatum . . . ole Tatum's daughter?"

"She alright. What you want to know for? Now, there's a example for you! She been my woman for goin on ten years now. We got two babies!"

"You marry her?"

Cool set the beer bottle down, "Marry? Man, you crazy or somethin? What's that?"

Joe turned away from Cool as he said, "Oh . . . then SHE got two kids."

Cool picked his bottle up slowly, "I recognize them boys. They my boys! I didn't try to lie! It's so straight, we ain't never even talked about it."

Joe turned back to Cool with a hard look, "You take care of them boys?"

Cool almost whined, "Man . . . I ain't got enough money for nothin like that. It's hard out here! It takes all I got to keep on goin on!"

"Course," Joe looked away and back to Cool, "it's prob'ly hard out here for her, too! Well, I repeat, SHE got two kids."

"Man, she manages! I go over there . . . ever now and then."

Joe snorted when he laughed, "And try to make another baby?"

Cool laughed, but not so loudly as usual. "Naw . . . I ain't gonna make no more babies. I give her a little piece now and then . . . cause I got to keep her a good woman," he smirked.

Joe smiled a sad smile, "I see your reasoning."

Cool fooled with his shirt collar and brushed over his pants. "You know . . . I think I love her . . . sometime . . . more than all the rest, on accounta my sons." He took a drink. "But not more than my new woman." He rubbed the brim of his "lucky" hat.

My heart was foolish enough to have a little hope for my foolish friend, Irene. But, at the same time, I knew her place in life would be flooded with tears and sorrow and want and need if she ever got this man.

Joe laughed a weak laugh and said, "Golly! She's lucky!"

But Cool didn't read the weak laugh, he believed Irene was really lucky. And that man had the nerve to tell Joe in a low voice, "Yeah . . . You know, I tried her sister out first. But she don't know that! Nobody do! The sister, Billie Jean, never did tell, bless her pretty lil soul. She got a ole man she don't want to go upside her lips if he knew. She wasn't so hot in the bed, noway. Not like little Irene. Irene was a virgin, man. That's alllllll mine! Bet I'm the only man in this town can say that bout their woman. A virgin. She my main stay!"

Joe threw his hands up in the air and shook his head, "Man, you got a hell of a philosophy! You go to church?"

"Joe, we ain't talkin bout church! Talk about church on Sunday. We talkin bout screwin now! I ain't tryin to get no religion. I'm tryin to get some 'givin,' man. You sposed to go to church when you sad. I ain't sad. My life is just what I want it to be! I got Irene, my two sons . . . every man wants a son . . . I got TWO! And I got a woman who gives me things so I stay clean and I get all the mojo I want! Now, what I got to pray for? Lord already done give me everything a good man needs!"

Joe seem to be just makin conversation now that all his preparation work was about done, but I knew, he knew, that I was interested in Irene. He said, "But what about them . . . the women . . . what do they have? What does the mother of your sons have?"

Cool smiled and took another drink of beer, saying, "Me! Me, man. But I can't be goin over there too much. Look what I'd be missin. It's too dead and borin over there. Ain't no excitement! And I am too young, too young to live like I'm a old man; sad . . . and through."

"Through what, Cool?"

"Through lovin women! Havin fun! Are you a fool? Gimme another drink, man!"

Joe went to get the fresh beer, saying, "Well, they say everybody knows what's best for themselves!"

I wanted Joe to ask Cool more questions, but the telephone rang. I was kinda glad when it rang because my leg was gettin numb tryin to stand still and not attract any attention to myself, and then, too, I needed to look at that food I had in there cookin that oughta be about done. I moved as Joe answered the phone and Cool was lookin in the mirror behind the bar as he smoothed his hair, setting his hat at different angles, saying, "Well, I sure do know what's best for me!"

I turned off all the fires cause I was rushin to get back to my listenin place in the dark. If somebody had to wait for this food, they just had to wait, because I was tryin to think of some way I could let Irene know, easily as possible, what kind of man Cool was, with the words comin right out of his own mouth! Now, you may not think that is bein a friend, tellin a woman somethin about her man. But I think it IS bein a friend, because, number one, who wants their friend to be treated like a fool? Forever? And, number two, who cares what you think?!

When I got back to my spot, Joe was off the phone and was tellin Cool, "That was a lady askin for you, but she didn't want to speak to you . . . say she was comin on over."

"Oh, hell, man. Who was it?"

"Forgot to ask . . . and she didn't say. But she sure got a sweet voice."

Cool smiled and preened in the mirror, setting that hat again. "I can't even get away for a little while to myself. The girls just won't let sweet daddy alone."

Joe laughed as he said, "When you got it, you got it!"

"Riiiiiight," Cool smiled at himself as he set the hat at a rakish angle.

Joe pulled off his apron as he asked Cool to watch the bar while he went to the rest room.

"Go ahead. I got to wait for the lady anyway."

As Joe came from behind the counter, he said, "I hope she ain't no 'mad' lady. Don't want no fightin up in here."

Cool laughed his cool laughter and said, "Man, ain't nobody wanta hurt me. They wanta keep me. Any woman I have . . . man, she mine . . . don't worry bout all that stuff you talkin bout!"

Joe reached back for his stick and was wavin it around. "That's good, cause I keep my peacemaker here for all drunks and fools. But, Cool, maybe you oughta worry bout somethin! Least about the one with your two kids."

As Joe left for the rest room, Cool hollered after him, "What are you today . . . the preacher? Man, I think about her. She is my ace in the hole. I know she is a good woman, a good mother . . . and all that!" Joe was in the rest room now, but Cool kept on talkin to hisself as he smoothed himself out for the comin lady. He finished his beer and leaned his elbows on the counter as he looked at hisself. Finally, after several moments, he spoke to his reflection in the mirror, "I'm gonna . . . I'm gonna marry Irene. I'm just savin her for the last. Cause I know she gonna be there. Ain't . . . goin . . . nowhere! with her little quiet self. But I might marry this new money woman first; long as she understands bout my sons, cause I might want to keep them myself someday."

Joe was movin behind the bar and heard the last few lines Cool said and answered, "Them quiet girls surprise you sometime! But I don't blive she will let you take them boys of hers."

Cool didn't even turn to look at him, just kept lookin at hisself as he said, "All kinda girls surprise you sometime! And them are MY sons! Irene ain't got nothin to say bout it, if I make up my mind. You got to learn more about women fore you can tell me anything." Then he turned to look at Joe, saying, "Hey, gimme another beer before she gets here, whoever she is, cause I ain't got enough money to pay for hers too."

Just listen at him! He says everybody givin him things and he don't have enough money to pay for one of them women's drink! A beer even! Humph! Well, I was gettin tired just standin in one place listenin to his bullmess and was just startin to tip back into the kitchen when Tan-Tan came in.

You remember, that's Rether's niece. I just had to wait before I moved because I wanted to look at her a minute.

Chile, the woman looked so tired and dejected, rejected and just downright lifeworn! I knew she was round forty-five, but Joe say she say she is thirty-four or -five. And she musta borrowed that wig she had on cause it didn't fit her head nor her style neither. And had on a black dress, a nice style and all, but a little weary from three or four days' wearin. And red shoes and a red purse (empty I bet). She walked in like she was lookin down at the bottom of the world.

Joe spoke to her first cause Cool was tryin to hurry his change back to his pockets. "Tan-Tan! What's goin on?"

She answered him with a frown, "Ain't nothin goin on! And don't call me Tan-Tan. My name is LaTanya!"

Cool mimicked her by sayin, "LaTanya! Miss LaTanya!"

Miss LaTanya threw him a mean look as she sat down on a barstool. "Don't bother me. Nobody say nothin at all . . . to me!"

Cool might not have said a word to her because she was one of those who was always flirtin with him, but when she said she didn't want to be bothered, he just had to bother her. "What's the matter, pretty? You look fine, but you don't sound fine!"

Tan ignored him and looked at Joe, sayin, "Gimme a straight shot, Joe. A double! And half is on you!"

Joe smiled, but said, "No, half ain't on me! I can't afford your habits, girl."

"Oh, yes you can! You make plenty money offa me!"

As Joe poured her drink, he answered with a serious smile, "Well, you know I must be standin back here for somethin, don't ya? I sure ain't here for my health."

Tan waved her hand in the air, "Well, comin here don't help mine either, but I come."

Cool laughed, sayin, "You come cause it's your business and pleasure to come! If you don't have someplace to get them lonely fools you catch, you'd starve to death on that waitress pay!"

She gave him one of them evil looks, said, "I ain't never tried to 'catch' you!"

Cool laughed as he looked in the mirror and primped his hair. "Not lately. You know you too old for a fine young man like me. I may be a loner . . . but I ain't lonely . . . and I ain't no fool either, darlin."

I know Joe butt in because he didn't want them to argue and I think he felt sorry for Tan-Tan. He is that kind of person. He laughed kinda softly and said, "You both loners . . . always by yourself til you catch somethin."

Cool didn't like him sayin that and said so, "Man, don't put me in her place! She ain't in my class. Sex is somethin she makes some of her livin with. For me, sex is somethin makes my livin worth livin. She got to make somebody go home with her . . . I got to fight em off!"

Then, because he liked Tan-Tan and maybe because she looked so sad, he said, "You my girl though, Tan—LaTanya, Miss LaTanya. I'll pay for her drink. Maybe someday you'll do me a favor!"

"I ain't nobody's girl! I'm a woman! And I don't do no favors in bed!"

Joe took the money Cool had in his hand before Cool could change his mind about payin. Said, "Right on, mama!" Then I wondered why Joe was so glad she didn't do no favors in bed. Was he foolin with Tan? But I would wonder about

235

that later when I got home, right now I had to keep listenin. So, this was the kind of stuff that people flocked to bars to listen to? Hmmm mmmm! A shame!

But Cool was talkin, "Fair exchange ain't no robbery! But you ain't got to think of me! I got more now than I can use! I'll be a ooold man fore I get to you!"

Tan was tired of the chitchat, "Leave me alone, Cool. I don't feel good."

And old kind Joe softened the atmosphere with his soft voice, "What's the matter with you, Tan? What is wrong?"

Tan answered with a tear in her voice, "It's my baby. My daughter."

Cool spoke up, "That pretty young lady you got? Comes down here to get you sometime? Sure is a fox!"

Tan took a swallow of her double drink. "Well . . . this fox of mine ain't smart like no fox! She done got pregnant!"

Joe lay his bar towel down and stepped back, "Damn! Another one down!"

I shook my head in sorrow for her. I knew that child.

Tan talked to the ceiling, "She thinks she 'loooooooooves' him . . . and I can't tell her nothin."

Joe leaned toward Tan, "Maybe they do love each other, Tan."

Tan shook her head, slowly. "I can deal with the baby. That happened to me, too. What I can't deal with is when we went over to his house to see what we was goin to do about everything . . . you know . . . the money and everything." She pushed her glass to Joe, who was standin there listenin. "Gimme another drink, Joe."

Joe was talkin as he got her another drink, "That's right! Get the father involved. It takes money . . . and everything!"

It sounded like tears in her voice as Tan continued talkin. "Well, we sittin there talkin . . . the kids get it together and everything . . . they want to get married. I like the young man, he's still tryin to go to school, even got a job after school, goes to church and all. So, I say, 'Fine, if that's what you want.' Then this jukehead man, his father, says, 'How do my son know that this is his doin?' And I got mad cause I know my daughter and this boy and I say, 'How do you know your son is your doin?' "

Cool laughed in agreement, said, "You sure laid somethin on his mind! Mama's baby, papa's maybe. But, one thing I sure do know is my sons are mine!"

Tan frowned quickly at Cool and turned back to Joe, "Well . . . that made me mad! Men always get so righteous when a baby shows up. THEN, they want a little integrity from a woman! But if they kept a little integrity on the tip of that thing they use to make them babies with, wouldn't nobody have to get unrighteous!"

Cool, as usual, threw in his smarts. "Don't forget . . . it was Eve bit that apple!"

Tan was up to it, "You ever make love to a apple?"

Cool shook his head proudly, "I don't have to!"

Tan had the last word, "And eatin apples don't make you pregnant!"

Oh! I wish I had been in there to say my few words! My feet were itchin to move, but I was holdin my lips tight to keep my mouth from openin.

At that moment two ladies came in. It took a minute or so for me to see them clear from my spot, and when I did get a clear look, my mouth dropped open. It was Rether and Agatha! In this bar! But, I noticed Agatha was holdin on to Rether, tryin to pull her back out the door.

Rether was steady, and strong, she was headin straight for the bar and Joe as she said, "Oh, come on, Agatha! We ain't gonna do nothin but order a cab! We have to, since your car stopped on us. What's wrong with you, girl? Don't try to ack like you ain't never been in no bar!"

Agatha answered, "There is a phone booth right on the corner . . . we can call our own cab from there. You just want to come in this club, Rether!"

Rether pulled free from Agatha, "This bar prob'ly got a direct line . . . so why waste a dime?" She reached the bar and looked up at Joe, flirtin. "Bartender Joe, can you call us a cab, please?" I knew she knew Joe from watchin him get grown, married and have his own children, so I knew she didn't mean nothin by battin her eyes at him. Still.

Then through the dark she saw her niece, Tan-Tan, and walked over to her to say a few words I didn't hear. They kissed cheeks, then Rether walked back over to Agatha.

I think Joe was amused at my friends, but he is always so friendly and kind. "Why certainly, ladies! Right away."

Agatha leaned around Rether to ask, "How long will it take for the cab to get here, Joe?"

"They usually don't take very long, Ms. Agatha."

Agatha sighed, "How you doin, Joe? How is your family?"

Joe, hung up the cab phone, answerin, "Just fine, Ms. Agatha, everyone is fine."

Rether was moving to the tables to take a seat. Agatha was turning to follow her and said, "It's dark in here! I can't see a thing."

Rether chose a table and laughed happily as she sat down, "What do you want to see?"

Agatha feeling for a seat as she spoke, "I like to know

238

what's going on around me. There is no tellin what's creepin round in this dark!"

Rether reached out to help Agatha to the table, said, "You ain't never known what was goin on round you, Agatha. Now rest yourself, everything's all right."

I don't know how well Cool knew my friends, him being so much younger than they were, but it's a small town so he spoke out to them, "Afternoon, ladies!"

I didn't really want my friends to see me, because I had just thrown on a clean cotton dress to come down to work in this kitchen and I don't think I looked too good, but I had moved, quietly, to a better place and I could see them without them seein me. After Cool spoke to them, I saw Rether put on a big smile (she showed me once how she made them dimples come, they ain't natural) and primp her hair.

Rether said, "Evenin!" And giggled! Yes mam, she giggled! Have mercy. But maybe I'm bein too hard on her; she got a right to giggle if she want to.

Agatha pulled herself together in her chair, held her chin up and her bust just naturally puffed out as she spoke, "Humph! You better quit speakin to people you don't know, Rether."

"Oh, for heaven's sake, Aggie. (She knew Agatha hated to be called that) Relax, girl. He ain't no stranger. You just can't see him too good with them bad eyes of yours! Just relax!"

But Agatha wouldn't quit bein a stuffy old lady. She was even makin me tired. She said, "How am I going to relax when I know I am in the devil's house?! And the good Lord is sittin somewhere wondering why I'm lettin you lead me out'a my own good mind!"

What the hell does she mean? I am in my nephew Joes club and you don't have to go to a bar to meet the devil, he sits right in your own house, if you ain't careful. But, I have to admit, I did know what Aggie meant.

Cool musta been enjoyin listening to them talk, because he spoke to the ladies again, "Would you ladies like a little taste on me? A soda or somethin? While you wait? It'll cool you off. That's my name, 'Cool.'"

Agatha foolishly gasped.

Rether blinked her eyes at him, then rolled them like she was thinkin, and smiled until, fightin their way through the wrinkles, her dimples showed up. Then she said, "Why, I believe I will, Mr. Cool."

Agatha seemed to be indignant, sayin to Cool, "Well, I sure believe I won't." She turned to Rether, said, "I don't do nothin like this, Rether."

Rether gave Agatha a pained, annoyed look. "I know you don't, Agatha. Cause it shows. But, maybe you shoulda, once in a while. Make a woman out of you."

Agatha never let up one bit, "Drinkin alcohol and talkin to strangers make a fool out of you, not a woman. Most you find in bars is crazy people and people with nowhere else to go! Just loners and looneys and losers!"

I kinda resented Agatha's words myself. I like a little drink now and again and I knew she did too. I come down to this place when I feel like it to talk to my nephew Joe. Not often, no, but just when I feel like it or I can help him. I ain't no loner nor a looney nor a loser. No mam!

Rether waved the back of her hand to Aggie, saying, "Lord, help me."

Aggie was gettin mean, she said, "You better call on somebody who knows you! Not the Lord cause He don't know you."

Rether was about to say something to Cool or Joe, but she stopped long enough to say, "Now you're an angel?" Agatha didn't say anything back because all three of us knew a few things about Agatha's past. We was close friends. She had not done many things at all, but just a few little things that made her human. A bit of a sinner. I cannot compare her with Rether, but God don't compare people either, we all go before Him and are judged one by one. Yes mam!

When Rether did speak, she said to Joe, "I'll have a sloe screw, please."

Agatha gasped again, "Rether!"

Rether laughed as she said, "Give my girlfriend one too! Please!!"

"No he isn't gonna give me no slow screw. He ain't gonna give me nothin!" Agatha started to get up, but Rether, laughing, grabbed her arm. "Sit down, Agatha. Have somethin else. It's hot outside. The drink will taste good and then the cab will be here and we can go."

Agatha sat back down, sayin, "Get behind me, Satan. Alright, but give me a tomato juice . . . with a little gin in it." She indicated a 'little gin' with her thumb and a finger held wide apart. "Rether, you get me into more things!" She smiled.

Rether smiled as she said, "Yeah . . . ain't you glad?"

Then Tan turned around and said to them, "Have the drink, honey . . . you may be dead tomorrow!"

Joe was putting the drinks on their table as Agatha leaned to look around him to tell Tan, "Miss LaTanya I wouldn't have a drink on my mind or in my hand if I thought I'd be dead tomorrow." Then she took hold of that glass and drank it right down, all of it, and I know Joe put a lot of gin in it.

Just then the cabdriver stuck his head in the door, saying, "Anybody call a cab?" Joe answered him, "Yeah! Be right out. Cab's here, ladies."

Rether picked up Agatha's empty glass, looking at the bottom of it. "It's a good thing. You might hurt yourself, Aggie." She turned to Cool, "Thank you, Mr. Cool."

Aggie couldn't let Rether's implication go by. "Don't lick the bottom of that glass, Rether."

Rether was gathering her things and answered with a frown, "Oh, Agatha, you always messin things up when I'm enjoyin myself. What's a little drink?!"

Agatha was movin to the door and spoke over her shoulder, "I'm the oldest and you look older than I do!"

Rether dragged slowly behind her. "Looks don't make me happy!"

"Well, if drinkin makes you happy, you won't be unhappy for the next thousand years just ridin on what you done already drank!"

"I wish you quit tryin to save me and let me live!"

Agatha reached back to take Rether's arm and pull her out the door. "You been living more'n sixty years! Don't you know you better get ready to die?! Come on here! Let's go by the church."

Rether went out, lookin back sadly. "Bye."

Tan called out to her, "Leave her home next time, Aunty. You deserve to get out sometime."

Everybody laughed after the ladies left. Tan said, "My mother sounds just like Aggie."

Cool laughed, saying, "That ole lady sounds like everybody's mother!"

Tan, thoughtful, said, "She had her points though."

Joe added, "She does look a lot better than Rether though. Bet she feels better, too."

Tan didn't laugh this time, "Okay, now, that is my aunt." Then turning to Cool, she said, "That was nice of you, Cool, buyin them two older ladies a drink."

Cool, back to lookin in the mirror at hisself, smiled, brushed his jacket sleeve and said, "Never can tell whether one of them old biddies have some money. You got to be nice to all women. Tan, your aunt, the fast one, might be comin back someday!"

I guess Tan wanted another drink because she didn't answer him. Or she already knew Cool couldn't get a dime from Rether; Rether might get his money if he wasn't real careful.

My legs were tired of standin still in one place. I knew I needed to do a few more things in the kitchen before I left, so I was just turnin to go back there when another lady came in. Well, you know me by now, so you know I waited to see who it was. Well, you could have knocked me over with a dead leaf! It was Irene!

It was takin her a minute for her eyes to adjust from the light outside so she could see in here, but I could see good! And just then Cool spoke up. "I wish the broad on the phone would come on in! I got things to do. I can't wait around all day!"

Joe could see behind Cool, the entryway. He said, "Maybe this is the lady."

Cool turned around to see and he was shocked to see Irene, too. "Irene! Irene, what you doin here?"

She could see better then and she was lookin at Cool, "I come to talk to you, Cool."

You could hear the annoyance in Cool's voice when he said, "Well, it sure coulda waited til I got out to the house to see you! I don't like you comin down here!!" Lookin back at Tan and Joe, he moved from his place at the bar to try to steer Irene to the doorway, outside.

My legs was sure ready to stand a little longer now.

Cool had his hands on Irene's arm, but she pulled gently away. Her voice was tired and strained. No anger in it. She even looked a little sad. "No . . . it couldn't wait. I tried to wait, but it's been a month now, and this just can't wait any longer because I didn't want you coming . . . over and bein surprised."

Cool looked over his shoulder at Joe and Tan again; they were lookin right at him and Irene. He took Irene's arms again, sayin, "Well, let's go. I'll take you to the bus stop and we can talk while we wait for your bus." Then her words must have sunk in and he asked, "Surprised about what?" He was so nervous he didn't wait for an answer, he turned back to Joe, "What I owe you, Joe?"

But Irene, gently, removed his hands from her body and moved away, deeper into the club. "I have a way . . . home. No, we can talk here, Cool."

Cool snapped his head around to face her, astonishment on his face. "No?! No? What you mean, no? Are you tellin me what to do? Woman, I'm your man! Don't question me!" He glanced over his shoulder to see if Joe had heard that.

Irene passed on around Cool and sat down at one of the tables, sayin, "Let's sit at this table."

Cool was utterly (I always wanted to say that word, but never had no occasion), utterly surprised. "What's wrong with you, girl?" Then he changed his tactic, sat down and said, "Well, alright. But only for a minute, I ain't got much time. I . . . uh . . . got . . . uh . . . a little job I got to do."

Irene smiled a little tired smile and looked a little amused as she said, "I think I'll have a drink, Joe. Something . . . pretty."

Cool spoke, "I ain't got much money, Irene, you know that."

But that did not faze Irene, she said, lookin at Joe, "Well, then . . . I'll pay for it. Somethin pretty, please, Joe. A Tom Collins."

Cool glanced at Joe and quickly said, "I'll pay for it! Hey, Joe, bring the little woman a drink." Turnin back to Irene, he asked her, "Where you get money for a drink? And what kind of ride you got? Who brought you here?"

She looked at Cool for a moment and started to answer, but didn't get to answer because just then Joe came with a pretty red and yellow drink with a colorful straw in it. Joe had a big welcomin smile as he said, "Well, it's little Ms. Tatum! I haven't seen you since you was goin to high school. How you doin?"

Cool answered for her, "She doin just fine! What kind of drink is that, Joe? What you put in it? She don't need no hard liquor."

Joe cocked his head at Cool and smiled, "It's just a nice, cool glorified Tom Collins with some gin in it."

Irene smiled and said, "Thank you, Joe, this will do just fine."

Cool didn't smile, "With a glorified price, I bet!"

Joe was about to answer when another person walked in. A man. When I see that it is Mr. Summer I am not surprised because I figured he was the one with the ride. Joe turns right away to Mr. Summer with a smile, saying, "Afternoon, Mr. Summer! How you doin, sir? Have a seat. What can I bring you?"

Mr. Summer took a seat at a table near Irene's and sat down, sayin as he smiled, "I'll have a Tom Collins, Joe. How are you and your family?"

Joe was already on his way back to the bar, "Fine, Mr. Summer, fine. Tom Collins comin right up!"

Cool didn't pay Mr. Summer much notice, he was talkin to Irene again as she sipped her drink. He tried to speak real low so no one could hear. "What is it, Irene? Now, I ain't got no money! I just gave you twenty dollars last time I saw you. It wasn't no month either."

Irene just sipped and slightly smiled. "Ten dollars."

Joe waved his hand at the air, "Was it ten dollars? Well . . ."

"Three months ago."

"Well, I still ain't got no more today."

Now Irene waved her hand at the air. "I didn't come for money, Cool."

Cool was taken aback, agitated, "Well, what is it then? My sons sick?"

All durin this time, Joe was servin Mr. Summer his drink and exchangin a few more words with him.

Cool paid them no mind, just kept talkin to Irene as low as he could keep his voice. "If my sons sick, what you doin out here at a bar? You oughta be home with them! Or at work. Not out here! . . . in no bar!"

Irene set her glass down, "The boys aren't sick, Cool."

Cool leaned back in his chair, satisfied as boss again. "Well, okay. I want you to take good care of my sons, Irene. I don't want them sick."

"Everything is alright, Cool. I won't let my boys get sick."

Cool sounded confused, "Well . . . what you doin comin down here to talk to me for? You sposed to wait til I get out there to see you."

"I had to talk to you today. I didn't know when I'd see you so . . . And every time I try to talk to you, you're runnin, so you don't have time to listen. You eat, sometimes hand me a dollar or two and then . . . you run out the door. It's been that way a long time, Cool. Since I didn't know when I'd see you, well . . ."

Cool's voice came up a little louder and I was glad cause I was strainin my ears. "Now, Irene, don't give me no speech bout no marriage. I told you I am goin to marry you . . . someday. But not now! I'm not ready to come out there in the country where you live and waste my life. I got to get ahead, while I'm young, and do somethin big for my sons. But when I gets bothered like this, you breaks my stride! I got a big business deal—"

Irene cut him off, "Cool, I want—"

Cool cut her off, "Irene, don't make me mad! I don't want to get married now! I have my life to live! Now you choose your way . . . and I'll choose my way!" I noticed he checked her face quickly to see if his psychology was workin.

Irene was gettin exasperated, "Alright, alright, Cool. Cool, stop a minute . . . give me a chance to talk."

"Okay, but whatever it is, I ain't got much time right now! And don't complain bout me runnin all the time. A man was born to go runnin. That's what he is; a man! A woman was born to stay at home and tend the house and his sons."

Irene stood up to leave, sayin "I . . . Cool, I just thought it would be fair to talk to you . . . if you're busy . . ."

He grabbed her sleeve and pulled her back down. "You done come this far, go head and talk, cause I ain't plannin on comin out there for a bit. I got a new . . . job I'm trying to do. Stop bein stupid! Just keep your voice down. I don't like people knowin my business. Hurry up, talk! But remember, I don't like my woman comin in no place like this! Don't come again! If it takes me a year to get out there, just wait! You know I'm comin . . . sometime!"

I think everybody was tryin to hear what they were sayin because everybody almost jumped when Irene hit the table with her fist. It was her first sign of any emotion. She hit that table and said, "Then be quiet!" Cool was so surprised his mouth dropped open and he hushed! "Now," she sat back in her chair and continued quietly, "I think I did everything I could to give our . . . love . . . a chance."

Cool spoke quieter too. "Irene, don't worry. I'm satisfied with you. You don't need to do nothin else . . . just stay out there in the country in that house and keep goin to work."

She ignored his words and kept speakin, "We . . . were happy . . . a lot when we first started all those years ago. Least-ways we laughed a lot. But I've been unhappy a lot . . . with you." Cool looked around to see who was hearin all this, but she kept talkin like she didn't care who heard her. And I can tell you this: everybody's ears was ten feet wide.

"And, Cool, that don't make me mean and mad at life, or you, anymore."

Cool patted her hand, "Irene, that's good, that's good."

But Irene wasn't through. "But, I believe in people bein happy . . . if they can . . . in life. That's why I never really bothered you." Cool smiled and nodded his head, sayin, "That's good, that's good."

Irene continued, "But, now, I want to be happy . . . all the time I can."

Cool pat her hand again, "Things gonna get better, Irene."

Irene waved that away easy like, "I'm not gettin any younger. And you always told me to live my life cause you was livin yours."

Cool leaned back and laughed softly, "And someday they gonna come together. Get it? Come together?"

Irene didn't laugh nor frown nor smile, she just kept talkin. "I know . . . there are gentle, nice, kind men in the world. Men who give love to their woman. I want to be loved."

"I be out there in a few days, Irene . . . be cool."

Irene just let his words fly on out in space. She kept talkin. "Men who love their children, their family. I want somebody . . . grown up, mature. Somebody who cares about me and our sons. You know, I'm learnin a lot from my sons. And I hope I'm teachin them somethin about life . . . and women and love."

"You a good mother, Irene, but you got to stay home to be a good mother! And don't you worry bout my boys and what they need to know bout women. I'm gonna teach them everything they need to know. They gonna be MEN when I get through with them boys!"

Irene looked down at her hands and smiled. "I want them to be tender and affectionate . . . like their father."

Cool's scowl changed to a prideful look of pleasure; if he had been standin up he would have strutted and preened his wings. "Why, sure," he granted.

Irene looked up at him, earnestly. "It's gonna be very important to them. See . . . I have learned that it's okay to kiss somebody's ass . . . but only if that ass belongs to you. See . . . Cool, some people can love . . . and some people can't. Those that can't are always lookin for some love to stuff into their own heads and pockets out from other people's hearts. While those who can love is always givin . . . always givin." She shook her head slowly and sadly, then, just as sudden, her face brightened up. "But when you get TWO givers . . . together, Lord, you really got somethin!"

"What you been readin, Irene? I told you to stop readin all that trash!"

"Cool . . . a lot of things start with mother's love . . . and father's love."

Cool laughed, happy to be on comfortable ground again. "I love my sons!"

Irene was lookin past Cool into her thoughts she was speakin out loud. "That's where you have to learn to love first, sometime." She looked straight at Cool then. "For a long time, I thought I loved you. People been tellin me they love me . . . while all the time I be tellin you I love you. They show me their love while I showed you my love and the people who love me suffer."

Cool's laughter had long faded. His face and his voice changed. "You been messin round on me, Irene?"

"Cool, I needed to see you." She stopped to take a long

swallow from her drink. "You've been by my house twice this month . . ."

Cool tried to sound angry, "I know! And you wasn't home! Where were you? I figured you was in church, cause it was late."

Irene took a sip of her drink, said, "I was, we were, going to wait until you came by again, but since I knew you were comin again sometime, we thought I better tell you before you did. I have moved anyway. I don't live there anymore." She smiled and took another sip of her drink. "I have a marriage now, Cool."

I liked to fell off my own legs. Yes MAM!

Cool, annoyed again, didn't seem to understand. "Now, Irene, I just got through tellin you that I . . . You moved? And didn't tell me? Where? And what you mean 'married'? I keep trying to tell you I ain't ready to get married."

She softly interrupted him by holding her hand up. "Not to you, Cool . . . to someone else."

Cool stood up (Mr. Summer did too). Cool knocked over his chair and asked, "Woman! Are you crazy?!"

Irene stayed calm, bless her little brave heart. She said, just as calm as could be, "Now, don't get excited, Cool, and we can talk. Otherwise, I'll have to leave."

Cool remembered the other folks in the bar and glanced around quickly. He pulled his chair back up and sat right down in it, leanin toward Irene, urgent like. Mr. Summer sat back down also. Cool was lookin angry, not so cool. He said, "You ain't goin NOWHERE!"

Irene's face was just as calm and bright, she still wasn't scared. "No. That's where I been. I ain't goin there no more. Now, I got some things to do so . . . let's finish this out."

Cool's eyes was all bucked when he said, "You damn right! We gonna finish this out! Who you been listenin to? Who been lyin to you? I ain't got to tell you, you know who your man is! You love me! All this shit you talkin . . ."

Irene held her hand up again, calmly. "Now . . . let me talk. We never have had much time to talk. When you come to see me, talkin ain't much on your mind."

"Well, who's the fault of that? You! You don't hardly let me touch you no more; you always sick . . . or busy . . . or the boys need somethin, or you got to go to your mama's house for somethin! It ain't my fault we don't talk . . . or nothin. Don't lay that on me!"

Irene turned her face away from all them words and held up her hand again. When she turned back to Cool, she said, "If we did talk, it was just games. Your games. Lyin games. You never took the time to think about if what you gave me was what I needed and wanted, or what I just took from you."

"Well, you was happy. And you loved me."

"I was not happy. And . . . I don't love you anymore. Not for a long time. Life with you ain't life."

Cool's face got ugly and he raised his voice in anger and indignation. "Well, in them nights when you used to let me be alone with you, you sure did seem to be enjoyin yourself!"

For some reason, nothin Cool said seemed to make Irene lose her cool. "Oh, Cool, the first few years there were times we could enjoy each other." She placed her hand over one of his. "But in the good times, I was burdened with all the things I had to try to understand." She moved her hand away from his and his hand lay on the table looking alone and forlorn.

Cool must couldn't think of what to say because he asked

a foolish question, defensively, "What did you have to try to understand?"

"Oh, Cool, you are way pass me. You have your own . . . dreams."

"You got that right!"

"I know."

Then he must have remembered, "What's all this about marriage? What you talkin bout? Who did you meet that would marry you?" He leaned back in his chair, gettin his manhood back. "And take care of my kids . . . my sons?!"

As cool as could be, she said, "Nobody."

In his joy, Cool laughed and said, "That's what I thought. Well, then . . ."

Irene held up that hand again. "Cool, let me talk and try not to interrupt me. This is not easy for me."

Cool stopped laughing, abruptly, said, "Don't say nothin you'll be sorry for! Cause I might not come to see you for another few weeks!"

Irene took another big swallow of her drink and a deep breath.

Cool, somehow feelin better and thinkin he is in control again, said, "Come on now. Have your say, then I got to go and you better get on home to my sons and stop talkin all this sh—mess!"

Irene started out talkin slow as she moved one of her fingers through the water drops on the little table. "You know I go to church, regular, because that is the place I choose to find my wisdom . . . find my way . . . to live by. And for years I been prayin for what I want . . . for what every woman wants, I think."

Tan had been listenin without seemin to, but now she turned a ear round closer.

Cool interrupted again. "Let's talk about this marriage you talkin bout doin, cause . . ."

Irene interrupted him back, sayin, "What I'm sayin is you are not enough for me."

Cool, right away, looked over at Tan and Joe.

Irene looked down at her lap, kinda in space with her thoughts. Even her voice seemed to come from a distance. "Ohhhh, I was lonely. So lonely. Many times I looked in that ole cracked mirror in my room and said to myself what a fool I was. So many things I wanted to do . . . with you . . . before the children and . . . even after the children." Then she raised her head to look at Cool. "I was young, I am young, and there were so many times I wanted to make love. In the middle of the night . . . or early in the mornin . . . or even in the afternoon, outside on the grass . . . in the rain . . . by the creek . . . in a tree. Not just sex, Cool . . . love. But, you wasn't there. You were with me when you wanted to be 'cordin to your feelings, not when I needed you . . . 'cordin to mine."

All I could say was, "Humph!" as my heart clapped in my breast for her.

Cool looked confused, well, he wasn't used to thinkin hard bout the right things, so all he said was, "Well . . ." Like he was tryin to say somethin smart back.

But Irene was not through doin her own thinkin. "Sometimes when you came to my house, you were tired. You came where I was so you could sleep . . . or eat. And when you wake up, you'd be on your way out."

Of all things, Cool asked, "What has that got to do with you gettin married?"

Still lookin in Cool's face, she answered, "It's the reason I found somebody else. I found out what real love is. You always ran your life 'cordin to your own music, now I can live my life 'cordin to the music I hear and feel. My own music. I can even touch it."

Well, that Cool jumped up again, upsettin his chair again, and his lucky hat fell off. Mr. Summer stood up, too. Joe looked a little worried and I knew he was thinkin of that gun Cool had in his pocket. But Cool looked over at Joe, then reached down for his chair and tried to look nonchalant, or somethin, as he sat back down, forgettin his lucky hat. But his voice forgot to sound easy when he asked in as low a voice as his anger would let him use, "Somebody else!!! What you mean? You been givin my . . ." He looked at Joe again, then he had to ask anyway, "You been givin my stuff away, Irene?"

"Not yours, Cool. Mine. I'm the one was born with it."

Cool scrunched his chair closer, "To who? When?"

Up came Irene's hand again, "If you're quiet, I'll tell you . . . if you're not, I'll go."

Cool's voice was low and sinister when he said, "Baby, you ain't goin nowhere!"

Irene leaned back in her chair and looked at Cool thoughtfully. "Cool, I know I ain't so good lookin . . . and I know fellas like the good-lookin kind. But I can't worry bout that cause I'm young, and I got a lotta feelings that I left up to you to satisfy for a long time. But, you didn't satisfy em. I don't feel like sleepin around . . . so . . . well, so while I was doin housework for some of the church members . . . I met . . . someone . . . else."

Cool sneered, "The preacher?!"

Irene smiled and looked at her hands as she answered,

"No. But a very nice gentleman, who was very kind to me, helped me in so many little ways, big ways too. He was patient with me, treated me like I was somebody special. And all the time it was really just love he was showin me."

Cool pointed his finger in her face as he said, with a sneer, "Oh, hell! They all do that to get what they want! You just a fool to go for that mess! Patient?! Hell, yeah, he was patient! Tryin to steal my woman on the sly!" Then he changed his tactic. He leaned in close to Irene's face, she didn't move, just looked straight in his eyes. In a low, husky-soft mannish voice, he said, "Irene, baby, you know what we have. We got love, true love. You know ain't nobody like me . . . for you, but me. We to-geeeeether, baby. Toooogether. We got babies . . . together. My sons. Listen to me, we a family. You got my sons, baby. You a fool to go for whatever he layin on your mind." He leaned back in his chair; satisfied that he had done his good job on his woman.

Irene looked at Mr. Summer, at least it looked like she did to me, as she said, "I don't think he is foolin me. And I know he is patient because I know he wants his family together and he didn't press on me when I had the first baby because he knew I still had some feelings for you. And he still didn't change. Even after the second baby. He still treats me in every good way . . . and it's been seven years now."

Cool stood up and the chair went over again. "Seven years! You been goin with me more'n that! You been foolin round with somebody else for seven years! I oughta kick your ass!"

Mr. Summer stood up and Joe come from round the bar headin for Irene's table. Joe told Cool, "Okay, Cool, don't want no mess in my club!"

Cool raised his hand for Joe to stop, "Ain't no mess, man! This bitch here . . ."

Then Mr. Summer said in his mannish voice, "Watch your language, boy."

Cool turned to Mr. Summer, sayin, "Sit down, ole man, this is my business. I ain't gonna hurt her, not now, anyway!"

Mr. Summer answered in a hard, strong voice, "See that you don't. It's my business to make very sure you don't."

Cool turned his back and waved Mr. Summer away, grabbed his chair and sat back down (smashing his lucky hat under his chair) at the table where Irene waited, patiently. Joe, slowly, went back behind the bar. He looked back at Cool a couple of times. I know he was thinkin bout that gun. And it's a wonder he didn't stumble over Tan-Tan's eyes cause they was stuck out all the way to Cool's table.

Cool took out a handkerchief and wiped his face as Irene asked him, "Cool? How many women have you had in six years? One year, even?"

He was breathin hard when he answered her, "That's different! I'm a man! But why did you do this to me? Me!"

Irene's eyes slid over to Mr. Summer just as easy, and she almost smiled at him, but I guess it wasn't the time just then. But, in a voice that was makin love to whoever she was talkin about, she said, "Because he showed me what it felt like to be a woman. To get Valentine cards and boxes of candy, birthday presents, soft underwear and nightgowns we could enjoy together. Somebody to rub you to sleep . . . to . . ."

Cool broke her reverie in a high voice I hadn't heard before, incredulous, "You been 'sleepin' with em?!"

Irene must didn't hear him, cause she smiled in a dreamy way as she said, "Somebody who make love to you like you're both there. Thinks of you . . . for no reason at all and stops by to see if there is anything he can do for you." She laughed lightly as she said, "Buys you perfume, not because you need it, but because he knows you like it, or pretty toilet paper even, not because you need it, but because he knows you use it. Makes you feel like you both somethin . . . not just him bein somethin."

Cool suddenly grinned, said, "Who is he? Who . . . is . . . the . . . sucker? The somebody-else's-woman stealer! Tell me who he is, cause I'm gonna tell him who 'I' am!"

Irene returned her gaze to Cool. "He knows about you. I told him about you a long time ago. How I wished you and me would get married . . . a long time ago, before the babies, and have a life together. After the first baby, I still thought maybe I wanted that, thought I could wait . . . until you had your runout."

Cool leaned back, satisfied, and you could see him feelin better as he glanced to see if Joe and Tan heard those last words. "What the fool say to that?!"

Irene looked at Mr. Summer again, "He never said one word about us, no matter what I said. I liked him for that. In fact, Cool, over the years . . . he's been there when the kids were sick, when they had to do somethin or, oh, just whatever came up about our sons . . . so that I piled up so much likin for him that it turned into love, kinda good and strong and . . . easy, without my even realizin it."

Cool came forward in his chair again and the high voice came from him in disbelief, "You love him?!"

Irene nodded and shook her head all at the same time and grinned, "I love him. Very, very, very, very much."

There was a moment's silence as Cool looked at Irene, then he asked, "You just think you love him cause I ain't been around . . . too much. But . . . I'm gonna be! Anyway, what you gonna tell my kids? My sons?"

Irene looked at Cool and smiled as she said, "I don't have to tell my sons anything, Cool."

Cool was silent a moment as he looked at her, his face all frowned up. Then he said, "I want them to know damn well who their father is."

Irene looked at Cool a moment, then her gaze passed to Mr. Summer. "They have always known who their father is. Their father knows them and they know their father. It's my fault they have been apart."

"What you mean . . . your fault?"

Now Irene sat up straight in her chair, looked into Cool's eyes and placed her hand over one of his. "Cool, I never told you those were your children. Your sons. You just thought they were because you thought you were the only man in my life. If you really look at them, they don't even look like you. You see what you want to see. At the time I had our first son, I should have told you then. But . . . I knew what kind of life you were livin, so I didn't feel like I was cheatin you any more than you thought you were cheatin me. And I just didn't know if I still wanted to marry you or not. And . . . their father told me to wait until I was sure what I wanted to do with my life, cause he could still love them and do for them whether you knew it or not. I waited, years, until I knew you were entirely out of my mind."

Cool stood up, lookin like he was goin to go out of his mind, chile. Yes sir! He was almost cryin, least his voice was when he was shouting at Irene. "Woman, Irene, don't you . . . shit on my life! Don't you take everything good from my life and leave the shit!"

Irene started to stand, but changed her mind and remained calmly in her chair. "But, we aren't your life, Cool." I could tell she was a little scared now, but still tryin to be kind. She went on talkin in a easy kind of voice, she never did holler. "Your life is out here where the . . . shit is. You brought the . . . shit into our lives. I didn't. You didn't even know my sons knew who their father was because you've never been close to them. Huggin and kissin is fine for a quick minute, but it does not put clothes on a child's back or food in a child's stomach. Or stand over them all night when they are sick or hurt. Or take them to a doctor or a dentist or even to school." She slowly shook her head and said, "We have a whole life apart from you and you didn't think enough of us to look and see it."

Mr. Summer was standin again and Joe was comin back round from the bar. Cool shouted at Irene, "You lyin! Why you take my money?"

Irene just shook her head slowly, "Because I had let you take my body at one time and I was still feedin you years later."

"You lyin bout my kids! Them's MY sons!"

"No, I'm not lyin, Cool, as God is my witness."

"Them's my kids, Irene. My sons."

Shakin her head sadly, she repeated, hard on each and every word, "No. They are not your sons. They are my husband's children. His sons. Our sons. They carry his name on their birth certificates. He was there when we made them and he was there when I gave birth to them." Irene took a deep breath and looked at Mr. Summer, then finished speakin to Cool. "It was more than a year since we had made love before my second son was born."

I can tell you this, and it's a fact! That woman was tellin the truth! Yes siree mam! And I could tell by the look on Cool's face that he couldn't remember when he had last made sex with her because he had been makin sex with so many women all his grown life. Even went out of town for em when he was out of em in town.

Cool lunged at Irene and struck her! Mr. Summer was round that table like a lightnin flash and Joe was there right after, holdin on to Cool, who was so mad that slobber was sprayin from his mouth as he screamed at Irene, who he thought was destroyin his life and now . . . his pride, in front of his friends. He shouted, "Don't you do this to me! Don't you do this to me!!"

Mr. Summer was lifting Irene up, brushin her off and talkin low to her while Joe held Cool. But she still stood up to Cool, still didn't holler back at him. That woman sure got patience!

Irene stepped back from the table as Mr. Summer picked up her chair and said to Cool, "I didn't do nothin to you, Cool. You always do everything to yourself. I have done told you now, so . . . I got to go."

Cool is so angry he is almost cryin, "You ain't goin now! You done come in here and . . . and strip me of everything in my life!"

Irene had started away from the table, but now she turned back and her voice had a little anger in it this time. "Everything in your life?! You never been IN our life. We wasn't nothin to you!"

The anger was leavin Cool's voice and a little pleadin was comin in as he said, "Yes, you was! Yes . . . you . . . was. I was goin . . . to spend my old age with you and them kids. Irene, Irene."

In a sad little voice, Irene said, "But they wouldn't be kids anymore, and I wouldn't be young anymore. The love wouldn't be the same because it's already gone from me to somebody else. Our dreams, if we had any, would be died out . . . or lost at some woman's place where you had laid em down and forgot em. Or you'd probably be sick, or wore out and through livin. I want to live . . . now."

Mr. Summer took Irene's arm and she turned, again, to leave, then turned back to Cool and said, "Take care of your-self, Cool."

But Cool lunged for Irene again and when Mr. Summer tried to pull her out of the way so he could step in front of her, Irene stumbled and fell to her knees. Cool raised his fist to strike her, Joe reached for his arm, and Mr. Summer pulled out a gun and put it to Cool's head!!! Jesus!! And said, "Don't hit her again, man."

Mr. Summer didn't seem mad and he didn't raise his voice, but . . . in a low, sure-serious voice he said, "I mean what I said, don't . . . put . . . your . . . hands on my wife ever again in your life."

Cool heard him, and backed up a bit, but he was hysterical, I guess. He could only see Irene. He screamed at her, "You bitch! You musta had everybody laughin at me! Whorin round callin it housecleaning! You don't know who the daddy of them bastards of yours is!"

Mr. Summer steps between Irene, who looks frightened

and shocked, and Cool. Cool finally registers Mr. Summer in his mind. I don't think he has seen the gun good. He says to Mr. Summer, "Get the hell away from here, man, I'm talkin to my woman!"

Mr. Summer holds the gun up closer to Cool's head and answers, "You are talkin to my wife. And I am not goin to let her be called another bitch out'a your mouth or I will put something in your mouth to stop it up."

Cool saw the gun then. He steps back, disbelievin, and says to Irene, "Your wife?!" Then he laughs at her (but he don't say "bitch"), "You married this old man?"

Irene answered right up, "Yes! The good Lord blessed me and my heart with a real Man!"

Cool must be crazy because he starts to reach for Irene again, sayin, "If I catch you with—"

Mr. Summer cocks his gun and even in all that noise, we ALL heard it. Cool, too. Mr. Summer said, "You gonna have to catch up with your head first, cause if you make one more move to hurt my wife . . . you gonna be lookin up at yourself from the floor through a hole in your head."

Cool is very aware of that gun . . . now.

Mr. Summer kept the gun cocked and kept talkin, "You need to pray that when you get my age . . . in a few years . . . you do as well as I have done. I have the woman I love . . . and my sons." Then he turned to Irene and said, "Come on, Irene, lets go get our sons and go where there is peace."

As they begin to leave, Cool hollers after Irene, "I'll marry you now, Irene." He reached his arms out to her, still shoutin, "Tomorrow morning, today! I'll marry you right now! Irene, don't, please, don't take my sons."

Mr. Summer has put his gun away, but he turns back to say to Cool, "We don't have to take our sons, they are already at home at their father's house. You need to understand, they . . . are . . . not . . . your . . . sons."

Before they get completely out the door, Cool shouts at Mr. Summer, "Take her then, old man. I had her first."

Mr. Summer stops and smiles, a little, as he says. "That's right. You did. But you didn't have the best of her. You didn't have sense enough to know how to get it. You didn't have sense enough to hold on to her. You maybe coulda had my sons, too . . . and I'm glad you didn't have enough sense for that either! It really was all your choice for the first year or so. But all that is pass. It's history now." Then he went on out the door to his wife, Mrs. Irene Summer, mother, wife and property owner. Now!

But Cool tried to get the last word. "Get on out'a here! Get on out'a here! You think you got somethin, but you ain't got nothin!"

Everything was dead quiet in the bar. Joe and Tan were dead still. Me, too. But, I heard Tan say softly, "He got somethin, Cool. It's you that don't have nothin."

Cool, in his extremity, does not hear anything, but he does remember Joe and Tan were witnesses to his loss and the beggin. So he says, "You see that bullshit, man? I didn't want to hurt that ole man! Shit! Who needs her? But them are my sons . . . my sons. She lyin, man! She be back. She gonna think of me and all them good lovin times we had. She gonna need me! But . . . I'm a loner, a player!"

His voice begins to break and his eyes are tearin up, still . . . he can't let anyone see that he is hurt. So he says, "But she be back! But I don't need her! I ain't gonna take her back!

When them kids grow up, they know who they real daddy is! Where is my lucky hat?"

He looks around the stools at the bar, forgets the hat again and says, "Gimme a drink, man!"

As Joe fixes the drink, Cool's body jumps as if he'd been shot, I guess it was the reality hittin him. He grasped the bar with his arms stretched out, and leanin on the bar, he sobs . . . deep rackin sobs as he slowly crumbles to his knees on the floor. Between sobs he says, "I . . . don't want . . . to be . . . no . . . loner. I don't . . . want . . . to . . . be . . . no loser!"

During all this time Tan has got up from her stool and looks for Cool's hat. She finds it crumbled up beneath the table. She walks back to the bar and picks up her glass and takes a drink, all while she is lookin at Cool in the strangest way; a cross between a grin and a smirk. Then she leans down to help Cool up. He lets her help him. She puts his lucky hat on his head as she tells him, "Come on, honey, you need some company . . . Come on with Tan-Tan." She does not say it like "everything will be alright." Just with a smirk.

As they slowly walk toward the door to go out of the bar, Tan looks back over her shoulder to Joe and smiles.

As they go through the door, Cool's lucky hat falls off again and rocks back and forth on the floor for a time. Joe comes from behind the bar, again, and goes to pick up the hat. He looks at it a moment, then opens the door, leans out and hollers to Cool.

"Hey! Man! You left your new lucky hat!!"

I untied my apron, came out that kitchen, hugged my nephew "good-bye" and went home and sat in my own red swing and thought about all that. Yes mam!

About the Author

J. CALIFORNIA COOPER is the author of five collections of short stories, including *Homemade Love*, winner of the 1989 American Book Award, and the novels *The Wake of the Wind, Family*, and *In Search of Satisfaction*. She lives in northern California.